MW00948156

BIG IN JAPAN:

Book One in the GAILSONE Series

***

A novel by Casey Glanders

Gailsone: Big in Japan

1st Edition

Copyright © 2010 by Casey Glanders

Written by Casey Glanders

Edited by Rebecca White-Glanders and Denise Huston

All rights reserved. No part of this publication may be reproduced, distributed, or transmitted in any form or by any means, including photocopying, recording, or other electronic or mechanical methods, without the prior written permission of the publisher, except in the case of brief quotations embodied in critical reviews and certain other noncommercial uses permitted by copyright law. For permission requests, e-mail the publisher at the address below. The cover image is a privately purchased image from www.dreamstime.com with all rights reserved.

Casey Glanders
cjglanders@gmail.com
www.gailsone.com

Ordering Information:

Quantity sales. Special discounts are available on quantity purchases by corporations, associations, and others. For details, contact the publisher at the address above or visit gailsone.com.

Orders by U.S. trade bookstores and wholesalers. Please contact Casey Glanders at cjglanders@gmail.com or visit www.gailsone.com.

This is a work of fiction. Any resemblance to any persons, living or dead, is purely coincidental.

No golems were harmed in the writing of this publication.

Printed in the United States of America

For Becca

Chapters

"Are you a good witch, or a bad witch?"

-Glenda

Prologue:

A New Line of Work

Then

***

'So this is how I'm going to die.'

The words flashed through Alice's mind as she braced herself against the steel walls of the ship's hallway. The vessel had just been rocked yet again by a massive explosion. Above her, a red flashing light pulsed in time with a blaring klaxon that signaled this ship was under extreme physical duress. For Alice, it meant something else entirely; the *Argent* was going down. Again, the thought of her death ran though her head as she tried to angrily push it aside.

Alice tried to get her bearings, but she was having trouble. Her black, skin-tight costume was torn from the blasts, her utility belt was spent from making her way through a small task force of UN soldiers, and her domino mask had been ripped from her pale, bleeding face. Alice brushed a strand of short, singed purple hair out of her eyes, and made her way to the main hangar as best she could.

She was the second-in-command, and right now, her first thought was of the crew. The *Argent* was a Super Destroyer class airship, designed to hold over 300 active personnel, many of whom she had trained herself. This was their maiden voyage, their destination being low-orbit over the eastern seaboard of the United States. She had known they would run into problems, but she hadn't counted on meeting such a massive offensive. It seemed that every hero or super-powered being in the USA was right there in Pittsburg, waiting for them. Alice gritted her teeth and braced herself again as the ship reeled from another blast. As she did, only one thing made sense as to why so much resistance was here; someone had sold them out.

It wasn't beyond question; they were villains, and sometimes people just became overwhelmed with the whole 'evil' thing and decided to turn tail. Alice had even considered it herself during the planning phases for this latest run, but she had kept her mouth shut. After all, Prometheus (her employer and leader of the criminal organization known as the Purge) didn't take kindly to dissent, even if it was from his most prized agent.

Alice struggled to keep her balance as the ship lurched a good 15 degrees to the left, slamming her against the starboard bulkhead. She was almost to the main hangar, and, from there, to the escape pods. Just past the next junction was her ticket to safety. Alice started running and then froze; from beyond the hallway, she could hear screaming and movement.

When Alice rounded the corner, she saw the main hangar in flames. The smoke was thick, but no one was fighting the fires. She looked from the railing of the hanger balcony to see Purge soldiers, scientists and workers running for dear life to the escape pods. Occasionally, she saw a soldier stop to try to put out a fire or save a ship, but then they would freeze, look at what they were doing, and run. Alice gritted her teeth and continued on.

Alice ran with her hand against the wall to steady herself. The *Argent* was at least two miles up, but that would change in a matter of minutes. On top of that, her boss had informed her just before dismissing her that he would "show the world the face of God," at which point he stripped naked and then immersed himself in the ships ergonomic sensory relay control pod. In other words, he had gone completely insane. Alice, while loyal, didn't feel like dying. As soon as she could, she casually left the Bridge and then ran as fast as her legs would carry her to the hangar. About 30 seconds later, the first UN task forces boarded the ship and the explosions started. Things had gone downhill from there.

Lining the halls of the vessel was a series of small pod doors that led to short range escape crafts. Each one could hold up to three people, provided they were small. The pods came with three days worth of rations and an emergency beacon, just in case. The pods could float, were air tight and had thrusters to help with descent, but that was about it. Alice had fought for their inclusion in the *Argent*, and now she was glad of it.

For a brief moment, the super-villain and manager extraordinaire was saddened by the destruction of the *Argent* and the loss of her troops. The vessel was a Gothic-styled super carrier that stood twelve stories tall. Alice had always thought that creating such a huge ship was a colossally stupid idea, as it provided a massive target. In contrast, Prometheus had said for the last year or so that being a target was the point. Alice had always figured that it was so he could take out large contingent of enemy forces at once. Now she was suspecting that the black hole cannon her boss had been working on wasn't so much a projectile weapon to be used against his enemies, but an expensive and large funeral pyre.

Alice quickened her pace to a nearby pod when she saw a young woman round the corner. Behind her were three Purge soldiers who were immediately engulfed in flames from a wall exploding on the portside. The young woman was thrown forward and slammed her head into the metal railing, which knocked her unconscious. "Allison!" Alice screamed to the young girl. Alice raced for the young woman and turned her over. Allison was one of her chief operatives in the field and her personal assistant. More than that, she also happened to be Alice's niece. Her long, auburn hair was blackened from fire damage and her red-rimmed glasses were cracked. Alice could see that she was breathing heavily, which probably meant a broken rib.

"Come on, soldier. It's time to get the Hell out of here," Alice muttered as she dragged the only person on board she would ever consider a genuine friend towards the nearest pod. As she did, she saw another figure round the corner. Alice couldn't make them out clearly through

5

the smoke and confusion, but the hangar was collapsing and in another minute, the person would be dead. Alice waved and screamed, "Over here!" Instantly, the person changed direction and charged for the pod. Alice grabbed Allison and dragged her inside as the third person, a woman in all black, leapt in. Without wasting a moment, Alice slammed the controls near the door with the flat of her hand. All three women were lurched against the pod wall as the craft rocketed out of the ship.

Alice took a moment to catch her breath. Beside her, the other woman was shaking and coughing from the smoke. Alice reached over and patted her on the back. "Easy now, we're safe. You...oh, hell."

Alice locked eyes with Blackbird, one of the chief heroines of the Collective Good, and one of her sworn enemies. Alice tensed, not sure what was about to happen. Blackbird looked terrible; her costume was a black singed mass of rubber, cloth and scorched carbon, her hair was a tangled black mess and her mask had a huge smudge across the right eye, but still stayed on (much to Alice's chagrin). Each woman looked at the other, ready to move, but then they heard the explosion and both turned to watch out the porthole.

The *Argent* was breaking up. She was falling in flaming chunks to the Earth, slamming into what Alice could vaguely make out as downtown Pittsburg. The bulk of the ship however, was collapsing in on itself. Both women watched in awe as a large, black mass appeared in the middle of the craft, sucking it into oblivion. The flames form the various parts of the ship bent around the hole, and the pull of the gravity well was such that the wreckage actually seemed to be falling in slow motion. The tendrils of flame from the burning debris were twirling up into the atmosphere and then were sucked in to a black, swirling void. It was awesome and terrible in its scope, and both Alice and Blackbird felt that they were seeing something that humans were never meant to glimpse.

Alice could swear that even as the hole was closing, she could feel a tug on her person. Thankfully, the void vanished after a few moments, but the ship was gone; the *Argent* was truly lost. Blackbird turned her attention back to Alice. "Dyspell," she hissed, "You are going to fry for this you little bitch, I swear it."

"Easy there, BB. We can't do much of anything until we're outta this pod. Besides, you'll hurt Allison." Blackbird glanced at the young, unconscious worker in Alice's arms and glared.

"She's one of yours. Why would I care?" Blackbird started reaching for the grapple-taser in her belt. The pod was small, and there was truly no room to maneuver. Without missing a beat, Alice reached over and put her hand on Blackbirds chest before the costumed hero could do anything about it.

"Stop." Alice said with a level voice. "Now listen, you know what I can do. If I wanted to, it would take me a moment to focus and rot this hand right through your chest cavity, and you know it. I could end you right here and honestly save myself a massive headache when we land and it wouldn't even make me break a sweat."

Alice could feel Blackbirds heart going a mile a minute under the suit. Alice, while being a gifted fighter and master planner had one thing Blackbird didn't; an actual power. Granted, it wasn't flight or super strength, but it was a magically-based entropy power. Alice had been born with the unique ability to rot, decompose or break down any substance known to man. While that alone was frightening, her unbridled mastery of it had been enough to earn her the title Deadliest Woman in the World, and Blackbird knew it.

"I could kill you super-fast, but right now...look, can you check her breathing? I'm at a bad angle here." Alice tried to shift a bit and took her hand off of Blackbird's chest. Blackbird stared at her foe for a moment, and then looked to the passed out girl. She leaned in and listened.

"It's ragged. She has a broken rib, possibly a punctured lung."

Alice closed her eyes and cursed. "You're closest to the nav pad. Find the nearest hospital and steer us down; she's going to need attention or she'll die."

Blackbird looked at Alice for a moment. "You want me to take you to a hospital? You realize there will be swarms of police, SWAT and God knows what else there, right?"

Alice looked at the unconscious woman. "Hey, bonus for you, isn't it? Please land the craft, Blackbird. My friend is about to die, and I think I've had more than enough of that today."

"Funny, you didn't seem to care about everyone else up there."

Alice nearly spit through her teeth. "Those were my men up there, dammit. Every single one of them was trained by me and my staff. I worked hard for them, guided them and gave them direction, a goal, purpose, and then... all this crap has to happen. You think I wanted this?" Alice gestured around her. "Prometheus gets it in his head to build a Doomsday weapon, okay, that's something that's almost routine, but it was never for actual destruction in the past. We worked for extortion, for profit and for advancement, not...God, not *this*."

Blackbird sat calmly, staring at the ranting villain. "You built a Doomsday weapon. What the hell did you *think* was going to happen?"

Alice glared. "It was a base *and* a weapon. It was designed for orbital defensive combat, not to fend off a massive surprise attack mid-launch. This wasn't supposed to fucking happen."

 "You think any of that matters to me, or that it will matter to the UN Judiciary Committee? You can dress it up any way you want, but you're gonna burn for this, Dyspell. You'll burn slow, and we'll all be there to turn your spit."

Alice leaned back and sighed. "Maybe, but that can happen tomorrow. Right now, she needs help and you're gonna be a hero and give it to her."

Blackbird considered the young woman in Alice's arms. She couldn't have been more than 20 if she was a day. "So, what's her story, and why do you care so much?"

"She's my niece. When her parents died, I made a promise that I would take care of her and I intend to keep it."

"And what about the others on that ship? What did you promise them?"

Alice closed her eyes. "Look, this... this is a bit much right now, even for me. Let's just deal with this when we land, okay?"

The pod was coasting down towards a hospital on the east side of Pittsburg, and Alice could see in the light of the setting sun that the auto-nav had guided them towards a back alley. Even if someone saw them land, they would have a few minutes. The pod opened behind Blackbird and Alice gestured to her limp assistant. "Little help?"

Blackbird looked again at Alice and then at the prone girl in Alice's arms, and sighed. "You really confuse me, you know that? One minute, you're trying to take over the world and the next... what is with you, anyway?"

Alice was about to answer when suddenly Blackbird convulsed and screamed, and then dropped to the ground, knocked out cold. Alice slumped under Allison's weight and had to readjust her grip, which was when she noticed her assistant was awake.

"Got her," Allison said, her standard issue taser still smoking in her hand. Alice smiled down at her charge.

Alice sighed to herself, thankful for the rubber insulation in her suit and for the split in Blackbird's. "Yeah, you did. I was wondering how this was going to go. Thanks."

Allison smiled up at her and then struggled to her feet. Alice looped her arm over her shoulder and leaned back in the craft to rummage in a small compartment by the door. "Here we are," she said as she handed Allison a small pack of clothes. "Put these on, we need to be civilians."

"What about your hair?" Allison asked.

Alice reached into the pod and took out a folded denim jacket and miniskirt. "I don't see it being a problem tonight."

Chapter 1

The Weight of the World

Now

***

"Alice? I'm ready for you now."

The chiseled, young-looking man was in his early 30's, and handsome by most standards. He had short, jet black hair, blue eyes and a physique to die for that was snugly hidden in a casual gray sport coat, the white shirt underneath undone at the collar. Alice noted that he kept his eyes steady on her face, which already earned him serious credit as she nervously stood from her chair in the simple, tidy waiting room and entered his office.

Alice was nervous. Actually, nervous was a rather low-key way of expressing her level of anxiety. To try again, Alice, while looking completely calm and collected on the outside with her face locked in a confident half smirk and her normally unruly purple hair forced down under a shoulder-length brown wig, was having kittens. She was terrified that the young man would notice her shaking in her black and purple business suit, but to his credit, if he did, he said nothing. With a well-practiced ease that came from years of acrobatics training, she deftly slid into the seat in front of his desk without having a psychotic episode right then and there.

This was Alan Tanner, THE Alan Tanner - known to most in the business world as "the sleeping dragon of Wall Street." He was the man who had single-handedly wrestled the economy of the entire East Coast back from recession through aggressive takeovers, insane business deals and an overwhelmingly strong push for a focus on American workers. He was feared on Capitol Hill as a possible contender for a House seat and maybe, in a decade or two, as a strong presidential candidate.

To Alice Gailsone, Alan Tanner was someone else altogether. Unknown to Wall Street, the East Coast and Capitol Hill (*most* of Capitol Hill, she reminded herself), Alan was also Blackthorne, scourge of the criminal underworld and one of the most feared and legendary heroes in the world. In a very short (and very violent) period of time, he had managed to (again) single-handedly save much of the East Coast from madmen like Dr. Edward Tolarius and his Tidal Cannon, the Moduloch frog-alien invasion of New York and, on countless occasions, from the super villain society Purge. Even *without* the help of actual super-powered heroes like Superior Force or the Red Guard, he had been able to hold his own, and the people loved him for it. Criminals, like the Purge, obviously had not.

The Purge had been defeated, their leader Prometheus sucked into a black hole several years ago when the invasion of Pittsburg turned even more ugly than it should have. Most of the Purge was rounded up, but many others were scattered, broken and defeated. Those that remained were pissed, exceptionally well-armed and looking for some payback. The situation had become so dire that people were afraid to leave their homes, and public transportation had suffered from fear of terrorist attacks. The country had reached a point where new options had to be explored.

Options like Alice.

It was Alan Tanner (as Blackthorne) who had suggested to the world's heroes that it was time to offer amnesty to those who were ready and willing to help rebuild. That maybe it was time to turn the other cheek and give the scattered forces of the Purge, and really all criminals, the chance to do the right thing. Alan saw an opportunity, however slim, for these criminals to use their abilities for the forces of good. It was his hope that these turncoat criminals – some of whom had powerful abilities – might give them the boost they needed to quash the tidal surge of violence destroying the city. Considering how most criminals and heroes alike generally felt, this did not sit well with either side of the fence.

Then Alan Tanner did something unexpected. He donated half of his multi-billion dollar fortune to a government-backed program designed specifically with known (and powerful) criminals in mind. The Open Hand Act, as the program was called, was designed to help willing criminals reform before reintroducing them to society. Even with Alan Tanner's generous financial backing though, the program was dead in the water — until the most dangerous woman in the world suddenly came forward to accept his controversial offer.

No one really knew why Prometheus' former second-in-command suddenly decided to switch sides, though the rumors and accusations flew furiously on both sides of the fence. Some said that she had been blackmailed by Blackthorne; others thought she'd been secretly good all along. In the end, only super criminal Dyspell, the Mistress of the Black Arts, knew for sure — and she was not inclined to share.

After that, the Open Hand act slowly gained steam. There were, of course, a few minor setbacks (after a military appointment, Infurnus the Living Ember had acted out his aggression on some non-combatants in the Middle East, but that's a story for another time). Overall, however, it looked like Blackthorne's initiative would be a resounding success. As the program gained public popularity, companies were tripping over themselves to hire ex-villains for use in advertising and promotions. For their part, the reformed villains didn't seem to mind the money or the attention.

Then there were the villains that wanted more, but couldn't let go of the street. There were the villains that had trouble seeing the line between what was allowed and what felt good, which were hard (if not impossible) to reform. And then there were those who didn't want more, who reveled in blood and chaos and the suffering of others. As it now stood, people were afraid to go out, the bad guys were reorganizing, and something had to be done.

Something like Alice.

Alice Gailsone was, by all rights, pretty lucky to be sitting across from Alan Tanner without any visible restraints in place. She was lucky in that she *should* have been in a maximum security cell behind a negatively charged ionic field to protect the guards from having their torsos blown out. She *should* be in a neutralizing helmet with her hands in a Polaris-level finger trap to keep her from moving or using her mouth. She *should* be trapped in a reverse singularity room, or at the center of a dwarf star locker surrounded by the Red Guard on 24-hour watch.

Instead, in the wake of the Open Hand Act, she found herself in the office of one of the greatest heroes of all time. Her nerves were on edge, and she wanted to blast something with a vengeance. Not because she wanted to do anything evil, necessarily, but it was either that, pee herself with fear, or scream. Honestly, the first one sounded like her best option — but first, she needed to know why the great Alan Tanner/Blackthorne had called her. Odds were it was nothing she'd enjoy.

"So, Alice," Alan started, his smooth, tan face pleasant and body language carefully neutral as he sat cross-legged behind his desk, "How are things? I hear the private sector has been treating you well."

Alice shifted slightly in her seat, met Blackthorne's icy blue gaze and calmly replied in her best please-don't-let-this-conversation-end-in-explosions voice. "It's been passable. I was actually starting to settle into things when I received your assistant's call. To be honest, I was surprised that you wanted to see me. Here. Alone."

"Indeed," Alan nodded slightly, his finger lightly touching the side of his face as his head rested in his hand, "I imagine that I'm the last person you wanted to deal with."

"When I came clean, you promised me that my record would be blank. That there would never be any repercussions."

"This is true."

14

"You promised me you would never go back on that deal as long as I kept my nose clean. That this would be a no-strings-attached deal, and that your friends would stay out of my life."

"This is also true."

Alice stared at Blackthorne from across the desk, trying to get a read on where this meeting was going. For Christ's sake, the man's presence seemed to take up the whole room, humming in the air and centering on those unnaturally blue eyes. She'd never understood how the city's business elite fell for his "normal businessman" persona , and she sure as Hell didn't get it now.

When she had volunteered to be the first recipient of the Open Hand Act, she had been promised up and down that she would never be held accountable for her actions prior, and that her identity would be kept a secret. She knew Blackthorne's program was in danger of failing, but it was a solid idea. All it needed was a powerful player in the criminal world to step up and get the ball rolling, and Alice was in prime position to do so. For two years, she had worked hard to keep herself clean and attempt a normal life. Despite even her own expectations, for two years she had succeeded.

All of that changed when she received a call politely (but firmly) demanding her presence at Tanner Tower with the big man himself.

"So...am I in trouble?"

An awkward silence settled in.

"Is this about your Munich facility? Because if it is, I am very, very sorry. I was young, it seemed like a good idea at the time, and we really didn't get that much of your net worth. You know, considering everything. If that's, you know, why I'm here, because if it is, I can send you the Swiss bank account number and it's all yours. Well, it was all yours. I mean, it's-- you can have it back. I've just been letting it accrue interest for about ten years so...it's...your interest? It's all yours."

15

Alan Tanner stared at Alice for a few moments in silence.

"Alice?"

"Yes?"

"Until this moment, I had assumed the Munich facility was robbed by the European branch of the Dead Talon."

Well, shit. Clearly, today wouldn't be one of Alice's better days. Tanner just smiled.

"You know, seeing you sitting here in that suit, talking to me like a normal, everyday person is quite possibly the most incredible thing that I've seen in years. I would have bet my fortune that nothing could have made this possible, and went double-or-nothing on you being this...scattered, but here we are."

Alice felt a bit of her nerves slip away. She hadn't been comfortable from the get-go, but now she was becoming agitated. Before the Open Hand Act, she had instilled fear and respect. She wasn't used to being treated this way, and it struck her as decidedly demeaning.

Alan sat up and casually opened a file that was on his perfectly polished oak desk. Alice noted the file was considerably thick, which made her assume that it was important - and probably hers.

"Annalicia May Gailsone, or Dyspell as you are known to the world at large," Alan read casually in a slightly more focused voice, "currently, you are listed out as being responsible for over 28 separate acts of terror against the United States and the European Union. You are suspected in no less than 13 kidnappings, 25..." Alan stopped to erase something on the paper he was reading and correct it with his mechanical pencil, "...26 robberies and have been noted as one of the most dangerous women in the world. Your powers are based in a form of black magic that seems to focus on entropy, making you considerably dangerous to all living things. You have escaped from nearly every super

16

villain holding facility on the planet, leaving the United States no choice but to list you as one of only 12 contenders on Earth for a special stay at our new Lunar Prison facility."

Alice sat and listened calmly. Inside, she was seriously considering throwing up. Until now, she hadn't even known there *was* a lunar prison. At worst, she thought, they would throw her in the Marianas Trench again. It wasn't like she hadn't escaped from there before, but still, the moon? Also, if they had a moon facility, why was he using a pencil and paper? Alice wanted to ask, but she was scared to interrupt. Also, she remember that this was the same man who tended to use a two-way radio in an age of smartphones. Alice figured he had a thing for retro technology.

"On top of all this," Alan continued, his eyes still on the page, "you have been noted as one of the top leaders of the Purge, considered to be second only to your now *hopefully* dead boss, Alexi Golonov."

"Huh," Alice said to herself. When Alan looked up sharply, she sighed. "Oh, well, we always just called him Prometheus. It's just odd to hear his real name out loud, that's all."

"Ah, I see." Alan continued to look through his folder quietly as Alice started to squirm. After a minute of silent reading, Alan gently closed the folder, clasped his hands together and leaned in a bit on his desk, staring again at Alice's eyes.

"Alice, even with the Open Hand Act, you're only about one misstep from being in a helluva lot of trouble. You know that, right?"

Alice nodded agreeably, using her peripheral vision to quickly scan the room for exits and potential weapons. The entire outer wall was made of nothing but standard double-plate glass. Sloppy, sloppy. She was a bit disappointed in Tanner, actually. From the 22nd floor, it would be a messy fall, but she'd survived worse...

"Calm down," Alan said, "I didn't bring you here to arrest you or renege on our deal. There are easier ways to ambush someone, and it took me years to get my office just right after the last incident. Plus, I happen to like this suit - and yours. I have to say, you clean up well, Miss Gailsone."

Alice sighed. She was still relatively young, in her mid-30s, with lustrous purple hair in what she considered to be a pretty rocking bob (despite it currently hiding under an itchy, brown wig). Her naturally deep violet eyes were currently hidden behind brown contacts. Her skin was strikingly pale, her frame tall for a woman with a slender yet athletic build. She had just enough meat on her bones to absorb a blow, and just enough in the front to distract a guard. Since the whole Open Hand Act debacle, she had often considered modeling - if not for the fact that she really, *really* hated having her picture taken.

She also didn't like it when members of her community hit on her. Oh, it was flattering enough, since heroes and villains had the tendency to be built like Greek gods. Still, she had always drawn the line between business and pleasure. With the villains, she never knew if she was advancing because of her skillset or because of her body; with the heroes, it made her wonder if she was winning due to her abilities, or because they were distracted by her rack.

The other female villains told her to suck it up and that, either way, it shouldn't matter. To them, winning was winning, and *how* you moved up the rungs of power didn't matter so much as how far you could go. Alice had never liked their mindset; her time sleeping on the streets in her youth had taught her pretty damn fast that there were lines you had to draw for yourself, otherwise you might get in more trouble than you could handle. Despite her questionable career choices, she wanted to be successful at what she did in her own right.

And now here she was, in the office of the everyman hero, being hit on.

The insanely rich, hot and available everyman hero that every single woman in a cape and cowl – villainess or heroine - had enjoyed discussing as the star of at least a dozen whiskey-fueled fantasies a piece. On top of that, Alice grudgingly admitted some truth behind that the little voice in her head screaming that her love life was as dead as a doornail and *dammit, look at him, woman*!

This was creating a moral dilemma for Alice, and as a rule, she abhorred morals.

"Did you bring me here for a reason, or is this some weird hero foreplay?" Alice asked archly. Her nerves had taken flight the moment his eyes drifted to her cleavage, and her rising anger was making her hands itch. Being under scrutiny for her actions was one thing – but the way his ice-blue eyes suddenly sparked as they reached her legs was another altogether. Insanely hot or not, this was becoming degrading.

The blow-everything-up-and-run option was once again starting to brew in her head.

Alan Tanner cocked his head and smirked. "Sorry, Alice. You're very attractive, but not really my type."

Alice relaxed a bit and sat back. "So I've heard. In fact, word around the campfire is that you have an on-again, off-again thing with The Blackbird."

Alan's smile left his face as his eyes shifted away momentarily.

Alice chuckled to herself. "Hey, don't sweat it. She looks like a Greek goddess in that jumpsuit, and she's had a serious crush on you for *years*."

Alan's eyes flicked towards Alice momentarily as he cleared his throat.

"I asked you here, Alice, because I need someone with your particular skills."

Alice allowed herself a relieved smile. 'Finally', she thought, 'he's not going to arrest me, he's offering me a *job*!'

"I need you to become Dyspell again."

Alice froze in her seat, her growing smile locked on her face. "I'm sorry?"

Alan sighed. "I need Dyspell, the second-in-command of the most ruthless terrorist organization ever to walk the Earth. I need the woman who led the Purge against the Collective Good time and again, and who held her own against me, Red Guard, Superior Force, Miss Major and every other hero on the planet."

Alice settled back into her seat again, her nervousness gone, she felt herself slipping into her professional mode. Now the Alice Gailsone who had successfully reformed herself into a world-class gem transporter and appraiser came to the surface. Alan noted the shift in her body language, from her posture to her facial expression. Now he was dealing with a business woman, a manager. Now he was getting somewhere.

"There are a lot of villains still on the loose, Miss Gailsone, and many of them don't believe the government when they say that all are welcome to the Open Hand Act. Most think it's a trap, others just don't see the point. We... I believe that given a chance, many of the world's villains could reform as successfully as you have. They all have amazing skillsets that could net them a fortune in the private sector and do some serious good for mankind, but I can't reach them. None of us can."

Alice nodded. She saw where this was going. "You think that I can convince them to turn over a new leaf? To forget their lives of crime? That's very flattering, and I do mean that, not in the bitchy super-villainess way but in the wow-you-considered-me way, but I don't think I'm the right person for the job."

"I do," Alan said, his voice firm. "You're one of the most feared and respected people in our community. When the Open Hand Act was first proposed to Congress, many said that it was dangerous to let certain members of the criminal world back into society. In fact, it was your name that was cited above all others. When you came to me, out of the blue and on your own, I had to fight to get your application approved. I promised the courts that I would let myself be held personally responsible if anything happened as a result of your pardon, and as far as I'm concerned it was the best decision I ever made.

"Now look at you, one of the first to sign and reform, and here you are, a wealthy, confident business woman in charge of her own worldwide corporation. You didn't earn that because you were a villain or because of your powers, you did it through savvy, confidence and intelligence. You did it because you are a leader, Alice Gailsone, and now you're proving it to the world."

Alice nodded slightly, but inside she was hopping up and down. It wasn't every day that your most feared adversary paid you the biggest complement you had ever received. Of course it was all true; part of the Open Hand Act had been to include a fresh start for all that wanted it. All Alice had asked for was that her name be purged from all records and databases. She wanted to keep her real name, but she wanted it fresh, and the government had grudgingly obliged by creating a 'clone' identity with a new social security number. While one Alice Gailsone was known for acts of terror, the other would be known for nothing more remarkable than a parking ticket or two. The Alice Gailsone who had once held entire cities hostage and defeated legions was gone forever In her place was Alice Gailsone, the common, ordinary every-woman with no criminal background whatsoever.

From that point on in her life, everything she had, she had built on her own. Her years of stealing rare gems had paid off in a big way, as her expertise was now considered second to none in the jewelry business. These were all things that she probably never would have accomplished while in the Purge, but they were things that made her proud. All things considered, Alice didn't think she minded being a clone.

Alice knew that the compliments weren't just to butter her up; he was right. She also knew that there were few people on the planet who could plan like Blackthorne, which meant that this conversation wasn't an erratic choice on his part. This was carefully thought out to the last detail, and while she was usually a good mental match for the man across the table, even she had to admit that outside of a jeweler's office or working with customs officials, she was a little rusty at this particular game.

"Mr. Tanner, what exactly did you have in mind?"

Alan smiled a bit. It was a smile Alice had seen before, but usually when wearing a skin tight purple jumpsuit and on a face covered mostly in nightmares and black cloth. Alice began to feel a bit uneasy.

"I want you to put a little team together, Miss Gailsone."

Alice paused. This was not what she had been expecting him to say.

"I'm...sorry?" was all she could get out. Smiling that same, devilish smile, Alan picked up a remote and clicked it towards a window to his left. Both parties turned their chairs as a screen dropped down, obscuring the sunlight behind it. From the wall behind them, a projector started its soft hum.

"It is my belief that the super villain community needs to see a familiar face come forward and work for the greater good. Most villains have reformed quietly, slipping into their private lives nicely. For those that can't, I propose a new team of heroes be created. You of all people can appreciate being offered a second chance, I'm sure."

Alice crossed her legs and settled in for the show. On the screen, newsroom archive footage of villains, some she knew, some she did not, flickered from fight to fight. She noted one in particular appeared in no less than three different clips.

"I never figured you for liking the Lotus so much. Asian ladies your thing, Mr. Tanner?"

Alan smiled, "I was hoping you would notice. Lotus, also known as Nanami Fukijima, is with whom I would like you to start. She's been cut adrift since the Dead Talon fell, and my sources tell me she's a strong candidate for reform."

"Nice use of whom. You never hear that anymore. Also, did your sources give you that name? Because I'm pretty sure that isn't her name."

Alan shot her a rather cross look. "I am quite sure."

Alice smirked, "Of course you are. Did your sources tell you that Nanami Fukijima is also the name of a wheelchair-bound bookstore owner in Nagoya?"

Alan stared at Alice as though she had just grown horns.

Alice let out a little laugh. "Oh my God, you didn't know? Nanami is her sister, and Fukijima is her name by marriage. Lotus borrowed it in case people like you ever came snooping around. She figured there was no way you'd ever believe Nanami was her."

Alan just stared.

"How could you possibly know that?"

Alice shrugged. "You may be the number one go-to good guy for info, but you forget, I was Prometheus's head lady for years. Who do you think was responsible for maintaining his global operations? The Lotus was part of our exchange program with the Dead Talon when we were making our push into Asia. I even ran point with her once on an art heist in Bangkok. You remember, the one with the Van Gogh? Yeah, I think that was you that was pursuing us..."

Alan scribbled something on a notepad, his voice devoid of humor. "This is all news to me. Again, my sources tell me that she is a prime candidate for reform and that if anyone should be recruited, it's her."

Alice shook her head. "Your sources might be full of it. Again, I've worked with Lotus before; we were on that assigned gig in Bangkok together about four years ago and I got a pretty good feel for her, then. She's strong, quiet and very, very not nice. She is honor-bound to serve the Dead Talon and can drink like a koi. She is about as Not Hero as they come, and she really has no qualms about killing anyone who says otherwise."

"Be that as it may, I would like you to cut your teeth on this one, if you don't mind."

Alice straightened in her seat, looked Alan in the eye and smiled.

"No, thank you."

Alan paused for a moment.

"I'm sorry?"

Alice nodded. "I said 'no thank you.' This is a generous offer, and I love what you're trying to do, but I have a life now. A real, non-super-powered life, and I've done what the government asked of me. I've kept my head down, followed the rules and contributed. I've contributed a ton. I see no reason to do this or any other super-related thing, and to be honest while you may be kind of hot, I see absolutely no sane reason to work with or for a man who I routinely tried to kill in the recent past."

Alan nodded.

Alice stood and straightened her skirt. "Well, this has been a very pleasant surprise. I honestly expected this to be a trap and was wondering if I had done enough stretching in the ladies room ahead of time to deal with you."

Alice extended her hand and briskly shook Alan's before turning towards the door. "To be fair, I'm woefully out of practice at what we used to do, but still, a lady should always put her best face forward. I was half-expecting a chemical narcotic or maybe an electromagnetic ray, or…"

"We can save your mother, Alice."

Alice stopped.

She didn't go rigid, she didn't whip around. She simply stopped in the doorway, her back to Alan as he continued.

"I've looked into your case more than any other. You didn't reform because you wanted to, or because you were tired of being a villain, you did it because three days before you came to me your mother was diagnosed with the early stages of lung cancer. For all of the crimes you've committed, you were afraid that you would be in prison when she finally died, and you wanted her to see that you were better than she had thought. You wanted her to die proud of you."

Alice stood silently.

"Alice, I've researched the cancer treatments available to her, and I can tell you right now, she is going to die. By all rights, her treatments should have caught it early, but they didn't and now... The medicine on the market right now is good and the money you've thrown at this is borderline insane, especially in your efforts to keep her at home instead of a center, but it can't reverse what's going on in her body. All she can hope for is maybe six more months before the chemo whittles her down to nothing."

Alice had a calm, unmoving stance that Alan had difficulty reading. It was beginning to make him uncomfortable.

"Alice, her insurance won't cover what she needs. Your mother needs..."

"I know what my mother needs," Alice said softly. "My mother needs a Phoenix. It's the only thing that could possibly save her, but they're all gone. Prometheus found each one and destroyed them, and I helped him. My mother is going to die, and it's my fault."

Alan nodded. "It's true that he found all seven, one for each continent."

25

Alice started to go again, not wanting to cry in the office of her greatest enemy.

"He never bothered to look for the eighth."

Alice stopped again.

"There isn't an eighth," Alice said. "There was only one Phoenix per continent, and they're all gone now."

"What about the Atlantean Phoenix?"

Alice turned around, locking eyes with Alan. Alan noted that there were tears running down her cheeks.

"There is no Atlantean Phoenix."

"What if I told you there was? What if I told you we had written records of it and the temple it was stored in?"

Alice took a hesitant step back towards Alan. His face was completely serious, and Alice noted that all the sarcasm and judgment was gone from his eyes.

"You found it? You actually found the Atlantean Phoenix?"

Alan shook his head. "No, but Poseidon thinks he knows where it is."

The Phoenix Statues, statues carved from an ancient meteorite that had crashed into earth centuries ago, were considered by many to be the greatest treasure on the planet. The strange gemstone that had been used in their carving was found to give all who touched it prolonged life and good health. They were known to cure all disease and were even known to heal the lands that they were kept in. They had been one of Prometheus's first targets as head of the Purge, as he didn't want mankind having any form of escape from his global plagues.

"Once it is found, the line of sick and wounded that will need to be cured will be huge. It will literally change the world, and my company is working to make sure that everyone on the planet who needs it will have access. Everyone, including your mother."

Alice looked Alan Tanner dead in the eye.

"Are you saying that if I refuse to help you, you won't let my mother be healed?"

Alan shook his head. "I'm saying that she's welcome to come like anyone else, but if her daughter would assist us in this project, she would be moved to the front of that endless line. Past the crippled and dying, past the children and scientists and gifted contributors of society, and everyone else that has just as much of a desperate and equally valid claim to the statue's powers as she does.

"The Phoenix can heal, but it takes time and exposure and it doesn't work on crowds. It has to be one on one, and I promised the leaders of the world that if we did this, if the Phoenix was real and brought back to civilization, that there would be no favorites, that it would be a true and fair first-come, first-serve as it was taken around the world to heal and mend.

"What I can offer you Alice, is the promise, my promise, that your mother would be wheeled to the front of the line. Even if you say no, I'll do my best to get her exposure as fast as I can, but I have been granted special authority from thew UN to go against policy in this one, special instance. Do this for me, and I can assure you she'll be cured the moment we have it back."

Alice stared down the most frightening man in her life as she weighed her options. She knew that Alan Tanner was a man of his word, that if he said he would help even if she said no, then he would. She knew that it was a big deal to be offered a chance like this, and that her mother did not have very much longer to go. She weighed all of this as she stared down the greatest hero on the planet and considered his offer.

"We can also pay you," Alan casually said, "I know this is asking a lot, taking you away from your day job and all. Have you ever wondered how much of a kickback heroes in the Collective Good receive?"

Alice shrugged, "I figured you were all too altruistic to care about money."

Alan laughed and scratched the back of his head. "Well, we are heroes, but we still have to eat. I'm rich, so I don't take a cut, but for heroes like the Red Guard, this is their primary source of income. By the way, it's a *helluva* income."

Alice stared at the ground as she thought. She thought about the man in front of her, about her life and why it was the way it was. She thought of how easy it would be to just slip right back into what she had done, to get as much money as she could and do it her way. She thought about how he was right, and that no matter what she threw at the cancer, it would do nothing but destroy her mother.

"I need some time," She said. Alan nodded and handed her his card. She smirked a bit and handed it back.

"Alan, I had your phone bugged for three years. I know your number."

Alan smiled and handed it back. "I know. It was a fake. I had yours bugged for four."

Alice Gailsone left the office of the world's most powerful man with the weight of the world on her shoulders.

Chapter 2

A Matter of Personal Interest

Then

***

With her niece propped under her arm and an unconscious hero lying in the alley behind her, Alice suddenly didn't care anymore about the burning remains of her airship, the smoldering tatters of her costume or even what would happen next. As they left the alley and hailed a cab in the bustling den of madness and confusion that was forming from the wreckage coming down in fiery waves a few miles away, Alice looked at her niece and came to a decision.

They quickly climbed into the cab and Alice provided an address for a hospital outside of Pittsburg. Nodding, the cabby headed north, keeping to the side streets to avoid the gridlock on the interstate. "I think it's time to retire," She said quietly to herself as the cab rumbled on, its occupants all happy to be heading away from the city.

Two hours later, in a quiet community on the outskirts of Pittsburg, Alice burst through the doors of the hospital, screaming and sobbing about how some Purge soldiers had tried to sexually assault both her and Allison.

"Oh my God, they, they pinned us down! They just kept hitting! Oh, please! Please help us, I think her ribs are broken!" Alice yelled and sobbed as she entered the emergency room entrance. Under her arm, she heard a mostly prone Allison start to snicker.

"Shut. Up." Alice mumbled under her breath. "Jesus, you weight a ton. Did you just eat bon-bons for the last two weeks?"

"I still have a taser. Say something again about my weight," the auburn youth replied quietly.

Instantly, the nurses on duty sprang into action and before long, Allison was in a hospital bed, an IV in her arm and her ribs being examined by a doctor.

"You say a man did this to you?"

Allison nodded while Alice waited in a chair off to the side. The doctor looked a bit closer.

"There are burn marks on your body," he said, his voice leaning toward disbelief.

"They... They pinned me against the side of a truck. It was running, and the metal was hot. Doctor, can you do anything for me?" Allison put on her best puppy-dog eyes. This time Alice had to cover her mouth to hide a snicker.

That night, Alice stayed in the vinyl chair beside her young assistant and tried to sleep, but she couldn't drift off over the constant noise of police sirens in the distance. Pittsburg was under lock down as Purge members were being rounded up and fires were being put out. The mayor had asked the President to declare Pittsburg a Federal Disaster Area, and the National Guard had been flown in. In technical terms, it was a complete mess.

Alice tried to watch the news, but the stations were all reporting the same story, how the *Argent* had crashed in Pittsburg and killed hundreds if not thousands of innocent civilians. Alice could only take so much of the footage of dead bodies piling up, of the ship exploding and then imploding, of her people dying, before she shut it off.

Alice sighed heavily to herself. All she could think was '*how could I have let it get this bad?*' It wasn't like she had really set out for something on this scale to occur; she had seen the *Argent* as a means for extortion and that was that. In fact, had she been able to do what she wanted, the *Argent* would have wound up in low Earth orbit to serve as a new orbiting base. It was designed for that, it was meant for that and most importantly *all* of its defenses were geared towards that. When the UN and Collective Good arrived and attacked before they had even gotten five miles up, it had been a slaughter.

Alice noticed that Allison was stirring. She went over to her charge and put her hand on the young girl's head. "Hey you, get some rest, okay? We probably need to bail come morning."

Allison, who had been playing with a small, white plastic card that she was slowly flipping between her fingers, looked to her boss and stared quietly for a long time. Finally, she spoke up in a quiet, tired voice and said, "You could have died up there, trying to get me out. Why did you save me?"

Alice looked at her for a moment. "Because I'm your aunt, dummy."

Allison shook her head. "I was awake when you were talking with Blackbird. Why not just tell her the truth? Just tell her you were done?"

Alice shot her a cross glare. "Because what the Hell good would that have done? You think that woman would ever give up a chance to see me hanged? You forget that where she lacks in powers she makes up for in sheer bitch-drive on a level that no one can match. It takes some serious steel make your way into the Collective Good without any actual superpowers other than kung-fu and a brain, and she did it. No way am I going to believe that she'd just be fine with us asking for a mulligan. Besides, it's not like I'm gonna start bonding with an enemy just because we nearly died together."

Allison closed her eyes. "You should have left me to die."

Alice looked at her for a moment. "That's the Vicodin talking. My job is to make money, serve our respective employer and do the best I can do with what I have, and nowhere in there does 'murder families' fit. I

31

don't know if you've ever noticed, but I rarely kill *anyone* if I can help it."

Allison sighed a little and leaned back into her pillow. "You always *were* a shitty bad guy. God, I hurt. I don't know that I can move."

Alice sighed and patted her head. "I know. I wouldn't, if I were you. Just get some rest, okay?"

Allison closed her eyes and tried to turn on her side. She clutched the small, white, plastic card from before in her fist. Her fingers covered the small green square in its center as she drew her arms as close to her chest as she could, only to be poked by the card. Allison opened her eyes and stared at the card as tears started softly falling from her eyes. "I'm sorry, Alice." The words were quiet, but Alice heard them.

"Shhh... hey, it's okay. You just get some rest, alright? You just get some good rest and tomorrow we'll probably have to shoot our way out of here, which will be difficult without guns, but we'll improvise. Now sleep. It's okay."

"Sorry..." Allison said again as she drifted off.

Alice watched as the younger girl passed out from a mix of exhaustion and Vicodin. She tucked in her niece and then finally the now former super villain settled into her chair. Despite still being keyed up, Alice closed her eyes and after a bit, let herself drift off to a blessedly dreamless sleep.

Now

***

Alice didn't go back to her work. She didn't call in to let her staff know what was going on. She walked right by her favorite diner and took the train away from her tiny but loved studio apartment and headed north to a tiny, cozy-looking brownstone on the Upper West Side. She used her key copy at the door, nodded to the doorman and headed up the four flights of stairs to the small apartment at the end of the hall.

The nurse was getting ready to leave when Alice opened the door. Alice noted the time, and knew that the night girl would be there soon. In the center of the room was a clean, sterile medical cot, and on it, in a fuzzy robe and connected to several machines, sat a small, wilted form that Alice had once recognized easily.

Mrs. Gailsone looked at her daughter and smiled a huge, warm smile. Alice instantly knew that this was the high point of her mother's day.

"Well, to what do I owe the pleasure? It's not every day that the world's best jewel appraiser comes calling at my door."

Alice took her mother's hand and sat down beside her bed. With a glance from Alice, the nurse knew she was not welcome for this conversation and headed to the next room to give the ladies some privacy.

"So what's up? Are you here to discuss that treatment center in Dallas again? Honestly, I don't think I would feel comfortable with..."

"No, no, it's not that. It's... a matter of personal interest."

Alice's mother eyed her for a moment. "A matter of personal interest? You make it sound so formal. Honey, tell me what's on your mind."

It took Alice some time to get her thoughts together before she was able to speak.

"Mom... I was offered a job today."

Mrs. Gailsone smiled and squeezed her daughter's hand. "Another customer? That's so wonderful to hear, dear."

Alice smiled and struggled to figure out how to word things correctly. As far as her mother was concerned, Alice had been on the street for years, not ruling it with an iron fist. As far as Alice knew, her mother considered her a delinquent who cleaned her life up in a big way, and she aimed to keep it that way.

"Mom... if you were given the chance to do something... something important, but something that you didn't want to do... how do I put this? I... If you were told you had the chance to do the most important thing you could do, but to do it meant giving up a lot of what you had worked for, would you?"

Alice's mother stared at her for a moment as concern started to cross her face. "Honey, is someone making you do something you don't want to?"

Alice sighed. "Yes...no...I don't know. This client could mean a chance at a new treatment for you, and that you might be okay. I don't want to get your hopes up, but this feels like a really good deal, but..."

Mrs. Gailsone sighed and cupped both of her daughter's hands in hers.

"You know, I always worried about you out there in the world. I always knew you had it in you to do something good and not that awful Purge work you were into for so long. You may not see yourself as a good person honey, but in doing what you've done, you've shown that you can be a *great* person. I just wish you could see that greatness. I wish you could see where that greatness could truly take you."

Alice smiled. "Thanks, mom. That means a..."

Alice froze, her eyes were as wide as saucers.

"Mom? Did you just say, 'that awful Purge work'?"

Mrs. Gailsone patted her daughter's head, and then gently removed her daughters wig. "Seriously honey, did you think I was an idiot? How many beautiful pale girls with purple hair are there in the world? Did you think a domino mask would hide who you were from me? I'm your mother; I know what my child looks like."

Alice sat in mute shock as her mother pointed past her to a bookshelf. On it were two oversized photo albums she had never noticed before.

"Bring me those, dear. I think it's time we had a talk. A very long talk."

"Mom...I...I don't..."

"Honey, cut the crap. I'm dying and I'm not proud of what you did, but I am your mother and you are my only living daughter and at a certain point, a parent has to suck it up and be supportive of their child's decisions, even if they don't agree with them. I just wish you would have told me, is all."

"Told you about my... You make it sound like I was busted for pot. There's a reason I never... Mom, I once held the city of Flagstaff hostage. There were buses full of school children dangling by a filament over the Grand Canyon. I did it because we had extra funds in the budget and I was trying to justify the hiring of some new help. That's who I was, mom. That was a Tuesday for me. Mom... Mom, I am *not* a good person."

"That's a load of bull. You're my daughter, and I know the woman I raised. You may have done some things that were wrong, but you stepped up when it mattered. How many of those children did you actually drop, dear?"

"Well...none, but..."

"And I don't think you would have, even if push had come to shove."

"You don't know that, mother."

"No, dear, but I know you."

Alice struggled for the words. For a woman who used to routinely address the nation via radio broadcast, Alice felt ridiculous. Her mother, without even trying, always seemed to have that effect on her. All at once, Alice felt like she was six and had to confess to smashing the cookie jar when she was reaching for it on the kitchen counter.

"Mom, I'm a killer, alright? I took assignments in the Purge all the time that required liquidation of targets. Believe me when I say I was, I am not... look, I was about as evil as they come, okay?"

"If that were true, you would have just dropped those children and been done with it. Don't bullshit me, dear. I'm dying, and my desire to play politics is non-existent. I'm sure you did have to do some awful things, but how many of those things were done because you didn't have a choice?"

Alice fidgeted, "But... mom, I was really, really good at it."

Her mother shrugged. "And I'm sure soldiers in the field are good at what they do, too. I wouldn't hold the actions of a GI accountable when they were in combat, so I couldn't do the same for you, now could I? Honey, I have always loved you, even when you were... not very nice."

"But... but you never..."

Mrs. Gailsone shrugged. "I figured you would tell me when you were ready, and I was so touched by what you did for me when you came forward that I was willing to forgive what had happened. Besides, at the rate I'm going I don't know how long I'll be able to have this conversation with you, so let's just have it already. Now bring me those two photo albums."

Dumbly, Alice stood and went to the bookshelf. As she picked up the albums, she remembered a time at least two lifetimes ago when she would stack her dolls and action figures on that shelf as they battled it out for world domination. Even then, her career path had been pretty obvious.

Mrs. Gailsone took the photo albums and patted the first one. "This," she said, a bit of a tremble in her voice, "I made when I realized that you were parading around as a super villain. I have to tell you, I was mad about that for a very long time. Not at you, but at myself. I blamed myself for the choices you had made, and I hated myself for it for years."

"Mom..."

"Hush, I'm bonding with you. Don't spoil it." Mrs. Gailsone opened the album and showed it to Alice. Inside were newspaper clippings of her battles with Superior Force, the Red Guard, Poseidon and the rest of the Collective Good.

"I tried to look at it as best I could," Mrs. Gailsone said, "I told myself, at least she can hold her own as an independent woman, and it's not everyone who can knock the world's heroes on their ears. Then you started dating that Prometheus and that...honey, what did you ever see in him?"

Alice bristled. "I never dated him. Ever. He was my employer, and I have a rule about getting involved with coworkers. Besides, he... he didn't prefer the company of women, mother."

Mrs. Gailsone stared at her daughter for a minute.

"He was...what word is politically correct now? Fancy?"

Alice sighed. "Sure, why not?"

Mrs. Gailsone shrugged. "Hmph. Well, I suppose that's his own business. I always hoped it was something like that. I always told myself you could do so much better."

Alice stared at her mother for a moment. "Mom, he tried to murder every man, woman and child in Costa Rica because someone there ran a news story about him, and you're focused on his private preferences? *That's* really what sticks out with you?"

Mrs. Gailsone shrugged and flipped through the album, looking with her daughter at photos of the most dangerous woman in the world. They kept looking, and as they did, Alice found herself telling stories she had never told anyone. She told her mother about team-ups and death traps, about drinking contests and situations where she had partnered with heroes out of desperation. Stories about time travel, about being in space, about what the heroes and villains were like behind closed doors. She talked about crushes and friends, about conquests and heartbreak.

They looked until the night nurse arrived, and even then Alice only got up to make them some tea. It was the first time since she had been 14 that Alice had just opened up to another soul. It was liberating. It was a slumber party. It was her confessional, and it was the single greatest evening she had ever experienced.

They read articles and shared stories until 1:00 in the morning, but to Alice, it only felt like minutes.

"I never in a million years thought I could talk to you about this, you know." Alice said as she sloshed the cold remnants of her tea.

"Honey, I never in a million years thought that you would. I prayed for it, but I never thought this would happen."

"Still, I'm just floored that you collected all of these. I would have… well, honestly if I had been you I don't know what I would have done."

Mrs. Gailsone looked at her daughter, and the look she gave her made Alice feel very young and very small. Even though her mother was powerless and immobilized in a bed as cancer continued to gnaw away at her, the grave look she gave Alice made her feel very, very small indeed.

"Young lady. I kept these because I wanted to remember you, and for years, this was as close as I could get. This book wasn't started out of pride, but out of desperation. I thought you were going to get killed doing what you did. And then you stopped, you came forward when no one else would and suddenly, you were at my door in that stupid wig, acting as if nothing had happened. Did you really, honestly think I never knew?"

Alice stared at her feet. "Kinda, yeah."

Mrs. Gailsone shook her head.

"Honey, there is only one thing that could make you come here tonight and start talking to me the way that you did. Someone asked you to put that costume back on, didn't they?"

Alice nodded.

"Well, who is it? One of your old co-workers?"

"No."

"Are you planning a heist? If you need money..."

"God, no. Mom, I'm rich."

"From the robberies?"

"No! Mom, the jewelry business. I'm making money hand over fist. It's not... no mom, I don't need money. I'm paying for your treatments, remember?"

"I know, dear. I was just worried. So...who's pressuring my little girl?"

"It's...it's Blackthorne."

Mrs. Gailsone's eyes widened. "Oh."

"He wants me to lead a team. He says it would be good for PR, and help some of the other villains step forward."

Mrs. Gailsone took her daughter by the chin and raised her gaze to meet her own. "And what do you want, dear?"

Alice felt herself starting to tear up as her mother held her face.

"I just want you better, mom. Blackthorne thinks he knows a way to cure you, and he's willing to pull some strings if I do this."

Mrs. Gailsone shook her head. "Do you want to put that costume back on, or not?"

Alice choked back a sob. "I don't know! I don't... look, that life was... it's incredible, mom. It's the ultimate rush. It's better than anything. Money, sex, it tops them all, and the power and control is mind blowing. I had to get out or it was going to kill me. You have no idea what it's like... once you go down that road... God, mom, I get why rock stars burn out, but this was 1,000 times more insane!"

"Are you scared that you'll go back to being what you were?"

Alice nodded. "I can't do that. If I do, you'll be alone, and I don't want you to spend your last... I don't want you seeing me as a failure. I want to prove that I can be better than that. I don't know that I can do it behind a mask."

Alice felt herself choke a bit as her mother wiped a tear from her face.

"Honey, you don't do a thing you don't feel comfortable doing. If you never put that costume back on and keep being the bright successful woman that you are, I will be proud. If you decide to do this and help the world's greatest heroes, I will still be proud. If you change your mind, and decide it's time to run the world, well, I can think of worse choices. I will be proud of you because you are my daughter, and because I love you. I have always loved you, and I could not be more proud of who you have become if I tried."

Her mother wrapped her frail arms around her daughter in a loving hug. While she would never, ever admit to it, Alice Gailsone always crumbled when hugged. Maybe it was because it just never happened to her, or maybe because the only person in the world who ever did hug her was her mother. Either way, in that moment, Alice felt stronger than she ever had and more frail than anything on the planet, all at once.

Alice stayed with her mother until she fell asleep. She prepped her mother's pills and tucked her in and logged the medications for the nurse. When Alice was ready to go home and had said her goodbyes, she finally remembered the second album her mother had brought down. Curious, she quietly slipped back into her mother's living room and opened the book.

It was another, smaller collection of news clippings and pictures, but this one didn't contain pictures of super heroes or villains. This one had articles about diamond traders and ruby exporters, and about a young woman who had gained fame with her meteoric rise in the gemstone world.

Alice quietly put both books back on the shelf and left without another word.

***

Alan Tanner was not a man accustomed to surprises. He was the Blackthorne, and as such, was always one step ahead of things in general. He made it his business to plan for every eventuality, for every surprise and unexpected situation that could come his way.

He knew that Alice Gailsone would be a hard sell, and that her pride alone would prohibit her from saying yes right away. He also knew that the pressure of the decision would sit with her for at least a few days before he received a call, and that the call would be short and direct, informing him on her terms that she agreed.

He knew this because that was what he had planned for. He was very good at reading people, and very good at planning around what he read. He knew his secretary would have his coffee ready for him on his desk when he came in at 7:15 a.m. He knew that his paper would be set slightly off center due to her holding it with her left hand as she placed the coffee on his desk. He knew that from the 14 seconds she would stay in his office, the area around his desk would smell slightly of lavender for at least 10 minutes as he read his headlines. He knew this because he saw patterns in everything, and prided himself on it.

This is probably why he was surprised when he opened his office door to find Alice Gailsone sitting in his chair, her legs propped up on his desk as she sipped his coffee and read his paper.

"Mr. Tanner," she said without looking up, "Are you aware that for years, the combination to your emergency office escape hatch has always contained a variation of one of three dates? I would guess they have something to do with your family or former sidekicks, but, honestly, I never really cared enough to do the research. Still, awfully sloppy of you."

Alan Tanner slowly straightened his tie as he surveyed his office. Everything seemed in place, but he did notice that the painting behind his desk was slightly askew.

"You noticed the painting behind me is slightly askew, didn't you? I took the liberty of rooting through your files to see what else you know about me. No, I didn't have the combination and yes, I did rot the lock off. You'll want to vacuum."

Alice held up her file, the contents half scattered on the desk. "I'm both flattered and embarrassed that my measurements are in here. Why are my measurements in your files, Mr. Tanner? Did you take them in my sleep?"

Again, Alan Tanner felt a bit taken off guard as he fumbled for an answer. This was not the morning he had planned.

Before he could offer a response, Alice tossed the coffee she was drinking at his face. Surprised, Alan raised his arm to block as Alice leapt over the desk with cat-like grace, spun around and planted her foot square against Alan's neck, slamming him against his door and pinning him as Alice stared him down, her eyes boring into him as she spoke.

"Mr. Tanner, I want you to promise me that my mother will receive care first. No forms, no waiting, no world leaders in front of her. I want her wheeled to the front of the line, ready to go. I want her to park there until every shred of cancer is gone from her body and she can stand up, lift that chair over her head and throw it out the nearest window. You will get her healed, you will pay her medical expenses and then you will fund a three month vacation to the most hedonistic island that money can buy, and you will personally make sure that her days are filled to the brim with cold alcohol and warm young men waiting to rub her feet, fluff her pillows and God knows what else. You do that for me, you heal her and make her happy, and I'll get you your team."

Alan Tanner smiled, but before he could respond, the foot against his throat tightened as Alice continued.

"I am not going to forget that you used my mother's health to get me to do this for you. I don't care how you dress it up or what you tell yourself; you used her sickness to manipulate me. It's what *I* would have done - but I was a *villain*, Mr. Tanner. I was expected to do things like that. So, let me do something else a villain would be expected to do. Let me make a threat.

"If you go back on your word, or if she dies...I will kill you, Mr. Tanner. It won't be quick, and it sure as Hell won't be clean. I will kill you and everyone you have ever loved, hired, spoken to or even *thought* about. I will hunt down your distant relatives, friends, teachers and even their pets. I will not be played, and I *will not* see her die. Do you understand, Mr. Tanner?"

43

Alice removed her foot and gave Alan a moment to catch his breath. After a moment of consideration, he nodded and extended his hand. "Thank you, Miss Gailsone. I believe we have a deal."

"I'll need something to wear," She said as she firmly shook it, "and call me Dyspell."

Chapter 3

Toys, Tasers and Confessions

Then

***

It was early morning when Blackbird, the most respected and feared female member of the Collective Good and scourge of the criminal underworld, awoke in a back alley with a screaming headache. At first, she couldn't remember what happened, but then she saw the escape pod parked in front of her and it all came rushing back. With a grunt, she pulled herself to her feet and limped down the alley to the nearby hospital.

With everything that had happened over the last 24 hours, it only took a moment for her to confirm her identity to the scattered masses of law enforcement on duty. After some moments of convincing the nearby medics that she was fine, she was given access to a police cruiser and started scanning the reports for something suspicious. Unfortunately, with all that had happened, this meant that there were no less than 17,000 different reports to comb through in the time period that she was looking in. She was beginning to think that she wouldn't find what she was looking for, but then she hit pay dirt; a report of two young women, one with rib injuries, reporting a sexual assault at a suburban hospital.

"Gotcha," Blackbird said to herself. She turned the keys in the ignition and gunned the accelerator, surprising the nearby police officers that were actually in charge of the car.

A few barked commands on the CB and in short order, Blackbird had every available police and SWAT member gathered outside the suburban hospital, armed, nervous and ready for the worst. The authorities waited on strict command for Blackbird to arrive, and once she did, a quick interrogation of the nursing staff revealed that two women claiming to be sisters, one pale with a bob of purple hair and the other with several broken ribs, had been admitted last night. After a quick call to the Pittsburg PD gathered outside, the lobby swarmed with armed officers, ready for a fight.

According to the front desk, the two suspects were currently on the third floor in a corner observation room. Blackbird and the rest of the officers came up the stairwell on the opposite end. After cracking the door, she signaled for the nurse on duty to come over and told her the situation. Quickly, every nurse on the floor was evacuated to the first floor. Blackbird watched them scurry by until all but two were accounted for. The other stairwell was covered and there were officers on the roof. Every road for 8 square blocks had been cordoned off. There was no way out, and a smiling Blackbird knew it.

"Okay, that should be all of them," the head nurse said. Several of the on duty RN's had been helping with surgeries and were still bloody, having literally just been pulled out of a completed operation. Blackbird gathered her thoughts and signaled the officer on duty. Even though she was a costumed fighter, Blackbird was considered a U.S. Marshal due to her membership in the Collective Good. As a result, she took point, armed with an automatic weapon provided by the somewhat nervous SWAT team.

With a signaled count of three, Blackbird burst into the room in question, followed immediately by a flood of SWAT. Every officer in the room pointed their guns at the two figures in the room and screamed for them to get down, only to realize they were already seated on the bed, their hands bound and their mouths gagged.

"Nurses. They got out with the nurses!" Blackbird nearly screamed as she pushed back through the flood of officers, the two captive RNs behind her mumbling in their gags and nodding frantically.

Two hours earlier, two nurses had decided to get off shift early. It was still pre-dawn, and there wasn't any reason to suspect that something was amiss about two young women in scrubs calmly walking out the front doors. No one had noticed at all in the early morning hours as two women casually hailed a cab and took off for parts unknown, and no one questioned it, as everyone was still focused on what was going on downtown.

The flight to Japan from New York was listed as 19 hours long.

Alice glared at her itinerary with a feeling of dread boiling inside her. She hated flying. She hated sitting in the same chair for more than 20 minutes. She hated filling out paperwork for her new job. Most of all, she seriously hated the looks her new 'coworkers' gave her as she was taken on the Tanner Tower guided tour.

Alan Tanner had converted the entire top 10 floors of his company's skyscraper into his own custom super hero facility. There were training rooms, holographic projectors, arsenal chambers, science labs and oodles of future-tech scattered all around. It reminded her of a living room on Christmas morning, if that living room had been in the home of Nikola Tesla's children, and Tesla had zero scruples about personal safety and infinite dollars to spend on his kids. She felt a wave of nostalgia for the old Purge tech centers she used to oversee. At least there the employees looked at you with fear and respect. Here...not so much.

There were a lot of dirty looks from a lot of breakable faces. Oh, they knew how dangerous she was – they just assumed she wouldn't be touring the great halls of Tanner's super dome if the Man didn't have her under his thumb. They were wrong, but she certainly wasn't in a position to demonstrate. It made Alice uncomfortable to the point that she caught herself nervously cracking her knuckles with her thumb, and she was not one to tolerate feeling uncomfortable for long.

Still, she reminded herself, this was work, and it was called work for a reason. While she may not like any part of it, she had always been a professional.

Overall, the tour was pretty miserable until she met a man who looked eerily familiar to her. In R&D, a young, shaggy, red-headed scientist popped up from one of the experiment tables scattered around and glided over to shake Alice's hand. Alice noted that he was actually gliding; his feet weren't touching the floor at all. The man was wispy, covered in freckles and had to move his goggles off his face to reveal two huge, brown eyes.

"Hi, I'm Steve," The young man said, "I've been put in charge of your gear. You know, the basics; making sure you don't die and all."

Alice shook the young man's hand. "Thank you," she said, "Believe me, I know the value of having some toys in the field, but I actually have my own power set. I don't know what all you were told, but I'm…"

"You're Dyspell, the greatest criminal mind of the 21st Century," said Steve as he glided/led her over to a table with a steel wardrobe beside it, "and you may have incredible abilities, but it never hurts to have some back up gadgets. Don't you watch any films? Good guys always carry gadgets."

"For one thing, this isn't a film. And wait, what about Superior Force? Isn't he just one big, indestructible flying tank with lasers? What does he need?"

"Well for starters, the guy can't breathe in space," Alan said from behind her. Alan seemed to be half paying attention to Steve and Alice, and half surveying his lab assistants as they worked in the skating rink-sized research room. "He keeps a compressed air supply in his belt for other-worldly trips. Steve has been assigned to you personally to make sure you're taken care of. He's studied you extensively, so I would pay attention to what he has to say."

Alice nodded and then paused.

"How extensively?"

Steve swallowed and abruptly turned to focus on his work station. "Here we have an all-new utility belt for you. I know your old belt was just a belt, but this one has some really cool stuff. For starters, there is a 2-way communication system, complete with GPS locator, located in the front side pocket."

Alice opened the pocket and took out the slick, black rectangle.

"Wow," Alice said drily, "I have one of these, too. It's called a phone. Brilliant."

Steve calmly took the phone and unlocked it. Then he pointed it at the nearest wall and pressed the ringer control on the side. A blast of electricity shot out of it, melting a hole in the wall and causing Alice to yelp with shock.

"It's a bit better than your phone. You can only do that once per charge, but it can be set to shock the hell out of anyone trying to make a call. You'll find the settings in the application titled PhoneBuddy. It can be voice activated, too."

Steve plugged the phone into a charging cable and pointed it at another spot on the wall.

"If it's plugged in, you can usually eke out another shot before the circuit board starts to melt. Ideally, try not to use this feature more than once per hour. PhoneBuddy," he called out, "Fire!"

Alan and Alice watched as precisely nothing happened.

Steve stood still for a moment, and then groaned. "I forgot to hold down the voice command button. PhoneBuddy! Fire!"

This time, a jet of electricity shot out and made a twin hole next to the old one.

"You really need to explore the options, and *be careful* what you ask PhoneBuddy to do," Steve warned as he put the phone back in the belt. "Now, look here. I've included several fun toys for you to use. You have several lock picks, a filament, an Infinity knife, rations for three days, flares, explosive pellets a miniature siphoning kit, and please notice the buckle."

Dyspell's old symbol, the purple diamond, was the centerpiece of the belt buckle. She noted with some satisfaction that it was an expertly-cut amethyst – and a gorgeous one to boot. As a former-villain-turned-jewel-expert, she abhorred faux paste gemstones. Anything of lesser quality would have been insulting, and would probably have ended up in a trash can. Clearly, Alan and his underlings had done their research.

"I approve."

Steve pointed to the gem. "This isn't a normal gem. If you turn and press it, it will emit an electromagnetic pulse rendering all technology within 15 meters useless. PhoneBuddy is shielded, but everything else not lined with lead is going to have a bad time."

Her eyes widened as she reached for the belt. "Niiiicccee," she said. *'Well,'* she thought, *'color me impressed. Maybe having some hero tech along for the ride wasn't such a bad idea.'*

"You can only use it once. After that, it has to be brought back here to be recharged."

"Awwww..." Alice said. Despite the seriousness of the whole situation, she *really* wanted to try that one out on a busy street corner during rush hour.

Admittedly, Alice wasn't *100%* reformed.

Steve handed Alice her belt and drifted over to the steel wardrobe standing next to his work station. Alice watched him, noting that he never once touched the ground.

"Do I get an antigrav unit like yours?"

Steve stopped at the wardrobe and typed a code into a numeric pad. The doors hissed open to reveal a slick, black jumpsuit with form fitting purple boots and gloves. A purple diamond was centered on the chest, and a slick purple stripe ran along the legs and arms. On the back of the costume hung a very short, ragged-looking cape that could have been mistaken for a shawl.

"No, this is purely for medical purposes. Besides, flying takes time and a lot of lessons, and frankly, the antigrav devices are a bit clumsy when it comes to high-speeds and maneuverability. We're just not where we should be, yet."

Alice barely heard Steve as she reached out and gently took the costume off its hanger. It was very similar to the one she wore as Dyspell, but a bit slicker. The fabric felt thicker, and unusually smooth. She recognized it from her Purge days as a semi-liquid Kevlar. It was good for stopping standard bullets and absorbing blows, and as long as you weren't stabbed head-on, it was pretty good about sliding a knife blade right past you. Plus, it could breathe really well, which Alice always approved of.

"This is nice," she muttered, letting out a low whistle.

Alan nodded as he moved up behind her. "I know you had a costume, but it didn't offer the protection this does. This fabric isn't just liquid Kevlar; it will self-heal minor tears and act as a makeshift tourniquet when exposed to blood. I've been saved by it many times; it'll do you well in the field."

"The whole suit is insulated, and I've made sure the outfit was designed to your measurements. The domino mask is in the left side belt pocket. It should completely cover your eyes, and it offers our latest night vision lense. You should be just fine for a nightly patrol."

"Cute," Alice said with a wry smile. She had worn something similar with the Purge, although this one felt lighter and smoother.

"Wait. Is this why you had my measurements in your safe?"

Alan gave a slight cough as both men remained silent.

"Oh my God. You're perverts. I knew it."

Alan blushed slightly and said, "I keep imformation on everyone, and you never know when it will pay off. Case in point; that outfit should fit like a glove."

"Yeah, a pervy glove. Geez…" After a moment of examining her new costume, she looked back to Steve, who was watching the whole exchange with obvious excitement.

"Steve, do I know you from somewhere?"

Steve looked at her wide-eyed for several seconds, then started to turn a bit red. Alice was starting to wonder if he was choking on something when he picked up a tablet from the desk beside him. He kept his attention on it as he spoke.

"Miss Gailsone, I'll admit…I've been a bit of a fan. I've been in your stores several times, pretending to shop."

Alan let out something that sounded suspiciously like muffled laughter. Alice stared at Steve indignantly. "You were *spying* on me?"

"I was doing field research. It doesn't hurt when your subject of study is also a hobby."

Alice smiled. *'Creepy. Seriously creepy.'* She thought to herself.

While Steve adjusted his glasses and tried to look dignified and professional, a woman walked up behind him. She had jet black hair that fell in waves to her shoulders, piercing green eyes and a trim build under her pressed, black business suit. Alice could tell from her body language that the woman didn't care for her in the slightest, which was fine. In her hands was a clipboard, and from the way she held it, Alice wondered if it was surgically attached.

Alan gestured to the woman and smiled. "Alice, I would like to introduce you to my head of public relations and all-around right hand woman, Ms. Victoria Green." The woman nodded and flashed Alice a very fake smile.

"Miss Gailsone," Victoria said, her voice clipped, sharp and extremely familiar to the former villainess, "My job is to set you up with your accounts and identity. Now, what would you prefer to be known as in Japan?"

Alice considered it for a moment and said, "Alice Gailsone."

Alice watched as Victoria let out an almost inaudible sigh. "We are attempting to give you a faux identity so you can maneuver covertly. We understand that your reputation might have consequences for this assignment."

"Oh, I'm hoping it does," Alice said in her sweetest voice. "I was head of operations for the Purge in Japan for years. I know every contact, dive and slum that isn't a slum. I know who to talk to and they sure as Hell know me. I was behind enough of the organized crime in the Pacific Rim that, retired or not, my 'reputation' had damn well better have some consequences. So thank you, but I think I'll keep my own name."

Alice made air quotes on reputation, causing Alan to snicker slightly. This earned him a sharp glare from Victoria, which caused Alan to immediately regain his serious demeanor.

"How can I possibly list you as Alice Gailsone? You're a known super-criminal. You can't even fly on a plane without that name raising some alarms."

Alice smiled. "I think you know how. I think you know already that Alice Gailsone happens to also be the name of a completely legitimate woman with a totally different set of perfectly bland records and a law-abiding history. Lots of people have similar names, so why not little old me?"

Victoria shrugged and proceeded to write on her clip board. "Fine, whatever you prefer. I will have your corporate credit cards, passport and itinerary waiting for you on your plane. They will be good for the duration of your trip only, so try not to use them any time after seven days."

"I get that you're worried, but trust me, I'm a pro at things like this. Besides," Alice said with a slight smirk, "I'm awesome. That's why I'm me."

Victoria rolled her eyes. "This," she handed Alice a manila folder from her clipboard, "is a list of the last known locations the Lotus was sighted. It's not a lot, but it gives you a reference point. Besides, an 'experienced' girl like yourself shouldn't have any problems, now should you?"

Alice was about to respond in a way that was decidedly unprofessional, but she held her tongue. She reminded herself that she was the former villain here, not these people, and she didn't know how her former life might have effected them. For all she knew, she might have (unintentionally) murdered this woman's family at some point in the past. In fact, when she looked at things in that light, the entire room was starting to feel incredibly uncomfortable.

Alan thanked Victoria and led Alice away as Steve continued to work in the background, thankful for having been forgotten. Silently, Alice wondered how many more vile looks she would get and when this parade would end. She wanted to leap out the nearest window and just forget about all of this, but she wasn't here for herself.

Alice considered praying for the tour to end, but had a sneaking suspicion God wouldn't really care what she wanted.

As far as her reason for being in Japan, Alan had that covered; Tanner Industries was looking at purchasing several distributors for LCD and crystal-based displays on their new smartphone lines and wanted to send the best, so he had chosen her. This gave her an alibi that could easily be backed up, and also a very vague and powerful title as an on-site purchaser for Tanner Industries.

The rest of her time was spent making sure her mother's caretakers were briefed on how to get a hold of her. She didn't call her mother directly; after all, "I'm going to Japan to track down a murdering villainess" probably wouldn't ease her mind.

Her only other stop before heading back to her tiny, uptown flat was her office. It was a small, side-street, yellow brick shop with a quaint front that read '*Rare Gems*' in Gothic, curved letters across the plate glass. Inside were several display cases and an appraisers' table. Alice rarely did business here; her work consisted of travelling to remote locations to inspect shipments and make sure purchases were what they were supposed to be. That aside, she often wound up staying there as opposed to her flat, as her niece lived above the store and Alice hated being alone.

Her entire store was currently run by three people; an older appraiser named Douglas, a young receptionist named Cindy and Allison that, as far as the rest of the staff knew, Alice had officially hired on as a jack-of-all-trades that was currently seeing a therapist for aggression issues. The rest of the staff, while not too pleased to be working with someone so abrasive, was at least happy with the fact that crime had virtually vanished from their city block and that local gangs tended to stay well away. In fact, the only issue that any of them could remember was when three local thugs had tried to rob the store four months ago.

Allison had taken personal offense.

One of the thugs was shot to death in the store. The police report listed 18 gunshot wounds, despite Allison only carrying her licensed Beretta. When asked, she admitted that she had taken the time to get a spare clip from behind the counter and then resumed shooting the corpse on the floor, "just to be sure." The other two thieves fled in terror, but one (who had pulled a gun on Cindy, Allison's favorite coworker) was found

56

the next evening hanging from a streetlight two blocks over. At least, the police assumed it was the second robber; it was hard to tell, considering the corpse had been burned to a cinder in a nearby dumpster. The third was left unharmed, but awoke the following morning to find the word BEHAVE written on his wall bedroom wall in what the police said was the second thugs blood.

Since then, Alice had made it a point not to ask Allison about her hobbies away from work, so long as she filed a police report and did her due diligence.

"Boss," Allison said in acknowledgment as Alice walked in the door. Allison hadn't changed her style much from her days in the Purge. She was a young, slim woman with auburn hair in a tight ponytail that came down to her shoulders. Her slender face was framed by her red-framed glasses that tended to catch the light when she moved. Allison was always dressed business-casual, to the point that Alice could not remember ever seeing the woman in anything other than a button-up blouse, vest and slacks. Cindy, the somewhat down-to-earth young blonde bombshell they had hired on six months after they opened, looked up from her desk and gave a friendly nod.

Douglas looked from his counter and offered a warm smile. He was in his favorite traditional black suit with a white shirt and black tie. He was sporting a rather bushy moustache and had longer, silver hair that he kept back in a short pony tail. Alice had often times imagined him as a lawman from an old western, but she doubted if Douglas had ever even touched a gun before. Alice nodded to each of them.

"I have to leave town for a bit. If you need me, you can reach me at my regular number. Try not to need me."

"Do you need any assistance?" Allison asked, her face neutral.

"No, no… I think I'll be fine. I'll be in Japan scouting for Tanner Industries, but I should be back by the end of the week."

"Seriously?" Allison asked with a snort, "Tanner? Is this some kind of joke? You know he's…"

"…A paying client who just gave me an insane amount of money up front to procure some new business. Yes. That is what you were going to say."

Allison stared at her boss and nodded. Alice knew Allison tended to forget that the others in the store weren't quite as familiar with the duo's former lives.

"Anyway," Alice said, "Allison is in charge until I get back. Allison, please do not scare the locals."

"Righty-o," Allison said, tapping a pen on the glass counter, her face still neutral.

Alice sighed a bit to herself and waved goodbye to her small staff. She had been a bit amused to see the looks Douglas and Cindy exchanged upon hearing that the scary one was now in charge.

That night, Alice made her way back to her small, one bedroom flat with the intention of showering, eating some take out and passing out in her own bed before having to head halfway around the world. What she had not intended on was seeing Alan Tanner leaning against the side of her building, looking as casual as a man in a $1200 suit jacket can.

"You know, most of the men I threaten to kill take that as a pretty reliable sign that I'm not interested," Alice said with a small smirk.

"I'm not a quick study," he said with a smile. "Buy you a drink?"

Alice stared for a moment. "What? Is this a trick? Am I on camera?"

Alan shook his head. "No tricks, just a drink. I wanted to talk with you away from the office for a moment, if you're up for it."

Alice sighed and shrugged. "Fine, but you're buying. After all, you're the billionaire."

There was a small pub a block down form Alice's apartment. It was a small, traditional brick eatery that boasted low, soft lighting with a long, redwood bar running the length of the establishment. Inside were about half a dozen patrons, all nursing their drinks, eating their dinners or watching the large flat screen propped up behind the bar tender.

Alan gestured for Alice to pick a seat. She chose one towards the back exit and took the booth facing the door. Alan shook his head with a small smile and sat across from her. Alice settled in and stared at the man across from her.

"Okay, what gives? I thought we had everything squared away from this morning," she said in her business voice. Alan nodded and gestured for a server.

"Oh, we did, but I couldn't pass up this opportunity," Alan said with a grin. "I've wanted to talk with you one-on-one for a long time now, and I saw this as my chance. Plus, there was something I've always wanted to know about you, and I figured, why not ask now?"

"Yes, why not ask now? This timing is a bit ridiculous, Mr. Tanner. We had all day. All. Fucking. Day. I am tired, stressed and I won't lie, a little nervous about what I'm about to do, so what was so important that you couldn't have broached it while we were playing Glad Hands with your staff?"

"I just wanted to talk shop for a while, that's all. I rarely get the chance to discuss work matters, especially with someone that used to work for the competition, so to speak. Also, like I said, there is something I always wanted to know."

The server, a young man with freckles and dark red hair, appeared beside them with menus in hand. Alan refused his and said, "Bourbon, rocks. Alice?"

59

Alice scanned the bar. "Blue Label, rocks, and bring the bottle."

The server nodded as Alan stared. "That's not a cheap scotch."

Alice grinned. "I know. Normally, I hate scotch."

"Then why order it?"

The server appeared with the bottle. Alice promptly opened it and poured a tiny glass. "Because *this* scotch is actually yummy, it's stupid expensive and because you just bought it."

Alan stared. "Ah."

Alice leaned back a bit, her glass in hand. "So, what does the great Alan Tanner want to know about the now dull and boring Alice Gailsone?"

"Why were you really in the Purge, Alice? I'm not talking about the standard villain answer. What made you join up with them in the first place?"

Alice stared at her drink for a moment and then reached for the bottle. She poured a healthy amount of alcohol and took a long, slow sip.

"That's not something I normally like to talk about, Alan."

Alan shrugged. "You're working for me now, and I like to know what I can about my staff. Besides, it just always felt... weird. You did the whole villain thing well enough, but you never really seemed *evil*, if that makes sense. So why? And why the Purge?"

Alice sipped her scotch and closed her eyes for a moment. When she started speaking, she still had her eyes shut. When she opened them, she kept them focused on her glass.

"So, pretend you're sixteen. Pretend you're going through your Hell raising years. Pretend... you are rebellious, into the whole punk thing and wondering why the Hell you're the only person you know that has purple hair and seemingly demonic powers."

Alice took a longer sip and set her cup down, her finger trailing across the top of the glass as she watched water droplets run down its side.

"Pretend you meet a boy. Pretend he makes you think you're special and loved and that you two are gonna go see the world and really make it and do all the stupid stuff that kids think they'll do when they're horny and confused and just wanting someone to accept them."

Alice paused and took another drink. She then slowly poured more scotch into her glass and set the bottle down, her eyes on the glass in her hand.

"Pretend you had a power. Pretend you had a power that could only hurt, as far as you could tell. Your family is somewhat religious, so you think your power is bad. Rotting is bad, right? And something like that had to come from God, right? So you grow up thinking it's evil. But here's this boy. This boy says you're not evil. He says you're beautiful and that he loves you anyway. Pretend you want so badly to believe it that you'll do anything."

Alice stopped for a moment. Alan debated prodding her, but simply sat quietly and waited for Alice to continue. The lighting was dim, and Alan couldn't tell, but it looked like Alice had tensed up as she was speaking.

"I had an accident when I was a baby. My powers activated, and my dad was holding me. I didn't know what I was doing. He didn't know, no one knew. It... it wasn't my fault, and I know that now, but it's a pretty big thing to have in your head growing up, you know? No matter what my mother told me, I always felt guilty that she was alone, that we were struggling. It *was* my fault, but not intentionally.

"Now, pretend you're with that boy. That boy who says he loves you so much. Pretend you're ready to do something you've been nervous and scared and anxious about that pretty much defines the turning point in your formative years. Pretend that accident is always in the back of your mind but you decide to do something anyway. Do you really *realize* how

61

nervous you're... when it's your first time? How much control you *don't* have over your body?

"I didn't realize it was happening until it was too late. I called 911, but he was dead on arrival at the hospital. He... My whole body, Alan. I didn't even know I could do that. My whole body activated and I didn't know how to stop it. I was terrified, and he... God, I saw the look on his face as it happened. That alone messed me up on romantic relationships permanently. "

Alice downed her entire glass and set it calmly on the table.

"I ran. I was scared and stupid and I just ran. I never told anyone what actually happened, not even mom. I just... I was found in a back alley in New York by Prometheus. He was recruiting for the Purge back then. It was a relatively new thing, but he wanted super humans. He had heard about a runaway girl that rotted the hands off of any hobo that tried to touch her. He bought me a meal, talked to me, made me feel safe. Let me tell you, when you're 16 and panicked, that can be a wonderful thing. He was the first person that had done that for me in a *long* time."

Alice turned her gaze from her shot glass to Alan and kept it there. Alan could feel the pressure of that stare as she spoke, and the steel in her voice sent shivers down his spine.

"I never actively set out to be evil, but I did love being accepted. He taught me how to use my powers, how to focus and how to never have another accident again. He made me feel valuable and important, and I started to realize that I could be someone special. He gave me responsibilities and I took to them, and I was *good*. Good God, I was good. I didn't even care what they were or how bad they were; I could do something in a place I belonged, and that was better than any drug, any sex, any rush I had ever known. It was... it was like being Home."

Alan slowly nodded, letting Alice's words sink in. "So why did you leave? Weren't you in charge once Prometheus died?"

Alice chuckled to herself. "You know, you're not the first person to ask me that. I guess... he had really gone bonkers, you know that? He totally was. When I met him, he was focused, suave and seemingly sane, but as we went on, he just... woooo. He went nuts. I don't know if it was the genetic experiments we would do, the stress of his position or just something wrong with him, but one day I looked at him and realized the man who had found me and helped me was completely gone."

"So why did you stay on after that? Why not just run again?"

Alice shrugged. "I had a good job, family, coworkers, and a purpose. People looked up to me and relied on me. I felt like I couldn't leave. There was just too much, and besides, where would I go? I was a wanted woman by then. When the *Argent* went down... I saw my chance and I took it. I had wanted out for a while and I just couldn't say no, you know? I was done. I am done. I... wow. You know, I never really told anyone that. Hell, I just had a huge heart to heart with my mom and I didn't tell her that. Did you drug me?"

Alan laughed and shook his head. "Your mom hasn't worked with you in a competitive environment for years. We're... well, I don't know exactly what we are, but I would go so far as to say peers. Maybe it's just nice to talk to someone about it that knows?"

Alice poured another drink and picked it up. "Maybe. You are the last person I ever imagined myself having a drink with, Mr. Alan Tanner. I hope I've answered your question, by the way."

Alan lifted his own. "I think so. I think so. I guess I was just curious."

The toasted and drank. "No, you just wanted to be sure I wouldn't relapse the moment I got back into that costume."

Alan pointed. "There was that, yes."

"And now?"

Alan considered the woman across from him. "I trust you, Miss Gailsone."

Alice smiled and finished her drink. "Then you're a damn idiot, Mr. Tanner, and thank you."

Alan walked Alice back to her apartment. It was now full-on night and Alice noted that it must have rained while they were in the bar. She could see puddles reflecting the yellow of the streetlights as they made their way down the cracked sidewalk to her building.

Alan and Alice didn't talk much on the way back, but as they neared her building, Alice said, "Sorry, by the way."

Alan glanced to his side at Alice, who was still looking straight ahead. "Beg pardon?"

"About your office. Sorry I broke in and... you know."

Alan nodded. "Ah. Well, I suppose it was for the best. I got a new employee out of it, after all."

Alice nodded. "I suppose you did. Meanwhile, I got an evening of toys, tasers and confessions that I probably could have done without."

"So, are you comfortable with all this? Working with the Collective Good, or at least with me? Being the Good Guy?"

Alice snorted. "Good Girl, Alan. And no, not really, but as long as you're okay with having a former criminal psychopath represent your foreign interests, then for the time being, I'm good."

Alan dropped his smile and stared. "You're not a psychopath. If you were, I never would have made the offer. You're employment history is extremely questionable, but Alice, I checked your record thoroughly and do you know what I found?"

Alice stopped and turned to Alan. "No, but I'm dying to know."

"Twelve confirmed kills in over ten years of criminal activity, and at least nine of them were in situations that could reasonably be argued as combat-driven or self-defense. For someone who was in charge of so many evil people and did her level best to paint herself as all big and bad, you seemed to go out of your way to be the opposite."

Alice shrugged. "Oh, I did it, but... Killing people is bad for business. You can't build relationships with people who are dead."

Alice looked up as they arrived at her apartment building. Sighing a little at the length of the day, she nodded to the doorman and then turned to Alan. "Thanks again for the drink, Mr. Tanner, and... I don't know if I should thank you for listening, but I do feel better for having told someone, you know? Besides, it's not like you don't know any of this. You're Blackthorne; you make it your business to know everything about everything before you even make a move. You just did this to see if I would be honest with you, and I'm not so stupid as to fall for such a shallow trick. Oh, and if you tell anyone about this conversation, if any shred of it winds up in your files, I will fucking. Kill. You. Don't think I can't find out, either. I always find out."

Alan nodded. "Tell you what; text time, you ask and I'll tell you whatever you want to know. Deal?"

Alice smiled a little and shook the billionaire's hand. "Deal."

Alice watched as he wandered down the street to a parked Bentley. Leaning against it doing a Sudoku puzzle was an aged man in a black suit with a cap. Alan nodded to the man as the chauffer opened the door for him. Alice watched him go and then headed up to her own apartment.

"Twelve confirmed kills," Alice said to herself quietly with a frown. "God, he keeps terrible records."

***

Alice left for Nagoya the next morning, her new toys in her carry-on, also provided by Alan Tanner. When she went through security, it showed as being filled with shirts and dress pants. Which, by the way, it actually was, once you ignored the costume and belt hiding underneath everything.

Alan had her name removed from the no-fly list and had even provided a private jet, but she still had to go through security, and the flight was still 19 horrible hours. Alice used the time to brush up on her Japanese, go over her contact lists, and learn how to use PhoneBuddy. To her surprise, the application could do just about anything she asked it to do. True to what she had been told, it was even tied to her current number, something she found equal parts disturbing and convenient.

Narita International Airport was clean, spacious and much nicer than she remembered it being the last time she had flown into Tokyo. That probably had to do with arriving as a civilian and not as...well...*her*. The ride on the Hikari Line was uneventful, and she even allowed herself to doze as the train whipped through the home-spotted countryside.

She always felt safe in Japan - well, in public Japan - and didn't really see a need for outright paranoia on the high-speed lines. Had this been New York, she would have clutched her bag with a wide-eyed predatory glare the entire time she was on the train car. Powers or not, on the subway people just didn't seem to care. Even if they were routine henchmen and knew who you were, Alice had found that the American subway system had an almost hypnotic effect on idiots that made them think they got a free pass when it came to crime. And that was how the Upper East Side Subway Massacre was inadvertently started five years ago, but that was a story that Alice had tried very hard to pretend never happened. Admittedly, it had not been a pleasant day.

Japan, on the other hand, was just lovely. The people had this nearly neurotic fear of invading personal space, which worked well for Alice, since she was a *big* fan of her personal space. So, while the subway here was indeed crowded, she never felt overly squished. She even managed

66

to get away with no one touching her person, although some fanboys on the train could not stop commenting on her pale skin and how incredible it was. Idly, Alice mulled taking off her wig and letting them see her purple hair, but she figured they would have a heart attack right then and there. At one point they whipped out a camera and took some photos, but seeing as how they actually refrained from touching her person, she let them live. She hated pictures, but she supposed a little worship was okay from time to time. After all, she *was* pretty incredible.

When she finally arrived in Nagoya and took a cab to her hotel, she allowed herself to promptly pass out in her tiny, yet clean, room. She only awoke to the sound of housekeeping knocking on her door, which informed her that she had slept for a jaw-dropping 14 hours. She knew she had been tired, but that was a bit above average, even for her.

After her shower, she was about half-dressed before she remembered the costume. It had been a while since she had worn anything under her civilian clothes, and she reminded herself again why she chose pants instead of a skirt for this trip. She took her time putting it on, getting a feel for it and trying it out. The fabric was cold and a bit constricting. She had never liked Kevlar in any form, and this was a little itchy.

"Nothing 50 runs through the wash won't fix," Alice mumbled to herself as she dug out some baby powder from her bag.

Once she was content, she started stretching. She knew that dealing with Lotus was going to be difficult to say the least, so she wanted to be ready. The last thing she needed was a pulled hamstring while engaging in combat. Besides, it felt good to do the old routine in a nice, new costume.

As Alice finished putting on a simple white blouse with a tan jacket and brown slacks over her outfit, she noticed something slightly out of place. At first, she had to stop and stare for a bit to confirm that she wasn't making it up, but after a moment, it registered in her mind why there was a small, green frog sitting on her nightstand, staring at her expectantly.

Alice closed her eyes and took a deep breath. "Okay, okay, I'll swing by tonight, alright? Just let me get settled in first? Please? I know the drill, I swear." She opened her eyes to look again, but the frog was gone. Alice cursed to herself quietly as she gathered her things and headed out the door. "One more goddamned thing to deal with…"

While Alan had provided her with a plane, a new uniform and an insane pay grade, the one thing his contacts had trouble with was tracking Lotus down. As a result, the good people at Tanner Industries had neglected to provide her with a proper starting point. Lotus had gone off the grid about a month ago and no one in the hero community had seen hide nor hair of her.

Alice however, did not operate in the hero community. She had done extensive dealings in Japan during her time with the Purge, and had even opened a branch office here a few years ago. She was pretty familiar with which businesses were fronts and which one were genuine establishments. One front in particular, an upscale bar in Nagoya Tower called the Red Bunny, was the perfect place to start.

As far as Alice could tell, the Red Bunny was specifically designed to repel women. At the door was a gigantic poster of a smiling young woman in a red, lace corset and panties sporting a set of red bunny ears on her head. Tied around her throat was a red, silk bow tie. The woman held a tray that listed out on a card the hand-written specials of the day.

The restaurant itself was far less impressive. There were only a handful of patrons when Alice arrived, most likely due to the lunch time rush already being over. There were a couple of businessmen, a young woman working on a laptop and an older gentleman reading a paper at the counter. Not exactly what one would call slammed, but not completely vacant, either. The staff, all young women, was dressed in black pants with white dress shirts and red bow ties. A very polite teenager took Alice to her seat at the bar and offered her a picture menu, which Alice turned down.

"I'll have a shrimp tempura bowl and an Amaretto Sour, and I would like to talk to Yoshi, when he's free." Alice said in spot-on Japanese.

The waitress smiled with a bit of surprise and nodded as she excused herself. Alice grinned a bit to herself. She had spent a lot of time in Japan, and while she hadn't had to use it in a while, she had become pretty proficient in Japanese. Plus, she had 19 hours on the flight over to give herself a serious crash course in what she had forgotten. Still, she thanked whoever was listening that the waitress hadn't asked her anything more, because even then she was still a little unsure if she remembered too much beyond that point.

After a minute, a young bartender with short, spiky hair and a warm smile came to Alice with a small drink in hand. He carefully placed it on a napkin and grinned at Alice as she grinned right back.

"Miss Alice, it has been a while." The man spoke in slightly accented English.

"It has, Yoshi-san. How's the bar?"

Yoshi smiled and gestured at the bar, half full with patrons enjoying a meal or a drink. "It is okay. We have a lot of new girls working here ."

"Really? What are they like?"

"None of them will sleep with me."

Alice laughed to herself. Yoshi was smart, average looking and when it came to the female gender, had no social graces whatsoever. It was almost endearing, in a really creepy way.

"Yoshi, I'm here on a bit of business and I was wondering if you could help me out." Alice said, taking a sip of her drink. Alice could smell the

Amaretto in her drink and winced a bit at the lack of Coke. With a mumbled apology, Yoshi capped off her drink with the spritzer.

"Anything for the Dragon Queen of the East," Yoshi said in slow but perfect English. Yoshi had learned to speak English in England, at Oxford no less. As a result, Yoshi was probably the nicest person Alice knew in Japan. When asked why he was always so polite to her, Yoshi had once told her, "People think Americans are the assholes of the world. No, Alice. I can tell you, the *English* are the biggest assholes of the world."

Not knowing how else to take that, Alice decided to read it as a compliment. That, or code for Yoshi had remained celibate on his educational travels.

"Thanks, Yoshi." Alice sipped her dink and nodded her approval. It still tasted terrible, but a little buttering up never hurt.

"Yoshi, I'm looking to hire and I need someone with skills, but I don't know how to get a hold of them."

Yoshi nodded as he started wiping the bar down. "Are you looking to set up shop again? I have heard nothing about a new business here."

Alice eyed Yoshi as he casually continued wiping the bar. "No, Yoshi-san. I'm not trying to step on any toes. In fact, I'm fully ready to meet with anyone who wants to discuss my business here, which will be brief, and hopefully non-intrusive."

Yoshi nodded as Alice watched him carefully. While a bit of a pervert and seemingly polite, Alice hadn't picked this place first out of a hat. Yoshi, despite his twenty-something age, was a chief operative for the Dead Talon, the father organization to the Yakuza. Alice knew that she had to be very careful about what was said here and the impression that she left, otherwise the trip could quickly become unpleasant.

"Yoshi-san, I wanted to speak with someone in particular, with the blessings of a certain party."

"Those may come, but that party would want to know who you want to speak to."

"I need the Lotus."

Yoshi stopped wiping the bar and glared at Alice, all pretense of friendship vanishing in an instant.

"The Lotus is not available at the moment. Maybe you would prefer another lovely girl?"

Alice felt the room drop ten degrees. She had expected a bit of friction; it was practically worked into the super villain handbook that opposing organizations had to give the other a hard time, but this was a bit more than she had figured on.

"Maybe I would in the future, but I have a need to see the Lotus when she is available. Will she be available, Yoshi-san?"

Yoshi took the empty glass from in front of Alice and started cleaning it with his rag. With a sigh, Alice saw his shoulders drop slightly. "She went missing a month ago. I do not know why. She was working as a bodyguard for Nakajima Toshino and then, nothing."

"The head of Nakajima Technologies? What did a tablet maker need with someone like her?"

"Apparently a lot, if something made her go missing. We interviewed him, but came up with nothing. She is gone, Alice. You should consider another lovely girl. In Nagoya, there are always lovely girls."

Alice stared at Yoshi as he continued to casually clean the glass she had been drinking from. Suddenly, she felt something familiar, and very, *very* wrong.

Alice dropped some change on the counter and stood.

71

"You know, I don't think I'm all that hungry, Yoshi. Why don't you have my tempura when it gets here?"

"Thank you, Alice. That is very generous of you."

Alice excused herself and left as quickly as she could. Yoshi watched her leave, as did the young lady carrying her food. With a glance from Yoshi, the young lady promptly headed back to the kitchen to dump the shrimp tempura in the trash.

Chapter 4

Falling Off the Bicycle

Then

***

Two days later, Alice and Allison stood in front of an old, small, abandoned-looking storefront in Brooklyn. The building was four stories tall, built from large yellow bricks and covered in graffiti. Alice walked around to the back to where a steel door was half-hidden by a dumpster. She typed in a security code on a small numeric pad hidden under a false brick and instantly the two women were rewarded with the satisfying sound of a lock opening up.

The inside was dusty and had a smell that made them both uncomfortable, but it was spacious, dry and unoccupied. "I don't remember this from the Purge hideout lists," Allison said as she looked around.

Alice felt around the far wall of the main room until she found a light switch and flicked it on. Only half the fluorescents popped to life, giving the place a dull, pale blue glow. "That's because it wasn't *in* the Purge records. I bought this myself under an alias several years back with cash on hand. No one knows this is mine. No one will come looking for us here... This is as good of a safe house as I can provide."

"Why not go to the country and just lay low?"

Alice laughed a bit. "Because we're two attractive young women with recognizable faces and I have purple hair. I think we'd be made pretty quick out there, but in Brooklyn? No one will even know we exist, here."

Allison pointed, "You could always dye your hair."

73

Alice glared at her. "You know my powers residually rot away the dye after a day or two. You think I want to go through that every other day? Screw it; I'll just wear the wig and suck it up like a big girl."

Allison shook her head. "Wigs are itchy."

Alice stuck out her tongue, "And you're bitchy, but I love you, anyway."

Allison glared as Alice smiled.

Alice walked to the back center of the main room and pried an old door open that revealed a dark, narrow staircase behind it. "There's a series of small apartments upstairs. Okay, more like dorm rooms, but still. Above that is a training gym and combat room. Merry Christmas, by the way. I had this place stocked with some clothes and some cash, but eventually we'll run out, and I'm willing to bet that the bank cards are being watched. We are officially on our own."

Allison turned to follow Alice up the stairs. "But... What about the Purge? What about Prometheus?"

"Didn't you see the big black hole that ripped reality in half earlier this week? Were you actually unconscious for that? He's dead, sucked into that... thing he made. It's over. The Purge is done."

"But, if he's dead..." Allison stopped short of the stairs. "Alice, wouldn't that make you in charge of everything?"

Alice stopped on the stairs and took a breath. "In charge of what? Most of our forces were killed with the *Argent*. Those that lived are either going to be rounded up or executed, and those that stay out will not like any additional attention. No hon, we're on our own from here on out."

Alice continued up the stairs while Allison stood rigid. "So we're done? We're going good?"

Alice pried open the door at the top of the stairs. Before her was a small, dusty hallway with several doors on both sides and a stairway at the end of the hall. "Hell no, but maybe… legitimate? Maybe legitimate. We need money and we're not doing anything stupid to get it."

"But… Alice! I have no marketable skills!" Alice turned to look at her charge to see she was starting to cry. Alice winced and shrank back, holding one arm with the other.

"Hey now, that's… not entirely true. I taught you sharp shooting, knife fighting, vault cracking… Oh God, I'm a horrible guardian. Okay, you're right, you have no marketable skills. So… let's work with what we both know. If we needed money, where would we start?"

"We would steal it."

"True," Alice nodded as she turned and opened a nearby door. A dusty, but nicely laid-out bedroom with attached shower greeted her, and she smiled. "Thank God, a shower. Okay, so, no stealing, but… wait. Wait, wait, wait."

Alice walked to the window and looked out. She scanned the block they were on until her eyes fell on the bank nestled on the corner and then started grinning. With a huge smile, she spun around and looked at her charge, who was looking concerned.

"Okay, we have a couple thousand saved up. I want you to go get some cheap food for us, and then you and I need to empty out some safe deposit boxes."

Allison sighed with relief. "Finally."

Alice shook her head. "They're my safety deposit boxes. We're going into business for ourselves."

The safety deposit boxes in question were loaded with gems. The first bank run taught Alice to prep her charge, as Allison let out a string of shocked curse words upon seeing the sheer amount of precious stones tossed haphazardly in the box before her. After that, they developed a quick routine of emptying out boxes, returning to the shop, dumping them off and repeating the process. It took an entire business day, but by the time they were finished both ladies were looking at nearly $6,000,000 in rare stones.

"We're rich," Allison said. "Oh my God, we're really rich. We can go anywhere, do whatever we want, we're..."

"We're just getting started," Alice cut her off and held up a gem. "Each one of these is hot. We need to recut these and then find some buyers. On that note, it occurred to me that the one business we know better than most is moving vast quantities of fenced merchandise, especially rare gemstones."

"What about security systems?" Allison asked.

Alice nodded, "Okay, we know those too, but we already know a pretty good network of people who would be willing to move gems for us, and who wouldn't mind using us to move them. This is a lot of money if we do a one-off sell, but can you just imagine where we could be in a year or two if we rolled on this and acted as brokers? We could be set for life, and we'd never have to...you know... evil things up anymore."

Allison looked to her guardian and asked, "But, don't you like what we did?"

"Yeah, kinda. I mean, of course I do. Did. Whatever. Of course, but... after what happened... those people were my fault, hon. All of that was my fault. I could have tried harder to convince Prometheus not to go forward with his plan. I could have taken control of the bridge and turned the ship around. I could have ordered an evacuation instead of just running for my life, but I didn't. I was in charge of the general troops, and how many people died because of it? I can't... I can't do that anymore. I know it sounds dumb, considering what we've done in the past, but I just can't, okay? That was my straw. I'm done."

Allison looked at her boss with a blank expression and said nothing. Alice, oblivious to this, continued to examine the gems in front of her.

"We are going to need a cutter," she said to herself. "Time to put out some feelers for an employee."

"You want me to run some background checks? You know, when we do get someone?"

Alice looked to her niece and shook her head. "Not the kind you're probably thinking of. Just the standard stuff; I don't think we have to worry about these employees potentially trying to kill us."

Now

***

Alice stood outside the building and steadied herself against the side as she focused. The drink had been poisoned. This was half-expected when dealing with Yoshi, but still. '*I just got here, dammit.*' She thought to herself. Criminals used to at least wait until pleasantries had been exchanged before trying to kill each other.

Alice shook her head and focused. The poison was fast-acting and very strong, but comprised of a multi-chemical mix to ensure a quick break down before autopsy. Alice turned her power inward, focusing on the chemicals in her blood. '*It's like riding a bicycle,*' Alice thought to herself, '*a painful, poison-fueled bicycle. Oboy...*' A light purple glow started to emit from her body and her brow broke out in a sweat. She forced herself to stay conscious as she aged and broke down the poison to its untraceable, non-toxic state.

"Focus...focus...don't die...not in front of the Red Bunny...I am *not* dying in front of the Red Bunny..." Alice silently chanted to herself in an effort to keep from convulsing and vomiting at the same time. The chemical was nearly gone, but she felt horrible. It had started to take a hold of her muscles, and it was all she could do to avoid dropping to the ground and screaming.

Finally, she felt the last shred of poison age and break down, and with a shaky sigh, she relaxed her focus. Her powers, while extremely effective, were more of a blunt tool. To focus them so carefully and to turn them inward was extremely difficult for Alice. Still, this was not the first time she had been poisoned, and it was not the first time she had dealt with Yoshi.

Slowly, Alice collected herself. She knew she was probably being watched, so she did her best to leave with some dignity as she hailed a cab and collapsed in the back. She wondered why they had been so direct with her. She also suspected that her meal had been similarly

78

poisoned. Had she actually eaten it, the combination might have effected her before she would have had a chance to react.

She was dazed, but not so dazed that she didn't notice the black sedan that had stayed three car lengths behind her. She knew she was being followed, but it was the middle of the day and the roads were busy. She was reasonably sure the people tailing her wouldn't kill her just yet. Idly, she scanned the passing businesses to see if there were any restaurants and involuntarily recoiled when she saw a little seafood market.

Great, she thought. She was shaking, hungry and developing a full-blown paranoia of *shrimp*. Scared of seafood while in Japan; this was a fantastic first day.

Eventually, she was focused enough to direct the cab driver to Oasis 21, the entertainment complex next to the Nagoya radio tower. Once there, she took a walk in the tower park to clear her head.

It took a full five minutes of wandering before it hit her: She had slept for *14 hours*.

"They drugged me and searched my stuff. That was how they knew. That was why they were so direct."

Alice dug PhoneBuddy out of her pocket and hit the contact for Alan Tanner. After four rings, a gruff, rumbly voice answered.

"Speak."

"I caught you at work, didn't I? How's things?" Alice forced her voice to be unusually cheery. Inwardly, she reminded herself to dial it down. Alan didn't need to know her day had gone as poorly as it had.

"What do you want?" The gruff voice barked. Alice jumped back a bit, and then grinned.

"You're with someone, aren't you? You only talk like that when you're trying to protect your secret identity. Who is it? The commissioner? Blackbird?"

"Tell me what you want or I'm hanging up." Alice quietly snickered to herself. In the background, she swore she could hear a small, feminine sigh.

"Fine. I need a favor, Blackthorne. I need a meeting tomorrow with Nakajima Toshino. You're going to want someone to examine his factories and make an on-site decision to switch your tablet screen maker from your Swedish company to his."

There was a brief pause. "Anything else?"

"Yes. Not to alarm you, but I might be changing hotels this evening."

"Fine," Blackthorne barked back. Alice shook her head and wondered how she had been so intimidated by this man for so many years. On the phone, he was downright hysterical.

Figuring that he wasn't the type to say goodbye, Alice hung up and decided to deal with the two men in suits that she knew were standing about 10 meters behind her. She felt focused enough to deal with things at this point, and after all, it was just two goons. Even if she had agreed to no killing, she was reasonably sure this would be a walk in the park.

Alice looked around and noted she was already *in* the park.

"Huh, half done already."

Alice debated her options. The Dead Talon knew who she was and what she could do. So, either these men were simply tailing her, or Yoshi figured the poison had hurt her worse than it had. Either way, Alice didn't feel like having an escort to her next stop.

Alice looked around until she saw what she was looking for. Casually, she strolled over to an intersection in the concrete paths that crisscrossed in front of the radio tower. There were several intersections in the area, but only one with a manhole cover. That told Alice all she needed to know.

Nearby, she could hear the music form an outdoor concert at the Oasis 21 center. As she slowly walked around the intersection, she tried to hum along with the random pop song that was playing, but couldn't seem to get it right. *'Any time now, boys.'*

Finally, the two large, well-dressed thugs approached her. They were your classic stereotyped Japanese gangsters, complete with generic sunglasses and slicked back hair. Noticing their arrival, Alice stepped back three spaces as they came to the center of the intersection, serving her purpose while making it look as if she were intimidated.

"Miss Gailsone," the first man said in thick, Japanese-accented English, "we would like you to come with us."

"Please," the second man said, "the Dead Talon doesn't like to be kept waiting."

"Can't," said Alice, apologetically. "Sinkhole."

"...What?" While she couldn't see his eyes, Alice was pretty sure the first man just blinked behind his glasses.

Alice pointed to the ground beneath them. At their feet was a small manhole cover that appeared to be dissolving into a red, flaky mass of rust.

"Sinkhole," Alice said again.

The men didn't have time to answer as the ground beneath them completely gave way.

People came running form across the park to help the two unfortunate souls who had been standing where the concrete, metal and earth had broken down to the point of opening up beneath them. Alice watched

81

for a moment, nodded to herself and casually strolled away as distant sirens whined to life.

***

Two hours, a change of clothes in a department store (Alice always treated herself to shopping after an attempted assassination on her person) and a sandwich later, Alice Gailsone found herself at the only real lead she had left to follow that day. After making doubly (and triply) sure that she hadn't been followed, she took the elevator in a run-down narrow apartment building to the second floor and knocked on the door of Nanami Fukijima.

After waiting several minutes and not getting an answer, Alice reached for her belt, but then stopped. Steve had given her lock picks, but it was still daytime, and picking a lock was always a pain to explain.

"Luckily, I happen to be awesome," Alice muttered as she ran her finger across the lock. She could feel the cheap metal dissolving and rusting away as she did. In a matter of moments, the lock and door handle fell to pieces as Alice calmly pushed the door open.

Alice had never actually visited Nanami and didn't really know what she looked like, but she had done her homework when working with the Purge. Nanami had been crippled in an accident since she was five, and while her sister had been sending her money for years to help keep her comfortable, Nanami had actually been supporting herself off and on as a sports writer while operating a small bookstore. The fact that she was a woman writing about baseball had actually given her column's sales a boost, and Nanami, despite being physically limited, had managed to carve out a cozy little life for herself.

That life was presently in shambles. Alice walked through the ransacked apartment, noting the classic signs of a failed search. Tables were overturned, books on the floor, dishes shattered, the place was destroyed. As Alice searched, something struck her as odd. It took her a moment to put her finger on it, but once she did, she became unsettled.

Alice had overseen nearly every aspect of the Purge, and that included interrogation and misdirection tactics. She had led seminars on the subject, and now, one of her lessons was coming back to her as she stood in the remains of Nanami's life.

The apartment was completely trashed. Every room, every cabinet, every surface had been attacked. It was too thorough, too complete – and at the same time, not. The drawers thrown helter-skelter all still had their bottom panels, and the throw pillows were superficially slashed but nothing had been pulled out. Sloppy, sloppy. This wasn't meant to be a search; this was meant to give the appearance of a search to anyone who came calling. Someone wanted people to think Nanami's apartment had been ransacked.

As Alice scanned the apartment, she could see where things had been. All the possessions, even the valuable ones, were still there. Nothing had been taken, and nothing showed signs of being forced open. There was no storage safe or important area of the apartment. From what Alice could tell, someone just decided to go nuts.

Alice went to the fridge and looked inside for the milk. There was also a small, plastic container that felt heavy, and when Alice opened it, she winced at the smell. There was old milk, there was cheese and then there was what was in that container.

Nanami had been missing for a while.

Quickly, Alice wiped her fingerprints off the container and the refrigerator and quietly left the apartment.

At this point, Alice was out of leads, ideas or directions and was about to call it a day when she remembered the frog on her nightstand. She stopped cold when she realized that she had said she would deal with it today, and as much as she wasn't looking forward to it, today wasn't quite over yet.

Alice had to check PhoneBuddy for the right subway route, but she knew the destination well enough that she could have walked there, given enough time. The park was small, just like every other urban park in Japan. It was nestled between a cell phone shop and a questionable adult DVD rental facility just to the north of downtown. The area was so small there was really only room for a park bench and a small sculpture in the middle of a micro rock garden, but there was grass and a pretty plaque describing the site's significance, so it technically counted as an actual park.

Alice wandered into the park and sat on one of the park benches while staring at the rock garden. She sat and waited for a good three minutes before she noticed a change in the air pressure around her. Something shifted just on the edge of her perception, but enough to be noticed if you were paying attention for it, and Alice was. Sitting on the bench with her was an older lady that a moment before had not been there.

Alice glanced at the older woman and took her in. She was small, barely five feet tall and severely hunched over. She was wearing a mish-mash of dark colored shawls that gave her a bit of a shell-like appearance, and her head poked out from underneath the cloth like a turtles Her chalk white hair was done up in a large bun with what looked like ornate chopsticks sticking out of it. She was reading a small paperback novel and looked completely engrossed, so much that Alice considered trying to slip away before the ancient woman said in a gravelly, creaking voice, "I was wondering if you would come."

Alice nodded slightly. "When the Spiritual Magistrate issues a summons, I generally try to heed it, Kappa-san."

The crone chuckled to herself and put away her book within the folds of her clothing. "Spiritual Magistrate? No one uses that tile anymore, no one. I just thought that you would have the manners to come and see me ahead of time before I had to send a friendly reminder."

Alice gave a slightly tense smile and shook her head. "Sorry, but my schedule was a bit thrown off. I can only guess that jet lag got me worse than normal, but I'm here now, and I'm checking in."

"As you should. As should anyone who is magically inclined when they visit my islands," the old woman said, her face in a toothy smile. "Shall we go inside?"

Before Alice could answer, there was a rush of wind and a change in light, and in a blink, both women had vanished from the bench.

Alice instantly found herself in a darkened room with a large, round wooden table in front of her. She was seated Indian-style on an old, flattened silk cushion and nearly gagged at the smell of incense in the room. Across from her sat Kappa-san, who was pouring out two small cups of tea from a dark brown ceramic tea kettle.

Alice glanced around as Kappa-san finished up with the tea. "Pocket dimension? Subspace? This room doesn't have any doors or windows, just us, this table and... are those walls? They keep fading in and out and I can't tell if it's the bad lighting or... come to think of it, where is the light coming from?"

The old woman ignored Alice as she set the tea kettle down. "You should have come to me, first." Kappa-san offered one of the cups of tea to Alice, who gingerly reached out and took it with a nod. She sipped the tea and found to her mild delight that not only was it not poisoned, but it was actually pretty good, as tea went.

"Sorry," Alice said after swallowing, "but this isn't something I tend to get involved with, if I can help it."

"If you can help it... Young lady, you are a magic user, and whether you like it or not, all magic users have to check in when they enter a new territory. This is not something that is negotiable. You *know* this."

Alice squirmed a bit, "You know I don't use that stuff if I can help it. It... doesn't sit well with me."

Kappa-san nodded and smiled. "Makes you puke your guts out, doesn't it? If you had studied or disciplined yourself, you wouldn't have this problem, you know. You could have been one of the greatest practitioners of our age, had you just bothered to give it the effort."

Alice shook her head. "I seriously doubt it, despite what people say, I just... it just doesn't click with me, you know? I can do my thing and that comes easily enough, but that's like flexing a muscle. The rest... It's not like I haven't read the books and tried things out. I know the spells and all, it just... It hurts."

Kappa-san shook her head and set her cup down. "When you were born, no living magic user could remember ever noting someone with as much natural aptitude as you had. Most of us have to work to form a connection with our gifts, but you... you were *born* with the ability. Do you even understand how rare and wonderful that is?"

"You're not the first person to lay this on me, you know. Yes, I know. I hear about it every time I have to deal with one of you Spiritual Magistrates. I'm so special, I'm so cool, but that doesn't change the fact that pulling a quarter from behind your ear would make me binge vomit. Look... just, am I in trouble? Usually, you don't send a frog-o-gram unless someone is in trouble."

"A frog-o-gram? What is...oh. Oh!" Kappa-san started cackling hysterically. That's...oh my, that's a wonderful name for them. I like that! Frog-o-gram. I'm going to use that, from now on. You are just so clever."

Alice stared. "So, am I in trouble for not checking in and announcing I was here, or not?"

Kappa-san shook her head. "Nah, you get a pass. The most dangerous woman in the world has graced my table for tea and conversation, and you did what you said you would, you let me know you were here. Now I won't be surprised when I sense foreign magic nearby. Won't have to send out any helpers to clean things up. No, you did fine this time. You can play… for a while, anyway."

Alice shifted in her seat. "For how long? When I was here with the Purge, you used to make me check in monthly."

The old woman shrugged. "If you're here more than a month, come by and see me again. Fair?"

"Then, can I go? Because I've had a day and I wouldn't mind going now…" Alice made to get up, but Kappa-san put her hand up.

"Not quite, my dear. First, all who come through should know their fortune, don't you think?"

Alice settled back into her seat and chuffed. "So I should know my fortune, or so that you'll know my future? Let's not beat around the bush; you're just using this as a way to pre-emptively keep tabs on me."

Kappa-san shrugged. "I used to take offense to talk like that, but at my age, I'm just impressed that you've got the stones to address a woman who could kill you with a word in such a manner."

Alice gave her a level stare. "I'm impressed that you still feel comfortable inviting a woman who could rot her fist through your chest cavity in five seconds into your home for tea. It's just a big ole' day of surprises, isn't it?"

Kappan-san stared. "I'm going to guess your bravado is due to your being nervous about the situation and not because you are acting like an ill-mannered bitch in someone else's home. Fair enough?"

Alice debated saying something, but opted instead for sitting quietly. Kappa-san looked at Alice and then took out a small, bent deck of cards. Carefully, and with shaking hands, she dealt out seven cards on the table, face down. When she was done, she offered the deck to Alice, who took the top card without asking and set it down, face-up in the center of the table.

The first card was a black pagoda, standing on a hill. Alice, who had never really put much faith or thought into divination, looked at the card and asked, "So, what is it?"

"The Black Pagoda is a symbol of focus, of power and control. There is something controlling your movements, something that acts as a focus. You have come here as part of something larger, Alice Gailsone."

Kappa-san gestured to the cards on the table and said, "Pick the next card." Alice idly pointed and flipped the next card over to find a picture of a rider on horseback greeting her. The rider was turned in his saddle and firing an arrow behind him. Alice noted there were several arrows in his side.

"The Pursuit," Kappa-san said, her eyes narrowed, "You will not find time for rest while you are on my islands, dear. Already, someone wants you dead, and very badly, I might add. There is something... personal about this." Kappa-san glanced to Alice, who turned over the third card. The image was of a woman combing her hair in front of a mirror. In the mirror was a skeleton, mimicking her reflection.

Kappa-san paused and stared at this one for a while. Alice cleared her throat lightly, which made Kappa-san look up and blink. "Oh. Yes, well. I just don't see this one that often. The Reflection is a sign of many things, but this early in the reading, it's hard to say. It feels like you'll meet someone who reflects parts of you that you wish were not there. It could also mean a glimpse into your darker half, or maybe that you'll meet your evil twin? Rather hard to say. I would go with the first, in this case."

Alice shrugged. "Considering who I'm here to see, that's not out of the question. Next?"

Kappa continued and gestured for Alice to turn over a third card. The next one featured a naked woman with a sword at her side. She was entwined with a man and lying on the ground. "The Lovers. Hmmmm... You will find yourself entwined with people you never thought you would. That, or you'll get lucky with someone in a situation that you will kick yourself for completely misreading at a time that will feel horribly uncomfortable, but hey, what do I know?"

Alice glared and quickly turned another card over. This one was upside down and showed a child standing on a mountain of dead bodies. "The Deceiver," Kappa-san said. "She will hide the truth from you. She will rely on you, depend on you, but you will not know the reason for her devotion. You may never know. Also... note the card was drawn upside down. This could be for you, or this could be about you. Hard to say. Hard to say."

Alice flipped over the sixth card. This one had an image of two hands, one holding a knife, the other a cup of tea. "The Negotiator. You will move something that has not been meant or suspected to be moved. You will do something no one ever through you could."

Alice flipped over the seventh card and saw a giant bird flying over a large fire. "The Phoenix," Kappa-san said, "Resurrection, death and rebirth, a change. For you... Something else. Do you remember this from before?"

Alice nodded. Every time Alice had ever visited a Spiritual Magistrate, the last card was always a Phoenix. It had started to become a bit annoying.

Alice stared at the cards on the table and then at Kappa-san. Finally she said, "So? What does all this mean? Am I going to succeed on this mission or not?"

Kappa-san gave her a level stare. "Your time here will be tumultuous. It has been already. This," she gestured to the table, "isn't just the immediate future. There is something at work here that is larger than you know. You'll feel it later, and it will become clearer as you travel your path... or not. You tend to not pay attention."

Alice sat back and scowled at the old woman as Kappa-san gather her cards together. "So great. This has been a colossal waste of my time. Thanks, Kappa-san, but I think in the future, I'll just send you a text letting you know I'm here, if I ever come back here. I..."

Alice stopped when Kappa-san held out her hand swiftly in an effort to silence her. Alice noted that Kappa-san was staring at something on the floor to her side. Slowly, the old crone leaned down and picked up an eighth card from the floor and stared at it. Alice regarded the woman for a moment and noted that her face showed serious concern. "What's wrong?"

Kappa-san came around the table and took Alice's tea cup and poured its contents out on the floor. Alice watched impatiently as Kappa-san stared at the bottom of the cup. Finally, the old woman looked at her and said, "If you go back to your room tonight, you will be murdered. There is no question, no change or uncertainty to this point. You are in extremely grave danger. I misread your cards, and I am sorry, Alice. You should go now."

"What? What's going on? How could you even know that?" Alice asked, a touch of concern now in her voice.

Kappa-san held up the eighth card. It showed a burning building with what looked like blood pouring out of the windows. "Good God, what card is that? I've never seen it before."

Kappa-san stared at her. "Neither have I. This card decided to make its way in. Your tea cup confirmed it. Don't question me on this; tonight, you will be murdered if you go back."

Alice paused. "My tea didn't have leaves. That stuff just dissolves into powder. How did you..?"

90

Kappa-san growled, "Are you seriously going to hover there and split hairs about magical techniques with *me*? Now shut up and listen; you have my permission to operate in Japan for the remainder of your stay. I hereby lift any barriers, laws or restrictions that may hinder or cripple you from acting to your fullest potential and so on. If you need to do something to stay alive child, you do it. There is a shadow following you, a shadow that means for you to die. It is dripping with hatred, a burning for revenge that can only be satisfied by your death. You are not safe here- the shadow can see you as you walk. You must hide deep, child. I think you know where I mean. You should leave here. Now."

Alice looked at the old woman. "Now wait a minute, you can't just say..."

There was a slight whoosh of air, and Alice found herself sitting on the park bench, talking to the empty space beside her. "... that I'm going to die and then... oh Hell."

Now out of leads, confused by her reading and not too eager to head back to what sounded like a compromised room, Alice considered her options. She couldn't go back to Nanami's apartment; that was just asking for trouble. Going back to the hotel and dealing with anyone who might show up could mean a miserable night of no sleep or even her untimely death, and sleeping in the street didn't sound appealing at all. She considered checking into a new hotel under a different name, but was hesitant with the Talon being on to her. She wasn't sure how well they were tracking her, and she didn't know if she wanted to take that chance.

Sighing, she headed to the only place she could think of that would be even remotely safe. Two cab rides and a bit of walking later, she found herself on the far side of Nagoya castle. While a fine tourist attraction and a great way to kill two hours, Nagoya castle was somewhat boring once you had been through it. The floors of the castle were a museum devoted to the history of Nagoya and Japanese culture in general. Alice had taken the tour once and found it mildly interesting.

91

It was the sub floors of the castle, however, that *really* held her interest.

The castle was getting ready to close as Alice bought her ticket and headed in. On the first floor, just to the right of a ceremonial weapons case was an old, wooden panel that seemed to have no function other than to be decorative. Alice looked around to make sure no one was watching, and then lifted it to reveal a security pad. Quickly, she typed in her old access code and breathed a sigh of relief as the case slid to the side, revealing an elevator.

The Purge had made a short-lived push into the Asian market a few years ago, but out of a desire to maintain good ties with the Dead Talon they had pulled out. Now Alice found herself in one of their main headquarters, abandoned but still with power and water, as it was tired directly to the castle above.

The hideout was spacious, metallic and laid out in a pentagon with a large, open area in the center that went down three floors. The idea had been to capitalize on open space to keep the feeling of claustrophobia to a minimum, and to house a ballistic missile in the center, just in case. They could never figure out a decent way to get the missile launch to work properly, but the center itself was a decent common area, and Alice was ready to find the living quarters and settle down for a nice, long sleep.

A sleep which would come just as soon as she figured out why the sound of chanting and drums was echoing from the center of the hideout.

As Alice approached the center area, she could smell the smoke from torches and hear rhythmic chanting. As she crept to the ledge overlooking a common area, she peeked over and saw that she was not alone in her old hideout. Below her were at least twenty people in thick red robes with hoods that obscured their faces completely. They were singing and praying in a ritualistic dance before a part of the hideout that had collapsed, revealing the rocky surface behind, and a large, cavernous opening. As Alice looked closer, she gasped at what she saw.

In the opening stood a stone giant that was at least 10 feet tall and extremely stocky. The body looked like it had been carved with only a vague idea of what a person actually looked like, with cylinder like arms and legs that ended in crudely carved boots and gloves. The face was round, with a simple mouth and two round eyes, but no nose. It was ugly, and large, and that moment it was the most beautiful thing Alice had ever seen.

There was a reason the Purge had excavated the area under Nagoya castle, and it had pained Alice at the time that the stories had apparently been false. Clearly, they had just given up too quickly - because there was one of the ancient Fudo golems, perfectly intact and ready to go.

Alice had studied these ancient monsters exhaustively when she was building this base, and to her delight, she saw that the activation kanji was already written on the top of the golems head. It was missing one essential character, but once there, it would be a nearly unstoppable force that would serve Alice and Alice alone.

Alice took off her outer civilian clothes as fast as she could and slipped on her domino mask. If she was going to take down Fudo Cultists to claim her prize, she wanted to be dressed for the part. Still, she did think it was odd that people would be down here praying to the thing. After all, any person who actually knew what that was would have fired it up by now and done some damage. As she flipped over the railing and somersaulted to the back of the crowd, she wondered what kind of people these were.

As she crept towards the closest cultist with the classic plan in mind of knocking him out and taking his robes, the cultist stiffened and whipped around to face her.

Alice blinked as a fox's black, beady eyes met hers, and a growl came from under the hood.

'*Huh*', she thought.

"Kitsune. Sure, okay, why not?" Alice said to herself as the fox-headed man howled, alerting the others to her presence. Alice took a moment to gauge her options, and then decided on the direct course and executed a roundhouse to the creatures face, knocking it out.

With a flip and a twist, she put herself between two others. In a blur of punches and spins, she proceeded to break one's arm while cracking the other in the face, putting it down as two more advanced. Alice was fired up, punching, kicking, grappling and twisting her way through the crowd.

Damn, it was nice to be back.

There was a science to fighting a group that most didn't appreciate. In a group, no one person likes to do too much; they just figure that the group will be enough to overpower one person and tend to slack when it comes to actual physical fighting. Mostly, people in a group opt to grab and contain, not directly engage.

Alice used to teach this in basic combat courses. She had used it to her advantage against riot cops, SWAT, angry mobs, pushy Girl Scouts, Black Friday mobs – really, any group she tended to interact with. The nice thing was that when harmed, a member of a group was more likely to back off. The group fighting mentality was that someone else would step up. As a result, Alice moved through the angry mob inflicting only two or three hits at a time, relying on the mob mentality to kick in.

Unfortunately, there were those times when the group got its act together and did manage to overpower a person, even if that person was fighting tooth and nail against them. Alice had taken down seven or eight of the fox men when they managed to pile on her, pinning her to the ground.

Alice felt strong hands grabbing her and hoisting her up to face a leader, a fox-headed man in a black robe holding a long, ceremonial knife. In a rough, bark-like shout, the fox man spoke in Japanese. Alice strained to make sense of what he said, as a fox's muzzle isn't the most ideal choice for forming words.

"Why have you come here, surface-dweller? You have disturbed our ancient rituals and angered the..."

'Surface dweller? Really?' Alice had already tuned the talking fox out. There was nothing here of interest; clearly these idiots had stumbled on the old hideout by accident and an earthquake had freed the golem from its resting place. While the whole kitsune thing was unusual, it wasn't the strangest thing she had seen. After all, she *was* in Japan.

While the cult leader rambled on about her imminent sacrifice to appease the dark stone god behind him, Alice considered her options. These people weren't sinister, just overly stupid and violent. Killing weres might not exactly count as killing actual people, but she imagined it would be a hassle. The place would smell and she would feel awful about it afterwards. At least, she thought she would feel awful. It was hard to...

Alice snapped back. *'Oops. Head fox is lifting his knife. Time to improvise.'*

Alice twisted her wrists around until she could clasp the wrists of the two fox men holding her in place, clamped down hard with her hands, and focused. In seconds, both foxes started yelping and screaming as their wrists rotted under her touch. Reeling, they recoiled, clutching their now withered, wrinkled forearms.

Before anyone could properly react, Alice tapped a spot behind her ear. Immediately, she reached into her proverbial bag of tricks and started chanting as she moved her hands in an ancient, mostly forgotten pattern. It was old magic, lost and banned (most magic anymore was, unless cleared by a Spiritual Magistrate, which she currently was), but it always came to her when she called. She felt it flow up her arms like a solid, icy breeze and she braced herself. The power was hers to command, but already she was not looking forward to the price.

As the kitsune watched, Alice erupted into purple flames. Her face slowly morphed into a glowing skull, and the walls rumbled when she spoke. The words were not Japanese or English, but the fox men dropped to their knees in fear as they felt the words from within.

"THIS IS NOT YOUR TEMPLE," she bellowed, "THIS IS MY TEMPLE. THIS IS NOT YOUR GOD," she gestured to the statue, "I AM NOW YOUR GOD. HE IS MINE, AND YOU ARE MINE, AND YOU WILL OBEY ME. YOU WILL OBEY ME NOW!"

Alice could smell her collective audience as they lost their bladder control.

The spell was an illusion spell, and against people it was generally pretty weak. It was primarily designed to intimidate animals, but on the rare occasion when Alice had run into a were-creature or an animal with elevated intelligence, she had discovered quite by accident that the spell resulted in pants-crapping terror on the part of the viewer. It also resulted in a susceptibility to suggestion.

Alice felt the spell leave her as the flames died down. While she loved magic while actually doing it, it was extremely taxing on her person - and her person had already been taxed as it was. Taking a moment to steady herself, Alice made her way to the kitsune leader and stood before him as he cowered on his knees.

"You there," she bellowed, "what is your name?"

The kitsune trembled as it answered. "Ma...Makoto."

"Makoto," Alice said, "you and your men will serve me now, understood?"

"Hai."

"You may stay here if you wish, but you will not worship this statue anymore, do you understand?"

"Hai."

"Good. Now, I want you and your men to go out and gather some information for me. Can you make yourselves look as men?"

"Hai."

"Wonderful," Alice felt a wave of nausea as her body reacted to the sudden surge of magic. "I want you to find me a cup of tea, something to eat and a decent bathrobe. Now, please."

The kitsune man paused. "H...Hai."

"Good boy. Go on, then." Alice raised her voice to the trembling kitsunes as they barked and yipped, and in a mad frenzy flowed out of the main chamber, carrying their wounded as they went. Alice waited until the last one was out of sight and listened for the sound of their footsteps to retreat into the tunnels of the base before she dropped to her knees and proceeded to vomit.

Alice reminded herself that she really needed to practice magic more.

After a while, Alice felt a foreign, yet not unwelcome, sensation. It was something she had not felt since high school, and it made her feel equal parts humiliated and grateful all at once.

Alice gave an internal whimper at the all-too familiar feel of someone holding her hair back as she continued to empty her stomach.

When she was done, she steadied herself, took some deep breaths and gathered as much dignity as she could to face her benefactor. Makoto was standing in front of her, looking a bit uncomfortable and now decidedly human as he held out his ceremonial robe, a cup of tea and a vending machine sandwich. Alice noted that he had taken the time to change into a faded orange tee shirt, gym shorts and some worn flip-flops.

Alice blinked and then remembered she had just asked for exactly what Makoto was offering. Gratefully, she accepted the robe and food while Makoto stood patiently.

"Thank you," Alice said as she took a shaky sip of her tea.

"Are...um...are you all right?" Makoto looked unsure about asking.

Alice let out a small laugh. "Ten minutes ago you were ready to carve my heart out and now you're concerned about my well-being? You, sir, have a way with the ladies."

Makoto blushed and looked away. "We weren't *really* going to kill you; we were just going to scare you away. This is our place, and that," Makoto gestured to the golem, "that was our new God."

Alice nodded to the golem. "It is impressive. I won't lie; the last time I was in Japan, one of my goals was to find exactly that. In fact, that's why this base was built. The fact that we missed it by about three meters is pissing me off a bit, but... why, exactly, were you praying to this thing?"

Makoto looked down in embarrassment. "This was supposed to have been carved by Mushiro Tohachi, the first kitsune. It is said that the golem gives you power over your form. Some of us have trouble..."

Alice nodded. She had worked with enough weres in her time to know that the transforming aspect came easier for some than for others. In fact...

"Makoto, how thoroughly have you and your men explored this place?"

Makoto shrugged, "Enough to know where the refrigerators and bathrooms are."

"Did you ever open the old R&D lockers?"

Makoto shook his head. "We couldn't. The doors were sealed. Wait..."

Alice looked at him for a moment expectantly.

"Your mouth," he said, "it's not matching up with your words..."

Alice nodded and pointed to a spot just behind her ear. "Before I cast my spell, I activated my universal translator. My Japanese is okay, but not good enough yet for steady conversation. This chip under my skin does a quick mental mulligan on whoever is around and converts linguistic brainwave patterns to match language."

Makoto just stared.

"I'm speaking English, but your brain thinks I'm speaking Japanese, and vice-versa."

"Oh. Okay." Makoto nodded slightly, his eyes now glued to the side of Alice's head.

After finishing her tea, Alice led Makoto through the twisting corridors that led to the old R&D wing of the Purge's Nagoya chapter. The door was sealed, but the keypad was still glowing. Without hesitation, Alice typed in an eight number sequence. With a gentle swish, the doors slid open to reveal a mostly empty, sterile, white room with lockers lining the far wall.

"Welcome to the now abandoned research wing for the Purge's Japanese branch," Alice gestured casually as she crossed the room to the lockers and immediately started rooting through the third from the left.

Makoto took in his surroundings as she did so; it was a large, white room with steel tables and cameras mounted in the corners. The west facing wall was covered in a giant mirror, which Makoto suspected hid a room on the other side. The room had a cold, ominous feel to it, and it took a minute for Makoto to realize that the tables were large enough for people, and all of them had leather straps where arms, legs and heads would normally be.

"What did you do here?" Makoto asked.

"My boss was big into genetic mutation and human experimentation," Alice said as she continued to search, "He would pick up drifters in the park, offer them a meal, take them here and play Jenga with their DNA."

Makoto stared at her back in horror as Alice started to whistle while searching.

"That... that's horrible... You would murder the homeless just for fun?"

Alice sighed. "No, *he* would murder the homeless for genetic advancement. This was... this wasn't something I had direct input on. In fact, there were a good number of genetic projects that he kept me in the dark about."

Alice shrugged, "Hey, it's all good. I'm a good-guy now, so no more of this," Alice gestured around her as she continued to root through her locker. "Nope, now it's all good-guy stuff. Nice, annoying, time-consuming good-guy stuff. God, I remember when we had a problem, we solved it with dynamite, or fire, or something loud. Now I have to play Miss Marple and be careful about that whole "law' thing and...ah! Found it!"

Alice closed the locker and held out a handful of what looked like wrist watches. Makoto eyed them for a moment.

"What are those?"

Alice grinned. "Makoto, you and your pack work for me now. Never let it be said that Dyspell doesn't keep the considerations of her employees in mind."

Makoto scratched his head. "Well, you were gonna kill us a minute ago..."

Alice made a tsk-ing sound and shrugged. "Ten minutes ago, and I didn't, and now I have tea and everybody is happy, and you have these," Alice handed the watches to Makoto. "They're molecule regulators. We made them for agents who had unstable molecule issues. They also do wonders for regulating were transformations. Granted, I've never used them on a kitsune, but I figure foxes are enough like wolves that these should work just fine. Give them to the members of your pack who can't control what they do as well, and they'll straighten up real fast."

Makoto stared at the not-wrist watches and blinked. After a moment, he said, "No one has ever done anything like this for us before."

Alice shrugged and headed for the door.

"Why are you suddenly being so nice?"

Alice stopped at the door.

"Makoto," Alice said, "I've been in Japan for one day. In that time, I've had to deal with three attempts on my life. I have a job that feels just slightly shy of impossible, my leads are gone, my network of contacts is worthless as they were the ones who tried to kill me this morning, and I am mentally and physically exhausted. I need you and your men, Makoto. I need a network and people on the ground. I have a job to do and right now I don't know that I can without help."

"You are compelled to obey me, but that will wear off. When it does, I want you to keep serving me by choice. Those regulators are my gift to your pack. In return, I need a favor."

Makoto straightened and puffed his chest out. "We always help friends of the pack," he said with pride in his voice.

Alice turned around to face Makoto and nodded, her face set in stone. "I need to know what happened to Nanami Fukijima; she's a paralyzed sports columnist who went missing not too long ago."

Makoto nodded as Alice took out PhoneBuddy. "What's your number? I want to be able to keep in touch with you."

Makoto fumbled for his phone in his shorts pocket and rattled off his number. Alice had to think through calling an international number, but on the second try, she heard a small tune come from Makoto's phone.

"Wonderful. Learn what you can and report back to me the moment you hear anything. Find her, and I will reward you and your pack greatly. Do you understand?"

"Hai."

Alice nodded, only wondering idly why the translator never seemed to convert the word 'yes'.

"Makoto, I'm tired and I still have some work to do tonight. Why don't you go and get some rest, and see what you can find on Nanami. I'll text you her address." Alice was already typing it into her phone as she spoke.

Makoto nodded and still clutching the regulators, he headed back to his pack. Alice watched him go and then looked back at the research room. She felt herself give a small shudder as she looked around one last time.

"So, I'm a good guy now."

Alice turned and left, the door swishing behind her as she made her way back to the main chamber. It was a full minute before she realized she was clenching her fist.

When Alice returned to the main chamber, it was empty, save for the golem. Even though she was ready for bed, Alice couldn't turn down the opportunity in front of her. She felt like a child at Christmas, and she had just received the biggest present in the world.

After a moment spent examining the golem and recalling proper magical procedure, Alice set down her tea cup, finished her sandwich and got to work. With no small effort (she was a bit exhausted at this point), she climbed the statue until she reached its head. Grumbling to herself, she took out her Infinity knife and proceeded to cut a small slit on her thumb. Before her glove could seal the wound, she used the blood to draw a kanji character on the head of the statue and leapt down.

At first it looked like nothing had happened, but Alice could feel the shift in the room. She was sensitive to magic, and the magic in the Fudo golems was old, and very powerful.

At this point, Alice really wished she knew what to do next.

Sure, she had read up on this sort of thing, but this was her first time with a golem. While she was sure she had just activated it, she wasn't quite sure where to go from here.

Alice shrugged, cleared her throat and called out to the statue.

"Hi, there. Can you hear me?"

The statue stood stock still.

"If you can hear me, and if you know I am your master, raise your arm."

Again, the statue stood stock still. Alice was starting to feel a bit silly, which quickly translated into mad at this point.

"I woke you up, which means you can understand me. I am your master, Fudo, and I command you to raise your damn arm!"

And again, nothing happened.

Alice felt herself give a small whimper.

"Please raise your arm?"

Slowly, the right stone arm of the statue raised into the air.

Alice felt a huge, dopey grin spread across her face as she started to giggle to herself.

"Oh. My. God. I have a pet golem."

The statue stood still, its arm in the air.

"Oh! Please put your arm down."

The statue slowly lowered its arm.

Alice started to hop in place. Up until that moment, the day had been absolutely terrible. Now, however…

Now here she was with a pet golem.

"Hmmm… What to do with you? You're going to be difficult to get out of here, but I think I have an idea on that. In the meantime, I can't just call you golem. While cool, it feels a bit generic. You need a name. Can you talk?"

The golem stared straight ahead.

"I didn't think so. No offense, but it looks like Tohachi-san didn't put much thought into conversation."

The golem continued to stare straight ahead.

"Rocky is too generic, and I don't want to call you something stupid, like Goldy… what does one call an ancient Fudo golem? What does… Fudo! Hey! Hey golem! I'm going to call you Fudo. When I tell you to do something as Fudo, you do it, got it?"

The golem stared straight ahead.

"Fudo, please step forward."

The golem took a lumbering step forward, shaking off ancient dust as it did. Alice felt the entire complex rumble a bit as the golem took the step.

"Wow, you're easier to program than PhoneBuddy."

Alice looked around and noticed that the kitsune tribe, while being trespassers, had kept the place reasonably tidy. Alice felt her stomach tighten, and upon looking at her watch discovered that it was getting pretty late in the day. Tired, still somewhat hungry and in need of a shower, she wondered if the kitsune had taken to stocking the break room fridge.

"That sandwich wasn't enough. Fudo, I am going to eat, shower and sleep. Please guard the base until I say otherwise."

The golem stared straight ahead.

"Fudo, please nod your head when I give you a command that you understand."

The golem nodded its ancient head as best it could.

"So cool..." Alice said to herself. "Please stand there and...well...guard things until I need you again."

The golem nodded. Alice tried to contain a small -squee- noise in her throat as she left to explore the facility. The break room fridge was indeed filled with food, albeit leftovers from what she assumed were their cult meetings. The showers were also working, albeit with poor water pressure and zero heat. Alice didn't care; she was full and she was clean and she was alive. For a first day on the job, she was ready to chalk things up to a win. Idly, she wondered if the golem would count as a team member. After mulling it over, she decided that it really didn't matter; no one was going to argue with a walking tank.

Her old room was the way she had left it, clean, Spartan and with a bed just waiting for her. When the Purge had abandoned this facility, she had insisted that they left it spotless on the off chance they had to return. Alice believed in always having something ready, just in case. Granted, the files had all been burned and the computers had been removed, but the furniture was all in place. Right now, that was all that was important.

With her costume neatly folded on her bare desk and her combed-out wig set neatly on her clothes, Alice rooted around her old wardrobe until she found an old tee shirt and some shorts. She glanced in the small door mirror – she looked like she felt, deep circles under her eyes, and even after a shower she could see that her naturally purple hair mussed and tangled from being trapped under that damned wig. Exhausted, she climbed into her old bed and set PhoneBuddy to wake her in 6 hours. While she wanted to sleep for days, her sense of professional pride wouldn't allow it. After all, she had a meeting to go to the next day, and she didn't want to be late.

Chapter 5

"They were hers"

On the other side of the world and three miles beneath the surface of the ocean, Chris Ellswood, also known as the man-god Poseidon, stood on the observation deck of the *Crystal Foundation.* Carefully, he guided his salvage teams through the twisted wreckage of the Atlantean temple district. The *Crystal Foundation* was the flagship deep-water drilling and excavation platform of the Ellswood Foundations fleet, and Chris Ellswood had poured a small fortune into its construction.

For the last three months, the Ellswood Foundation's fleet had slowly crawled its way across the floor of the mid-Atlantic in search of the now-destroyed high temple of Poseidon (the God, not the hero). Now, after several false starts and bad leads, Chris was feeling tense with anticipation. At this very moment, his submersible crew was removing the last crumbled pillar from the front of the temple's antechamber.

Chris watched on his monitor spread as the robotic arms of his submersible crew slowly and carefully did their jobs. Behind him, his team of operators and technical advisors guided his crew in their task. Chris found he was holding his breath as the last pillar was lifted out of the way and the antechamber door was slowly forced open.

Chris had spent many years searching for Atlantis, like countless mortals and immortals before him. When he finally found it just three years ago, he hit the closest thing that a hero can to a mid-life crisis. Able to breathe underwater and gifted with superior strength when in the oceans, Chris had always hoped that it was due to some lost lineage. If there were any others like himself, they would be here. When Chris finally stumbled upon Atlantis, he discovered to his dismay that it was completely deserted, and that he was (as far as he knew) the only one of his kind.

Then, Alan Tanner discovered lost texts that detailed the existence of an eighth Phoenix. These ancient texts indicated that it might be located in the temple of Poseidon. While it was a shaky lead, it gave Chris something new to focus on. From that point forward, Chris had devoted his resources towards excavating the lost city, block by block.

Now, after all the searching and all the resources spent, Chris was about to find out if his search had finally paid off, or if he was to come up empty again. Eagerly, he watched as the team sent in their robotic mini-subs to do reconnaissance.

Chris took the mike from its terminal and flipped the switch for the main crew's channel. "There should be a narrow hallway with statues on either side leading to an elevated altar. Please be careful of the statues; the legends say their eyes are actually emeralds."

"You want us to collect some before we move forward?" a voice squawked back over the speakers.

Chris smiled, "How about afterwards? Just note if you see any for now. It would be nice if this treasure hunt could actually start paying for itself."

While not the billionaire that Blackthorne was, Chris was by any account, extremely wealthy. He had spent years collecting the riches from sunken cargo holds all over the world, and had amassed a fortune larger than the holdings of some small countries. This entire expedition was being paid for out of his own pocket; not that he minded, of course. Chris loved being underwater. If he had to stand on the dry, metal deck of a command platform instead of gliding through the depths, it was worth it to be able to talk to people.

Chris was in his 60s, and now knew that he was the only one of his kind left alive. After wasting the majority of his life searching for something that was apparently never there, he was tired of being alone.

Eagerly he and the rest of the bridge crew watched the monitors as the mini-sub reached the area of the temple where the high platform would have stood. As the sub slowly glided over a fallen piece of ceiling, Chris saw the barren pedestal and instantly felt a pang of dread. For a moment, he envisioned yet another failure, and that cold knot of anxiety started to grow in his stomach.

"Hold on, the sensors are picking up something behind the pedestal."

The entire bridge crew held its collective breath as the mini-sub crept over the pedestal and focused its camera lights downward.

Beneath the silt, a beautiful, purple light faintly shimmered back.

The bridge erupted in cheers as the mini-sub used its robotic arm and silt vacuum to slowly pry the Phoenix Statue, amazingly intact and unharmed, out of the debris. Chris felt his entire body loosen at once as the sub put the statue in its holding cradle and slowly backed out of the antechamber.

As the submersible crew returned to the wet-dock beneath the *Crystal Foundation*, they were met with cheers and applause. Chris nearly ran onto the submerged catwalk leading to the mini-sub and its storage cradle. Half submerged in subzero waters, he easily freed the statue and held it high to the ecstatic hollers and shouts of his team. After years of searching, false hopes and dead ends, the most important discovery in the history of mankind was theirs.

***

That night, all duty rosters were scrubbed. A facility-wide party was ordered as Chris broke out every ancient keg and bottle he had brought on board just for this occasion. The PA system was hijacked by a tech worker who decided it was put to better use by playing dance music, and the common room, usually used for TV, ping pong, and reading, had been converted into a dance hall. As Chris watched his team eat, drink, kiss, drink and drink some more, he idly wondered to himself what the future would now hold.

Chris stood to the side, sipping a glass of 200-year-old wine that they had found in a wreck last month and mused about what would come next. As he stood lost in thought, a young, blonde intern with large, green eyes bounced over to him with a smile. He noticed wryly that her jumpsuit was zipped up just enough to keep her out of trouble and not a millimeter more. Apparently, he wasn't *quite* as old as he had thought.

"Hey, you wanna dance?" The beautiful young woman asked, her pony-tail bobbing as she moved her head to the music. Chris couldn't help but notice she didn't seem to be wearing anything underneath the jumpsuit.

Chris smiled. "Sure," he said. "I don't recall seeing you before. Did you come on board with the new shift last week?"

"Yeah," the young girl said, her head bobbing lightly to the beat, "I shipped in with the crew from Boston. I'm Anna."

"I'm Chris."

"Well, yeah. I know," Anna said, giggling as she moved with the music, and then against Chris.

Chris suddenly had a very good idea of what the immediate future would hold.

After a few minutes of dancing, Anna leaned in and whispered in Chris's ear, "Hey, you wanna get out of here?"

Chris looked at the young lady, considering his answer. He was an older man, with admittedly loose morals when it came to physical pleasure, and he didn't want to lead her on. On the other hand, she was built like a supermodel, this was a party, and he honestly could not think of a single good reason to turn an offer like this down.

Quietly, they slipped away from the party and back to his quarters.

Later, as Chris lay in bed basking in the afterglow, he watched Anna stand naked at the view port to his room. The perimeter evening lights were on, illuminating the blackness of the Atlantic just outside with a dark, blue glow. Anna was silhouetted against it, and Chris marveled at the soft, indigo outline of her figure.

"That was wonderful, by the way," Chris said. He meant it, too. It had been a while.

"Thank you. I've been looking forward to this for a long time, you know." Anna collected her clothes, turned back to Chris and made her way back to where he lay. Carefully, she placed her folded jumpsuit at the foot of the bed.

"Really?"

"Oh yeah," Anna said as she leaned in to kiss him, "and it was totally worth it."

She continued to kiss Chris as she eagerly climbed on top of him. Beneath him, Chris barely felt a slight rumble.

"Did... did you feel that?" Chris asked.

"Are you kidding me?" Anna said with a half-laugh.

The bed rumbled again, this time with a bit more force. Chris tried to sit up. "There it was again. That was the base. Anna, something's wrong."

Anna nodded and reached behind her into a mussed pile of her clothes at the foot of the bed. "I know."

Before Chris could react, Anna brought out a curved, jewel-encrusted knife from the pile and plunged it into his chest.

111

Chris screamed as Anna smiled down at him. Around them, the base vibrated with a strong shudder as an alarm claxon sounded in the hallway.

"You know," Anna said as Chris gargled back some blood and clutched at his wound, "I honestly didn't think this would be that easy. Seriously, you're old enough to be my grandfather! For a hero, your moral compass is waaaaay off."

Anna grabbed the knife and twisted it in the wound, causing Chris to scream and clutch at her wildly.

"I will admit, you are a prime specimen of manhood, but as far as being a cautious hero, you failed miserably. Do you really just jump in bed with any young thing that grinds on you? Who do you think you are, James Bond?"

Anna hopped off of Chris as he started to convulse. Casually, she picked up a towel and dabbed the blood off her chest as she hummed to herself.

"Who...who are..." Chris managed through the blasts of pain.

Anna turned to answer, but instead let out a yelp as the entire station lurched to the left and started to lean at a slight angle. Chris clutched at the bed as he began to slide off.

"That would be Totallus. I told him to have some fun, but I figured he would take it easy until we knew for sure you were down."

Anna slipped her jumpsuit back on, this time zipping the front all the way to her neck. She walked to where Chris lay at the edge of the bed, leaned over and spoke softly into his ear.

"The knife is a cursed Infinity blade. It won't come out until your heart stops beating and your body grows cold. Your team is dead; all of them. The moment we left the room, I dropped a vial of airborne nanite toxins behind us. They were dying while we fucked. Anyone who was in the wet-dock working or studying the Phoenix was killed by my shock troops when they boarded the station. And Totallus," Anna gestured towards the window, "he's been waiting out there for *days*. We moved the second you got the Phoenix on board."

Angrily, Chris tried to get up, but Anna pressed the knife down, through his chest with surprising strength, and pinned him to the bed.

"There," she said, "that should hold you until you're nice and dead. I have to say, I half-expected a long, drawn-out fight, but as you've already experienced, I'm flexible."

Whistling to herself, Anna half-skipped out of the room as Chris's heart stopped beating.

***

In the wet-dock stood a team of eight shock troops in wetsuits, laser-sighted pulse rifles in hand. Their faces were completely covered by opaque, reflective masks, their breathing echoing against the metal walls of the docking bay.

In the middle of the soldiers stood a humanoid figure, easily eight feet tall, wearing black, skin tight pants held up by what looked like a large, circular silver belt with the symbol of a flame in the center. His top half was covered in a V-necked black and purple, skin-tight shirt that showed off his figure, and the skin that was visible had a metallic sheen to it. His forearms were clasped in silver gauntlets, and his face was long, with sunken, black eyes and a smooth, bald head.

"Totallus," Anna said to the humanoid as she entered the wet-dock, "report."

Totallus responded in a deep, rich, reverberating voice, "The crew is liquidated. The Phoenix is in our possession." Totallus gestured to a large, black duffle bag held by one of the shock troops. "We may evacuate at any time, Mistress."

Anna smiled to herself as she took the duffle bag from the soldier. "I want Poseidon's personal sub yacht. You didn't destroy it yet, did you?"

"Not yet, Mistress," Totallus replied, his face devoid of emotion.

"Good boy," Anna nodded and then turned her attention to her troops. "Set the charges for five minutes and then clear out as fast as you can. Meet back at the northern diving bells. It will take a good 18 hours to decompress, so I hope you brought something to read. Get a move on!"

The shock troops scattered without a word. Anna nodded and turned to Totallus, who tossed her a set of keys. Anna caught them and stared for a moment.

"For his sub," Totallus rumbled.

"Excellent, you can ride with me."

"The vial, Mistress?"

Anna snapped her fingers and nodded. "Thanks. You know, I almost forgot about that… now where…aha!"

Anna pulled a small vial of dark blue liquid out from her belt and went to the water docks edge. Carefully, she poured the thick, viscous chemical into the water.

"And we're sure this will work?" Anna asked the giant behind her. Totallus nodded.

"It was made specifically for this purpose. The Master does not fail."

"Yes, yes, the Master does not fail. Except when he does. Ah, well, I guess we'll just have to wait and see, won't we?" Anna shrugged her shoulders and smiled at the emotionless behemoth as she dropped the vial into the water and strolled down the dock to the massive white submersible yacht parked at the end.

Poseidon had the sub yacht built as a tool for business use. Personally, he didn't need it; he could swim just as fast and as deep as the yacht could go. His clients and business partners, however, could not, and Chris very quickly learned to appreciate the luxuries of comfort that the yacht provided.

Anna let out an impressed whistle when she saw the yacht's interior. The walls were a glossy black with running lights along the bottom and under the wooden railing that ran the length of the cockpit. The control panel was an LED maze of lights and dials, and the carpeting was a soft, fluffy shag. In the back was a giant, round mattress under a huge, golden clamshell. Anna rolled her eyes. It was an 80's spy movie brought to life.

"This is… I don't know whether to be disgusted or impressed. A thousand showers will not remove that man's skeeziness," Anna mumbled to herself. Quickly, she placed the bag with the Phoenix off to the side in a storage bin and took the controls. Beside her, Totallus strapped in silently.

A quick check of the controls confirmed that the sub was prepped and ready to go. Without a word, Anna released the docking clamps and guided the sub downward, hitting the running lights and gunning the propellers. After a solid minute, she reached into her jumpsuit and pulled a small, square device with a switch from the front. Without looking, she flicked her thumb over the switch.

Behind the sub yacht, the *Crystal Foundation* erupted in a massive explosion of bubbles and a momentary flash of light before completely imploding on itself.

Anna gripped the controls of the sub as tightly as she could, fighting the shockwave and then the suction from the blast. Totallus watched her as he steadied himself in his seat. After a few moments, the sea calmed down and the echoes of the blast subsided.

Anna stayed tense for a minute or so longer, and then relaxed as she realized she had been holding her breath. After punching in the autopilot coordinates, she turned to Totallus and said, "Take over for a while. I'm going to find the shower and get the Poseidon off of me. Oh, and radio in that we have the Phoenix, and that, unfortunately, we lost the team in the skirmish."

Totallus stared at her.

Anna sighed. "Look, I would have had to pay them a huge bonus for completing that job, and really, they killed, what, four drunk guards? I was the one who planned the operation, snuck on board, killed the crew and slept with the geezer. My job, my effort, my bonus."

Totallus continued to stare.

"Fine. They were hers, okay? They may follow my commands now, but what's gonna happen down the road? They weren't reliable for me, and I can't have that if I'm going to give orders."

"As you command, Mistress. You are in charge."

Anna strutted to the hatch leading to the rest of the yacht, her eyes focused dead ahead.

"That's right," she said to herself as the hatch hissed open. "I'm in charge."

Chapter 6

Living the Dream

Then

***

Alice was busy looking over her books for the week when the door chime alerted her to a potential customer. *Rare Gems* had been in business for six months and already was earning a solid reputation as a reliable mover of jewelry merchandise. At times, Alice wondered at the meteoric climb to success her business had experienced, but then tried not to read too much into it. After all, she and Allison knew their stuff, so why wouldn't they be this good?

The blonde woman standing in her shop was young, attractive and somewhat overdressed. Alice recognized that this was the young woman who had phoned about the receptionist's position the night before. Alice looked her over for a moment and then approached her, all smiles. "Hello, and welcome to *Rare Gems*. I'm Alice Gailsone," Alice offered her hand, which the younger blonde eagerly shook. Alice noted the pretty white smile and wide, eager eyes.

"Hi, I'm Cindy Berkshire? We spoke on the phone?" Alice nodded and gestured for her to come around the counter to a little desk she had set up. Alice offered Cindy a seat and then took the one across from her.

Alice stared at the young woman for a moment and said, "Cindy, this job that you called about… Look, we're a small firm. A *very* small firm. We need someone who can work a customer and take an order. Are you a people person?"

Cindy nodded, "Oh yes. Back in college I…"

Alice held up her hand. "I'll make this brief. You're desperate, cute and seemingly polite. You can speak English and make eye contact, so I'm guessing you fit the bill. Would you like the job?"

Cindy stared at Alice for a moment. "I'm sorry?"

Alice pointed to Cindy's clothes. "That is the only suit you own. There is no way you would wear that to an interview unless you absolutely had to. It's nice, but it's too flashy for what you're trying to do. You walked in with high energy because you needed to be noticed, and you're underweight, Cindy. There's a difference between dieting and living off of Ramen. Plus, when we shook, I felt your hands. You've been busing tables and washing dishes in the evenings to get by, haven't you? I could see the stains from the diner on your shoes. You'll need new shoes. In short, you need this job, I need someone to man...woman the store, and I think you're desperate enough to do it, so welcome aboard."

Cindy bit her lip and said, "I'm sorry, this was a mistake. I... thank you for your time." Cindy stood up and Alice stood to meet her.

"Cindy, stop." Alice held out her hand and smiled. "None of that was meant to be harsh. I said it because if you're going to work here, you need to look the part, you need to be tough with clients who will take advantage of you, and you need to understand that I do not miss things, Cindy. I may not seem like it at times, but I swear to you, I notice everything. I'm offering you a job where you'll be handling a small fortune in gemstones; you need to know why I'm offering it to you."

Cindy nodded, "I get it, still... that was a little harsh, ma'am."

Alice nodded. "Okay, point. It's a holdover from my last job."

"What was your last job?" Cindy asked.

"Human Resources Director. Now, you take this." Alice grabbed a small purse from her desk and fished out several hundred dollars. She then put it in the stunned girl's hands. "Go and buy yourself some nice, business-casual suits, skirts and pants. Yes you will wear skirts occasionally; some of our clientele are more easily swayed when greeted in the lobby or at the airport by a pretty gal with good legs."

Cindy eyed Alice. "Isn't that sexual harassment?"

Alice shrugged. "Not sure, but It's the truth. We're a small firm, and aside from Douglas, we're all women. Don't worry about Douglas; he's our gemstone cutter, and he's old enough to be your grandfather."

Cindy kept staring at Alice. "How could you not know that's sexual harassment and have been in Human Resources?"

Alice sighed. "I wasn't a terribly *good* Human Resources Director. Now, take that money, buy some nice clothes, eat a big meal and be here by 7:30am. You'll open the store with me and shadow me for the day. Then you'll shadow Allison for a day. Then if you still want the job, you can stay."

"How do you know I won't just take this money and run? This seems awfully trusting of you," Cindy said. Alice gave her a level stare and held up her resume.

"First, I know where you live. Steal from me and I will kill you. I really don't budge on that point. Second, you're too smart if you went to college and too desperate if you've been bussing tables to throw away a quality job with benefits and a pay scale by taking a few hundred from an irate business owner, or am I wrong?"

Cindy shook her head 'no'. "Um, did you just threaten my life? I really don't think that..." Alice smiled and held up a hand to stop her.

"It was... figurative. Of course. Third, it wasn't that long ago that I was homeless, near-broke and directionless in life. We smell our own, and honey, you *reek* of desperation. Just show up, do good work and do you do drugs?"

"Oh! No, no ma'am."

"Great. Welcome aboard. Now go eat and get some nicer clothes. You start in the morning."

"Great! Thank you so much!" Cindy said, her face a huge grin. Alice was worried the young woman would start bouncing up and down.

Alice shook her head. "Don't thank me yet; you haven't shadowed Allison. Now get out of here and come back looking more… not the way you're looking, which is fine and all but…just go buy something new."

Now

***

Alice awoke from a messy dream to the sound of PhoneBuddy chirping wildly from her metal nightstand. With a groggy, incoherent string of curse words, Alice groped from under her covers until she found the offending phone and lobbed it at the nearest wall. PhoneBuddy promptly stopped chirping as Alice sighed to herself.

Alice hated waking up mid-dream, and this one had been about the old days; a job at Madison Square Garden that didn't go as she had hoped. She didn't know why, but it stood out for her and wouldn't leave her mind, even as she attempted to take one more (extremely quick) cold shower before dressing. That had been a pretty routine heist with a fantastic helicopter escape, but nothing more than her usual. Still, Alice had learned a *little* about magic, and one of those lessons had been to pay attention to her dreams.

After mulling it over, she decided that it wasn't that important. She had bigger concerns, namely the big concern quietly guarding her secret base. Fudo hadn't moved one inch since Alice had left him standing there the night before, and for a moment Alice felt bad about it, but then she shrugged it off. He was a golem, after all. What did he care?

"What to do with you?" Alice said as she adjusted her bath towel and marveled at her new toy. While not a giant, the golem was 10 feet tall and that meant it wouldn't exactly blend in on the street. Alice considered ordering it to just charge out the main entrance, but that would cause a scene, destroy part of Nagoya castle and probably get her in trouble. She just wasn't in the mood to start her day off poorly.

Then Alice remembered the kitsune tribe. They had left pretty quickly the night before, and Alice wondered how they had managed before she remembered that the base had service entrances connected to the city sewer system. These in turn connected to a vast underground shopping mall beneath central Nagoya.

121

"Okay, we can get out that way. Now... how do I disguise a ten-foot-tall stone monster without arising any suspicion?"

Alice shivered as she noticed a draft, mentally amending her to-do list.

"And buy some clean clothes, get some breakfast and have a corporate meeting?"

The golem stared straight ahead.

"You are not helpful, Mr. Awesome Engine of Soulless Death."

Alice sighed as she considered her options. Money was not an issue; even if Tanner hadn't provided her with a credit card, she had her own. She was, after all, pretty well set financially. Clothes weren't really an issue either. She knew of several stores that carried fashions that she liked, and there was a TokyoHands ('the WalMart of Japan', as she called it) nearby. No, her biggest concern now was that she had only one move she could make, and the people who had tried to kill her yesterday were the ones who had provided it.

Alice knew it was most likely a trap, but she did find it odd that Yoshi had taken the time to let her know about Lotus before trying to kill her. To be fair, she downed the poison before he had told her, but that was just splitting hairs in her eyes.

Alice straightened her towel and headed back to her room for her outfit and suit. She had to get dressed, do some research, get some breakfast and move a golem. Alice headed to the stairway that led to her quarters and stepped around some metal debris that had no doubt been a result of the earthquake that freed Fudo. About midway up the stairs, Alice paused, turned around, and stared.

"Wait. I'm in Japan."

And just like that, Alice knew what she had to do.

***

The crowds in the Nagoya mall were small in the morning, and the fact that it was a weekday meant they weren't crowded at all, which made things easier for Alice. Honestly, she didn't know if she could handle a large crowd snapping photos of her without slipping into villain territory at this point. Still, she was impressed at her idea's mind-blowing level of awesomeness, and mentally patted herself on the back for a job well done.

In the middle of the mall, its (his?) head barely clearing the ceiling, stood Fudo. He was wrapped in sheet metal from head to toe that had been appropriated from the Purge compound. With some added spray paint that Alice had found in a storage closet, her golem looked very much like a large, slow-moving robot.

At first, Alice wasn't sure how to get Fudo to put the costume together correctly. She tried describing what she had in mind three times, but Fudo had been asleep for a long time, and had never watched modern television. The concept of a giant robot was simply lost on him. Finally, Alice dug some paper and some colored pencils out of an office desk she found in the working quarters and sketched a rough draft of what she thought a giant robot should look like. Fudo stared (Alice assumed he was staring - it was kind of hard to tell with his eyes being stone), nodded and began bending metal around him until he had what a three-year-old with brain damage might mistake for a robot. At a distance. At night. During a thunderstorm.

At first, Alice was scared that her cunning plan was going to blow up in her face, but 30 seconds into leaving the service tunnel and emerging from a false store front (the sign said 'closed for renovations'), she knew she had hit gold. Children squealed, adult men clamored around and adult women walked quickly away. It was perfect.

For added effect, Alice bought a stereo unit with some portable speakers from a nearby electronics outlet. Then, she ducked over to a media outlet and grabbed several Anime soundtrack CDs. After ordering

Fudo to stand in the middle of the mall, she put the stereo at his feet, popped in a random soundtrack and hit play.

"Fudo, please move your torso and arms at random and wave at people."

The golem stared straight ahead.

Alice became exasperated. "Here, just... watch me, okay?" Alice began her own awkward rendition of the Robot, but very slowly and with some added jerking in her movements. Around her, the audience began to snicker and point. Alice seethed.

'Not a villain. Not a villain. Do not kill the mall. Do not kill the mall. Not a villain....'

Alice found that soothing mantras were helpful in times of stress.

To the audience's delight, the robot/golem started moving in time with the music, copying Alice as she moved.

"Good! Now, please just keep that up while I go shopping. I'll be back in a bit. Please don't be afraid to improvise!"

Alice patted Fudo's side and scurried away, mindful of the Yen coins the audience was tossing at the robot's feet.

"Eh, why not?" Alice said to herself as she headed to the nearest clothing outlet.

Two hours, a dozen card charges and one quick meal later, Alice was in a new suit and had a full belly. Upon returning to Fudo, she found a large crowd gathered around him as he moved in time with the music. Then, to Alice's horror, Fudo picked up a small child with one large hand, lifted her above the crowd and set her down on the other side.

The other children in the audience cheered and clamored to be next.

Alice pushed her way to the front as parents and kids gave her disapproving looks.

"When I said improvise, I meant do an extra wave or turn, not pick up children! They're tiny, and very, very squishable! You could have squished them! What do you think you're doing?!"

Fudo stopped as he reached for another child and looked in Alice's direction as she fumed.

"Fudo, please go to the stairs, now. We are going outside."

Alice rubbed her temples and sighed. The golem *had* done what she had asked, and admittedly, the children didn't seem hurt. While Alice wondered if she or the golem would eventually get blamed for any accidents, she figured that either way, murdered children would not go far towards her staying off the International Most Wanted lists.

Slowly, the golem lumbered towards the exit as the crowd cheered. Alice waited until they dispersed, and then quickly gathered the coins the crowd had tossed on the ground.

Topside, Alice checked PhoneBuddy for directions to Nakajima Tower. It was 12 blocks through city traffic, and she couldn't exactly call a cab. After mulling it over, she shrugged, smoothed her gray, pinstriped pants and suit jacket, checked her red silk blouse and made sure her new black pumps were scuff-free. She made sure her wig was firmly attached, and then ordered Fudo to put her on his shoulder. Once there, she had Fudo pick up her shopping bags as she put on her large, white $800 Gucci sunglasses and held onto the side of Fudo's head.

Alice smiled to herself; it felt good to dress up, and while sexy and professional, this outfit hid her other work clothes nicely. The only piece she wore outright was her belt, which matched her loose, oversized purple tie. Her new Prada purse held her boots, wallet and Infinity knife with room to spare. It was quickly becoming a good day.

As they made their way down the sidewalk, Alice's phone rang.

"This is Alice," She said.

"I received a notification from the bank saying you racked up $3,200 dollars on the credit card." The voice wasn't as gruff as it had been before, but it was still stern. "What exactly are you up to?"

Alice leaned against Fudo's head as he rumbled his way across an intersection. A passing motorist was busy watching the spectacle and rear-ended a compact.

"Livin' the dream, boss."

"Alice, this isn't a party. I sent you because you have a reputation for being professional. I sent you because you were supposed to be the best."

Alice sighed, her smile fading from her face. "I had two attempts on my life, fought a were-cult, created an underground spy network of kitsune and got a golem. That was day one. Now I'm on my way to a meeting that you hopefully didn't forget to set up."

There was a pause on the other end of the phone.

"Isn't Japan great?" Alice said.

"Your hotel had an incident last night," Alan said, "every single person staying on your floor was found dead; their throats were slit open."

Alice felt a knot in her stomach and an unexpected surge of anger. There had been a family with three children in the room next to her. The pig-tailed little girl had actually said hi to her, which at the time had freaked her the Hell out. Now, they were all dead. Apparently, the Dead Talon didn't like being embarrassed.

"It wasn't me," Alice automatically said.

"I know," Alan said, his voice losing a bit of its edge, "local authorities are calling it a cult slaying, but this smacks of the Dead Talon. Alice... look, I thought this would be a simple recruitment assignment. I didn't expect to throw you into the deep end so soon after being out of the game. If you want, I can pull you and we can have someone else take over."

Alice thought back to the day before, and how quickly everything had escalated. She thought about Nanami and her apartment, and about the hotel.

"Mr. Tanner, quitting mid-game isn't how I became the most dangerous woman in the world. You wanted Dyspell. Now you have her, and she is getting more and more agitated as this assignment continues. I don't like being targeted, and I don't like mysteries. I want to know what's going on and I'm going to find out. I'm going to eat well *and* dress well as I do, and you will pay for it."

"Alice, you're rich. Do you really need to rack up my company card?"

Alice smirked, even though Alan couldn't see it.

"By the way," Alice said, "How goes the Phoenix hunting?"

Alan paused. "We received a message yesterday that Poseidon's team located it, and then nothing. We've been trying to raise them for hours without any luck. I've alerted the Coast Guard and put in a call to Superior Force, so we should know something soon."

Alice took a moment to compose herself before speaking, trying to tamp down her growing rage. When she spoke, it was in a cold, clipped tone.

"So. You *lost* it."

"We don't know that," Alan said, concern in his voice. "Chris...Poseidon was heading the team. If there were any problems, I'm sure he would have been more than capable of handling them."

127

"He's over 60, and can be easily defeated by a miniskirt."

Alice swore she could hear a small sigh from the other end of the line.

"So, Alan, what you're telling me is there's a good chance that you never had or are no longer in possession of the Phoenix."

The short silence from the other end was her answer.

"Alan, do you remember when we were in your office and I took the job?"

"Yes?"

"You know the clothes I bought this morning?"

"Yes?"

"I left my corporate card in my hotel room."

"Uh . . . I'm sorry?"

"I used your private card, Alan."

Alice hung up before Alan could answer.

***

The dealership was small and crammed between an office building and a tempura shack, but it had several nice models of sports car to choose from. While foreigners normally had a difficult time purchasing a vehicle of any type in Japan, it definitely helped to have Alan Tanner's personal Black card. Alice hadn't really cared which one she bought as long as it was the most expensive. She ran her 'borrowed' card, bowed to the sales associate, drove the car exactly one block and then parked in front of a hobo sitting near an alley way.

Alice walked up to the scruffy, smelly man and tapped him on the shoulder to wake him up. The sleeping bum snapped awake with a sputtering. Alice, still leaning over, smiled at him and held out the car keys.

"The title is in the glove box. Consider this a gift and remember to pay it forward. Thanks!"

The hobo stared with disbelieving eyes at Alice. Alice waited for the man to take the keys, but he refused to move. After a moment, Alice stopped smiling and said, "Look, do you want a shiny new car or not? No strings attached, I swear."

The hobo eyed Alice and then looked past her to the shiny red compact sports car behind her. After a moment, he grinned a crooked, toothy grin and took the keys from her hand. Alice smiled and waved as the hobo drove off, veering wildly into traffic.

"Well, now I feel a little bit better," Alice said to herself. She had already outlined a mental to-do list involving Alan's credit card, but now that list had compounded by a factor of 1,000 upon hearing that he had found and then lost the Phoenix. As Fudo lumbered up behind Alice, she nodded to herself and climbed back on his shoulder. After patting him on the head, she continued on her way to her meeting.

Nakajima Tower was easily the tallest building in Nagoya, and was responsible for the employment of a staggering 15% of the local population. Nakajima Toshino had been the primary innovator of a new type of dry cell battery that could recharge in a matter of seconds, paving the way for revolutionary advances in cell phone and portable device technology.

In just five years, his enterprise had grown to include distributors in Russia, Holland, Germany and Dubai. The United States was in the final stages of approving his devices for use on their networks. According to Business World, Nakajima Toshino was the #1 entrepreneur to watch for the coming year.

Alice parked Fudo half a block away in front of a micro-park, instructing him to act like a robot statue unless she called. To Alice's delight, Fudo nodded and then stood stock still. Alice found a public locker set and stored her new clothes, straightened her suit and entered the impressive front lobby to Nakajima Tower.

A young woman with a short skirt, white smile and prim clipboard greeted Alice as she entered the facility. To Alice's surprise, the young lady spoke perfect English.

"Miss Gailsone? I am Megumi. I will be your escort until Mr. Nakajima arrives. Please follow me."

Alice let Megumi lead on as she took her to a large elevator nestled at the end of a bank of smaller elevators. With the swipe of a key card, the doors swished open. Megumi stepped aside and allowed Alice to enter, and then followed. Once the doors closed, Megumi pressed her thumb to a black panel, causing it to light up with a soft green glow. Alice felt them moving down.

"Megumi? Out of curiosity, shouldn't we be going up to Mr. Nakajima's office?"

Megumi nodded her head slightly. "Yes, but first Mr. Nakajima wanted me to give you a tour of our facilities. Here, please put on a protective mask before setting foot on the factory floor."

Alice took the mask and put it on as the elevator doors swished open, revealing a massive underground factory. Under the tower was a huge warehouse-like environment, filled with line after line of tables covered in electronics parts. Sitting at those tables were hundreds of men and women in white coats and masks, busily piecing parts together and putting them in blue bins. Alice noted that the parts seemed to be coming at a semi-steady stream from side doors, behind which Alice could hear the sound of heavy machinery.

"We have worked hard to make this facility the top producer of cell phone and electronic devices in all of Japan," Megumi said with pride. Alice nodded; the facility was indeed impressive. With a gesture, Alice was led to a side set of stairs that led to the far end of the facility. There, she was taken to a smaller room that looked like a makeshift conference room. A smoked glass sheet served as one entire wall of the room. On the conference table in the middle sat five devices.

Megumi took off her mask, gestured to the devices and smiled. "Miss Gailsone, Mr. Nakajima is a very busy man. He wanted to see if I could answer any questions about these devices for you before you met him."

Alice gave Megumi the eye as she took off her own mask and then turned her attention to the phones on the desk. She had been wondering what was going on when she wasn't taken directly to see Nakajima, and now she knew; she was being tested. They didn't buy that she was there as a representative of Alan Tanner, and now they wanted to prove it.

Alice strode over to the table, picked up the first phone and studied it for a moment. Without a word, she dropped in on the table and idly turned to the others.

"That was a cheap Korean knock-off. The screen was plastic, not quartz, and the battery pack fit poorly."

Alice scanned the other devices. Of the remaining four, two had plastic screens. The other two were tablet-phones, but one seemed a bit off. Alice picked it up and flipped it over, studying the device. After examining it closely, Alice brought it close to her face and sniffed. With a calm demeanor, she smiled and turned to Megumi.

"Why, Megumi. I can't seem to power this particular phone up. Would you be so kind?"

Alice offered the phone to Megumi, who smiled and let out a small laugh.

131

"That is quite alright, Miss Gailsone."

"Please, call me Alice. After all, if you're going to try to kill me, we might as well be on a first name basis."

Megumi paled as Alice offered the phone again.

"There's a slit near the power button on this device. It's big enough for a needle, and the casing has the smell of carbon tetrachloride. While it is used in some factories, I doubt you're making fire extinguishers."

Megumi backed away as Alice advanced, still holding out the phone.

"Do you have any idea what it takes to keep yourself from dying of carbon tetrachloride poisoning? Do you even know what the chemical byproducts are when that crap breaks down? I should make you eat this goddamn thing on general principle!" Alice moved for the young woman, who was now backed against the wall.

"That won't be necessary."

The voice on the intercom speaker was crisp and halted, and Alice relaxed. She turned her attention to the smoked glass wall and nodded. "Mr. Nakajima, or should I say Nakajima-san? How Western can I go before you take offense?"

The glass wall slid apart to reveal a nicer office behind it, and standing before it was a short, older man with white hair and a sharp black suit. Without looking at Megumi, the man said, "Megumi-chan, you may leave."

"H…hai." Megumi bowed deeply and quickly left the room. Alice didn't bother to watch her go. Casually, she gestured to the table behind her.

"Was all this really necessary?"

Mr. Nakajima smiled and turned back towards his office. He headed towards a minibar off to the side, which Alice noted was packed to the gills with exotic beverages.

"We've had a surprising number of corporate spies down here. One of them even had your same story. I wanted to be sure."

"Really?" Alice moved to sit on a large, leather sofa that was facing Nakajima's desk while her host mixed drinks at the bar.

"Yes. You would be amazed at the parties that try to get in here. We have had to go to extraordinary lengths to keep things quiet. When we heard from Tanner that he wanted a meeting, and that you were already here, we were a bit gun-shy. And please, be as Western as you wish."

Mr. Nakajima turned to Alice and offered her a drink in a small, porcelain cup. Alice nodded her thanks and took a small sip. After a moment, she nodded and smiled.

"Thank you for the drink, Mr. Nakajima, and thank you for not adding to this one. I've had some dubious experiences with liquor since arriving."

Nakajima paused and considered the small woman in front of him before continuing.

"I need to know why you are here, Miss Gailsone," Nakajima said as he sat at his desk and sipped his Sake.

"I thought you knew. I'm here to review products and decide if you're a good fit for Tanner Industries."

Mr. Nakajima shook his head and smiled a huge, toothy smile.

"No. I need to know why Dyspell is sitting in my office, lying to my face."

Alice sighed a little. Having a reputation could bite both ways, she reminded herself.

"What I told you is true; I am here acting as a representative for Tanner Industries. Mr. Tanner is looking to expand into the Asian market and he knows about my familiarity with how things operate."

"You expect me to believe that Mr. Tanner would hire someone like yourself?" Nakajima emphasized the 'Mr. Tanner'. Alice wondered if she was supposed to act surprised that Nakajima knew about Alan Tanner's extra-curricular activities.

"Mr. Tanner hired Alice Gailsone, one of the leading market experts in gemstones and crystal appraisal, to personally inspect Nakajima Industries and see if your next generation of LCD and touch screen crystal would be up to American standards. He also hired the number one independent trader of precious stones in the International market to transition her skills towards tech, which has been a quite comfortable fit, to tell the truth."

Alice had been considering the validity behind her backstory, and the more she thought it through, the more it made sense to her. She was an expert, she did know international shipping and she could negotiate even without a death ray. Already, she was considering exploring Vodaphone options once her work for Tanner was finished.

"And what, exactly, would any of that have to do with our mutual friends at the Red Bunny?"

Alice tensed slightly. Nakajima knew more than he was letting on.

"On a personal level, I'm looking for a former acquaintance and I believe you may know where she is," Alice said, her voice as level as a calm pond.

"And who would that be?"

"A young lady that up until recently was in your employ. You knew her as Lotus, the chief assassin for the Dead Talon."

Nakajima's eyebrows went up slightly in mock surprise. "Miss Gailsone, I am surprised you think me so base. What would I be doing with such company?"

Alice gave a light shrug. "I really couldn't say. It's none of my business why she was here, but I do need her for a little side project. Her former employers seem to think she was working as a body guard for you. In fact, they were dead positive. Of course, I suppose they could have been mistaken..."

Nakajima glanced at Alice with a smirk and nodded. "Yes, I knew her. I had her in my employ for a brief time, but then she vanished. I already told this to the Dead Talon. Tell me, when did you start doing their dirty work, Miss Gailsone?"

Alice shook her head. "I don't. Like I said, this is something I'm working on independently."

"And Mister Tanner is comfortable with you doing this?"

Alice smiled a bit. "Mr. Tanner only cares that his interest in the Asian market are represented professionally. Japan is his area of concern, so as his newest employee, it is my area of concern. I came here to negotiate licensing. The fact that Lotus was recently here is a happy coincidence."

Nakajima swished his sake cup lightly in his hand as he stared at it. After a moment, he started speaking while examining his drink.

"Miss Gailsone, I keep a very close eye on potential business movements in the technology market. I can tell you the trends for the next 24 months - who will profit, and who will not. You could call it a gift; it is my business to know my business, and believe me when I say that Tanner Industries has no interest in moving into my arena. They have made no inquiries, no purchases and have done nothing to feel out the market, and I doubt that they would start by hiring a former criminal and then beg for an impromptu meeting."

Alice let out a small sigh. She knew her plan had been flimsy, but now she just felt like an amateur.

"Miss Gailsone, if all you wanted was the Lotus, you should have just said so. While I am insulted by your deception, I am impressed that you were able to have Alan Tanner contact me personally to arrange this meeting. As I don't feel like being bothered again, I will tell you what I know. Like I said, she vanished. She was supposed to show up for work and simply didn't appear. I haven't seen her since. No one from the Dead Talon has seen any trace of her, either. It's a pity, but sometimes help just doesn't work out."

Alice shook her head again and smirked. "No, I don't think so, Mr. Nakajima. With someone like Lotus, it isn't a simple matter of things 'just not working out'. The Lotus is an expert fighter and master of stealth. If you were keeping her in your employ then you must have had a damn good reason to need someone like her. If she up and vanished, then whoever could have made that happen would have then made you very, very dead."

Mr. Nakajima nodded a bit and sipped his sake. "I suppose that would be true."

"Why was the Lotus working for you, Mr. Nakajima?"

"If you must know, someone made an attempt on my life. I checked around, but no one would come forward to claim responsibility. I was nervous and I wanted protection, and the Dead Talon offered it. Once she went missing, they decided that I wasn't worth the trouble."

Alice nodded to herself. "No, I suppose you wouldn't be, would you? After all, is it ever worth it to lose a good employee?"

Mr. Nakajima shook his head, "You are a very forward woman, Miss Gailsone."

"I try," Alice said, laughing a little. "Tell me, are you excited about this weekend's match-up?"

Nakajima laughed a bit. "Of course I am. I even have a little riding on Koruga."

"I thought you might. I did some reading on the way over here. Koruga is the favored wrestler for the weekend match-ups, but what about Yamahoshi?"

Nakajima snorted, "He hasn't been the same since his knee went out."

Alice nodded. "True, but I thought I read that he was looking into some experimental surgery. Something to do with carbon fibers?"

Nakajima shook his head. "That article jumped the gun, I'm afraid. Yamahoshi was turned down for the surgery at the last minute."

Alice tsk'd at Nakajima. "Did someone pull a few strings behind the scenes?"

"Like I said, I have a little bit riding on this weekend, Miss Gailsone."

Alice nodded and set her cup down on a small, glass coffee table as she finished her drink. "As do I, Mr. Nakajima. Thank you for the lovely drink, and I apologize for bothering you about your former employee. I hope you continue in your good health."

Alice bowed slightly to Nakajima, who returned the bow and smiled. "Miss Gailsone, if Mr. Tanner is actually serious about doing business with Nakajima Industries, then I could not think of anyone who would handle his affairs better."

Alice smiled and managed a blush, which on her pale face was extremely noticeable. "Thank you, Mr. Nakajima."

Nakajima pressed a button on his intercom. "Megumi-chan, please see Miss Gailsone out."

In an instant, Megumi was in the office, her face still in a smile. As Alice stood, Mr. Nakajima raised his cup to Alice. "Continue in your good health, Miss Gailsone."

Alice nodded as Megumi led her out of the office.

As soon as they were gone, Mr. Nakajima walked back to the bar and poured himself another drink. Without looking up, he said in crisp Japanese, "*Kill her.*"

Behind him, Nakajima noted a wisp of movement.

In the outer office, Megumi led Alice to a door on the other side of the conference room. "This will take us through the factory. It is a shortcut," said Megumi.

Alice let Megumi lead as they entered a long, white, brightly-lit concrete tunnel. The path seemed to lead slightly downward, and at the end was a service elevator with a small utility door to the side. Alice followed calmly until they reached the end of the hall. Once there, Megumi pressed the button for the elevator door. With a clunky swish, it slid open.

"This is a double-door airlock. It's silly, but it is the fastest way to the factory floor."

Alice nodded and stood still. "Megumi, I wanted to say I'm sorry about the phone thing, earlier."

Megumi nodded and flashed a huge smile. "It is quite alright. Now, please, let us continue to…"

"Masks."

Megumi paused, her smile still in place. "I'm sorry?"

"The last time you took me onto the factory floor, the first thing you did was hand me a mask. Where is your mask, Megumi?"

138

Before Megumi could answer, Alice decked her with all her might. Megumi went flying backwards and cracked her head hard against the concrete wall of the tunnel, knocking her out cold. Alice waited until she slid to the floor and then proceeded to rummage through Megumi's coat. After a moment, she found her keycard. Smiling, Alice started to stand, and then she stooped back down and sighed a bit.

"Sorry about this, but I need one more thing. Honestly, this isn't what I had in mind and I might have considered carrying you, but this is the second time you've been a bitch to me in 20 minutes, so... yeah. Sorry."

Alice leaned over and grabbed Megumi's thumb by its base and started to focus her powers.

As morbid as it was, from experience, Alice knew exactly how much power it would take to rot the young lady's finger off. For a moment, she considered how many times she had done things like this in the past and how easy it was. She didn't owe this woman anything, and if she had the chance, Alice knew Megumi would probably push her down an elevator shaft while smiling and waving.

Alice knew her type.

Still, Alice was stuck with a moral dilemma. She knew hauling around a hostage would slow her down and prove difficult, but she also knew that severe mutilation was usually frowned upon in the superhero community. She almost said the Hell with it, until she remembered why she was being a hero.

Alice knew her mother would not approve, and for once, Alice knew she was paying attention.

She couldn't explain that to her without feeling like a disappointment.

"Hell, is this what being good feels like? I think I'm starting to get why all the heroes look like they just want to up and snap; this is harder in practice than I thought it would be."

Alice made a mental note to find a gang and take out her aggressions, provided she lived through the next ten minutes.

Megumi woke up with a jolt as Alice pulled back and slapped her as hard as she could.

"God, I hate doing that. It reminds me of interrogating, and I hate interrogating. Oh, well," she shrugged as Megumi clutched her face and let out a convulsing sob.

"You...you bitch!" Megumi screamed out between sobs, "You're dead, you hear me, dead!"

"No, I'm not, and neither are you," Alice said as she opened the utility door. Behind it was another passage. "Megumi, tonight you go home and you look in the mirror. Think about how the woman you tried to have killed twice was nice enough to leave you with not only your life, but the rest of your fingers. You think on how I could have put my hand through your face or through your chest. You think long and hard, and you thank whatever God you pray to that I'm a good guy now, understand?"

Megumi glared at Alice as the former super villain grabbed her and dragged her into the side hallway.

As soon as the door closed behind them, Alice took off, hauling the uncooperative Megumi behind her. She sprinted down the hallway as fast as she could with her unwilling charge while she scanned the walls for an exit. She figured Megumi had led her into a trap with the elevator That being the case, this was probably her way out.

"Does this passage lead out of here?"

Megumi looked at Alice for a moment.

"*Wakarimasen*," Megumi said in a chipper voice.

"You damn well *do* understand, you two-faced, little…" Alice considered deploying various methods of torture as she rounded a corner and saw a set of white double-doors. With a heave, she kicked them open found herself back on the factory floor. Around her were hundreds of calm, zoned-out workers piecing electronics together like high-priced Legos.

Alice glanced around quickly and saw a coat hanger on a nearby section of wall. On it were the factory standard white coats and helmets that Alice saw each of the workers wearing. Alice let out a small sigh of relief and drug Megumi over to them, a plan already forming in her head. She would put these on and (in her clever disguise), ride the elevator back up, knock Megumi out, and kick her in the head a few times, just to be sure (but *not* because she would get any sort of personal satisfaction out of it- she *was* a good guy, after all). Then she'd walk right out the front door, collect her golem and figure out who to beat up next. It was a simple plan, and in her experience those were always the best.

As soon as she had settled the hard hat on her head, she heard a familiar, high-pitched whirring sound. Without thought, she spun away and down as a throwing star sung through the air and missed her, embedding itself in Megumi's neck with a wide-arcing spray of blood. Megumi let out a choked gasp as she collapsed onto the polished concrete flooring, a pool of crimson already spreading from her torn throat. Alice bit her lip as she watched Megumi collapse.

"Crap. Sorry about that, Megumi."

Alice refused to comment on whether or not that had been completely accidental.

As she whipped around and scanned the factory, Alice caught sight of a female figure with a white robe and white fox mask crouched on a railing across the workroom. The fox mask showed only the woman's mouth, which seemed to be forming a moue of disappointment at having missed her target.

"Lotus," Alice cursed, as three more throwing stars whizzed at her. She dodged the first two, but the third embedded itself in her thigh, drawing a cry of pain and nearly dropping her right there.

"Damn, damn, double damn…" Alice limped as fast as she could to the coat rack. She yanked another helmet and a lab coat down as a fifth throwing star embedded itself in the wall behind her. It had been a long time since she had been stabbed. Breathing shallowly, she realized that was one part of her old job she *really* didn't miss. But Alice (one-time Dark Witch of Entropy and Queen of Pain) could handle battle wounds nearly as well as she dished them out.

That's what she told herself as blocked the pain from her mind and limp-sprinted for the far end of the factory to the double doors where the bins of electronics were heading out.

Alice didn't have to look behind her to know that Lotus was hot on her trail. For a moment, Alice mused that she had at least found who she was looking for. Admittedly, she had imagined more talking and way less blood at their initial encounter.

Alice collided with a worker, spilling all of the newly-assembled phones from his box as she rolled past him. Slamming into the double doors, Alice realized she was heading into a warehouse-sized shipping area with towers of electronic pallets stacked in a labyrinthine maze of aisles. Smiling at her luck, Alice ducked down the nearest aisle, grabbed a pallet and started scrambling up it for all she was worth.

Once she reached the top, Alice turned her attention back to her leg. She was leaving a blood trail, and the star in her leg was cramping her mobility. With a grimace, she reached into her purse and pulled out her Infinity knife. She bit down on the hilt and braced herself. With a gargled cry, she grabbed the star in her leg with the edge of her shirt. Quickly jerking it out, she applied pressure to the gushing wound. She shot the bloody, discarded star a dirty look. *'Serrated blades'*. She'd have to thank Lotus later for her thoughtful attention to detail.

After a moment, she spit the blade out onto the pallet beside her, breathing hard. She started ripping strips off her shirt to bind the deep, ragged cut and stop the bleeding. She kept waiting for her uniform to self-seal, but to her dismay, the fabric wasn't closing nearly as fast as it should have. Grumbling, she kept an eye out for trouble while she tended her wound. "This is the second time in two days I've had a bad meeting, nearly been killed, had to climb something and oh-my-God-I-am-an-idiot." Alice closed her eyes briefly in frustration before ducking further back between two stacked pallets to regroup and focus her thoughts.

***

Outside in the main assembly hall, Mr. Nakajima stood over Megumi's slumped body with a look of mild disdain on his face. Behind him, Lotus stood, waiting for his orders.

"*You did this?*" Nakajima asked in Japanese, glancing at the Lotus.

Lotus nodded slightly.

"*...You missed?*" Nakajima asked.

After a beat, Lotus shrugged.

"*You're supposed to be the best,*" Nakajima said through clenched teeth.

Lotus turned her head to face Nakajima. When she spoke, her voice was clipped, but strong. "*This is not a woman to take lightly.*"

Nakajima grabbed the bridge of his nose with his fingers and sighed. After collecting himself, he went to a nearby wall and activated a control panel. Behind him, two workers and a janitor got to work on removing Megumi from the factory while the workers behind them carried on, seemingly oblivious.

Nakajima pressed a button and spoke into a small microphone in the wall. With a short pop and whine, his voice was echoing throughout the factory.

"Attention distinguished employees; there is an American intruder in the production area. Anyone who sees and detains her will receive double their salary this week as a reward."

Behind Nakajima, the employees at the electronic tables glanced up, now not so oblivious to their employer.

Alice cursed to herself as she continued to focus. She felt dizzy and a little sick from blood loss, but she did her best to ignore it. If she couldn't do what she needed to in the next two minutes, she suspected that she would wind up very dead, very fast.

The double doors to the shipping area burst open as workers poured in, looking around frantically. Among them, Alice could see Lotus calmly wandering in and staring towards the floor. Alice mumbled some choice words as Lotus bent down, examined some blood splatters on the floor and then looked right in her direction.

To Alice's complete shock, Lotus then proceeded to casually drift to the opposite side of the warehouse and examine a stack of pallets that was decidedly Alice-free.

Before Alice could process this, she felt a small rumble. After a moment, the workers beneath her noticed it, and with a scream, they headed for the nearest entrance to brace themselves.

"Earthquake!"

Alice felt the rhythmic pounding and almost starting crying with thanks.

The wall next to the closed garage at the far end of the warehouse exploded inward, revealing Fudo.

As the factory employees scrambled in terror and alarms began to sound, Alice leapt down, careful not to land on her wounded leg. As she raced towards Fudo, she heard a familiar whizzing sound and noticed three more throwing stars fly past her head, narrowly missing her and embedding in the pallets beside her. From across the warehouse, she saw the Lotus begin to give chase.

Without pausing, Alice charged at Fudo and leapt into his arms. Clumsily, Fudo raised Alice to his shoulders as several factory workers attempted to charge him. As soon as Alice was secure, Fudo swung his arm out and swatted the factory workers away like flies. Lotus paused as three workers sailed past her and crumpled to the floor. After considering the golem, she looked at Alice before giving a slight nod and slipping into the shadows.

As Fudo carried Alice back through his impromptu doorway, Alice glanced back in time to see Nakajima watching from the double doors, his face a mixture of shock and anger.

Alice waved cheerfully as she and Fudo left.

Chapter 7

"Please take 'em down!"

Alice did her best to keep Fudo to the back alleys as they made their way towards Nagoya Castle. For the first 15 minutes, Alice enjoyed the illusion that she had managed to give everyone the slip. Then, she heard the familiar wail of sirens and knew that she'd soon have some more "official" visitors.

In her old career, she would have welcomed a fire fight. But this was a different situation, and Alice wasn't sure that her status as a representative for Tanner Industries meant that much anymore. At a loss, Alice looked around until she saw what she needed – a convenient subway entrance located less than a block away.

"Fudo, please head to that subway entrance as fast as you can." Before the words had even finished leaving her mouth, Fudo had taken off at a jolting run towards the subway tunnel, cutting across traffic. Alice held on for dear life and shut her eyes as a compact car plowed into Fudo's side, but Fudo didn't so much as falter. Amazed, Alice watched as her golem grabbed the car with one giant, stony hand and tossed it out of the way.

As they entered the subway tunnel, Alice ducked to avoid hitting her head and looked behind them to see the police screeching to a stop in the street just beyond. Alice then reached up, focused, and let her hand trail along the ceiling as Fudo continued down the stairs. The familiar warmth of the magic winding through her fingers caused a shiver to course down her spine.

"Clear the entrance! Earthquake! Earthquake!" Alice yelled at the people as they continued on their way. Instantly, they rushed out of the

146

tunnel, panic on their faces as they yelled for help. As the last person cleared the tunnel, Alice gave one more massive push with her power, so much so that the tunnel pulsed with a faint purple light before giving off a loud rumble. The police officers at the top of the stairs felt it and paused just long enough to see the tunnel in front of them completely collapse, cutting them off from their target.

Alice knew that they only had moments before the police made it to the other side of the street and entered through the cross tunnel. Quickly, she guided Fudo to the rails and steered him onto the track.

"Fudo, please destroy the center line before a train kills us," Alice said. Fudo immediately bent down, grabbed the center rail and squeezed. Instantly, a shower of sparks erupted from the line as a loud, static popping noise echoed throughout the tunnel, causing the lights to flicker. Once he was done, Fudo stood and proceeded to march into the blackness of the subway tunnel and away from the eyes of gawking pedestrians.

It took some time (and wall smashing), but eventually they found a route that took them close enough to the underground mall. From there, they were able to find a side entrance to the service port that led back to the base. As soon as they arrived, Alice collapsed in a nearby steel chair and did her best not to have a mental breakdown at the day's seriously screwed up turn of events.

While he was busy saving her life, Fudo had accidentally dropped the shopping bags full of new clothes that Alice had spent the morning picking out. Somewhere out there, some Japanese teenager was probably having a really great day. Unfortunately, that meant the only clothes she had left were the torn and bloody business suit she was currently wearing and her costume. Alice noted that her leg had stopped bleeding, and that the costume underneath her dress pants had finally self-sealed over the wound. Silently, Alice gave thanks for the good people at Tanner Industries. They may not like her, but at least they were useful.

Upon returning to the base, Alice parked Fudo in the main chamber. She had just climbed down from his shoulder when she heard a shuffling sound from behind her. Alice whirled around, ready to face whatever else this day had in store, only to find Makoto standing there in a black shirt with tan cargo pants. He was wearing a hideous, neon-orange backpack, scratching his head and grinning nervously.

Alice nearly collapsed from a heart attack right then and there. "What the Hell are you doing?! You do not sneak up on a girl, do you understand me? Do you have any idea what kind of day I've had?"

Makoto held up his smart phone. On it, a news video was playing back Alice's escape from Nakajima's factory. "I have an idea, yes."

Alice sighed. So much for keeping this from Alan Tanner. She had been one of the most organized, accomplished villains in the world, so why was this hero thing so incredibly hard? She wasn't used to things that didn't go according to plan – and, frankly, she didn't like it. She didn't like it *at all*. Alice wanted to cry, scream and drink, all at the same time.

"So what do you want, Makoto?" Alice asked. Makoto reached into his backpack and pulled out a newspaper that was folded open to the sports section. He handed it to Alice, who strained to read the Kanji. She didn't have to read all of it to notice the name of the author.

"For a girl that's been missing for a month, little Nanami-chan has certainly been a busy bee." Alice mused.

Makoto nodded. "She's been putting out articles every day for a month, without fail. Her paper says they get them via e-mail; no one's actually seen her."

"Have they talked to her?"

Makoto shook his head. "It's not for lack of trying. They've been trying to set up a meeting about her continued employment. Apparently, they're looking to fire her."

Alice handed the paper back. "Let me guess; her sports reviews and predictions have been way off this last month, haven't they?"

Makoto nodded. "She's even missing the big matches that should have been easy calls. A lot of people are saying her articles are a good way to predict winners, if you pick the person she says is going to lose."

Alice cringed and rubbed the bridge of her nose. "Makoto, have you or your pack been able to find any physical trace of Nanami?"

Makoto shook his head. "Not yet, but we're still looking. She can't hide now that we have her scent."

"You'd be surprised," Alice said as she sniffed her outfit and noticed her own body odor. "I'm going to take care of the bleeding hole in my leg. I'll be back in a bit, okay?"

Makoto nodded and looked at Fudo. "I'll just stay here with him, if that's okay?" Makoto said. Alice nodded, and Makoto sat down near Fudo and started playing on his Smart phone.

Without clothes and supplies, and now wanted by the police, she headed to her room. Alice slipped into a clean tee and some shorts and made her way to the infirmary. While her powers were fine for rotting things away, they did little for healing open wounds. After digging through the medical cabinets, she found some iodine and gauze.

As she gritted her teeth and disinfected her wound, Alice glanced at her phone and noticed she had one message. Well, she had to face the music sometime. Once she finished bandaging her leg, she picked up PhoneBuddy, hit play and listened. The voice on the other end was that of a very angry Mr. Nakajima.

"You have murdered my assistant, sabotaged my factory and committed an act of terror in my city," the business man said in a calm, hard tone. "If you leave Japan now, I will let you live. However, if you choose to stay, I promise that you will not live to see tomorrow. This is my last warning, Alice Gailsone."

Alice sighed and hit erase on the message. "God, did I sound like that when I used to threaten people? That was just awful." Alice checked her phone memory and realized that she had not received any other calls. Concerned, she dialed her shop.

"Good morning, and thank you for calling *Rare Gems*. This is Cindy; how may I direct your call?"

"Good morning, Cindy, it's me, Alice."

The voice on the other end perked up. "Good morning, ma'am. How are things in Japan?"

Alice looked at her bandaged leg. "About how I thought they would be. How is the shop?"

There was a pause. "Things are fine."

Alice straightened up. "What happened, Cindy?"

There was a longer pause. "We had a buyer back out. Dalatan Ltd. Wants to go with another vendor."

"What?! That's impossible! There are no other vendors that handle the volume of gemstones they need!"

Cindy's voice was a bit shaky, "They said their parent corporation made the call. They said it was non-negotiable."

Alice closed her eyes and counted to three. "Cindy, who is their parent corporation?"

"Nakajima Industries, ma'am."

"Of course they are. That's just...dammit, they were 15% of our projected income for the year. What did Allison do when you heard?"

There was a longer pause. Alice asked again. "What did Allison do, Cindy?"

"Allison said she was heading to Dalatan's headquarters in Stockholm to discuss the matter. She left yesterday, saying that it damn well was negotiable."

Alice shrugged. "You know what, why not? Hell, what's the worst that could happen at this point?"

"She might kill their CEO?"

Alice snickered. "I've always liked your sense of humor, Cindy."

"I wasn't joking, ma'am. She told me if it didn't pan out, she was going to murder their CEO. I'm really not sure if she was kidding."

Alice shook her head. "Well, we can't fight all her battles for her, now can we? Don't worry, Allison is a big girl; she can behave like one while representing us abroad. Everything else going well?"

"So far, ma'am."

"Good, just keep me posted if anything changes, and let me know if I need to post bail. I'll talk to you later, Cindy."

Alice hung up the phone, and for a moment had an image of Allison standing on a table in a board room, surrounded by scared, balding, round German executives that were begging for their lives while she pointed a rocket launcher at them. Sadly, she didn't know whether to feel guilty or start laughing.

After a moment, Alice dialed another number on her phone. After four rings, the line picked up, and Alice heard a clipped voice on the other line. "Gailsone residence."

"Hi, this is Alice Gailsone, Ms. Gailsone's daughter? Are you the nurse on duty?"

"Yes, this is Catherine." The voice was professional, but a bit detached. Alice did not care for this woman, but knew she couldn't complain about every nurse that tended her mother.

"How's my mother doing, Catherine?"

"She's fine. She's had her medicine and is still sleeping. I just checked in an hour ago, but she hasn't stirred since I got here. Do you want me to wake her up?"

"No, no," Alice said, her disappointment creeping into her voice, "that's okay. Just tell her I called?"

"I'll do that, Miss Gailsone," the nurse said in a distracted voice. Alice definitely did not like this woman at all. Alice mumbled thanks and hung up the phone, sad that she didn't get a chance to speak to her mother. Still, she wasn't about to wake her up; she deserved to rest.

Alice put her phone away and headed back to Makoto in the main room, who put his Smart phone away the moment she entered. "So what now?" he asked.

Alice thought for a moment and considered her options. "I need to finish what I came here to do," she said. "Even if she says no thank you, I want to know why I'm still alive and why Lotus quit. And I want to know what happened to Nanami. And I want to kick Nakajima's ass. And I want a shower. Yeah, I'm taking a shower. Makoto, thank you for your help. I may need you and the pack tomorrow. Will you be available?"

Makoto nodded. "I think that can be arranged. Just call, and we'll be here." With that, he nodded and took off down one of the darkened tunnels that led back to the subway system.

After freshening up, Alice reentered the main area where Fudo was keeping watch. She was in a set of gray cloth shorts and a tank top and was still tending her hair from the shower. Her leg was wrapped in a thick set of clean bandages and she had a slight limp, but aside from that, she felt much better.

Her plan now was to put Fudo on guard duty and get some well-earned sleep – at least, until the ceiling above her head exploded.

Alice dove for cover as chunks of concrete and debris rained down around her. Through the dust, she could see what looked like eight figures in black dropping down on cables, each with what appeared to be an automatic weapon. One landed just in front of her. Before he could get his bearings, Alice charged him, slamming him in the throat with the palm of her hand and slipping the arm with the gun between hers and pulling down. Even over the din and yelling, Alice could clearly hear a bone crack.

Alice took the gun from the screaming solider and cracked him in the helmet. She noticed that he, like the rest of the soldiers, was wearing a gas mask. She sniffed the air, but didn't smell anything off. That meant she probably had a few seconds before things got went from bad to worse. Sure enough, several of the soldiers dropped canisters to the ground as they landed. Alice saw a thick, yellow gas come shooting out as she ripped the mask off the now unconscious solider and slipped it on.

Alice took the gun and hunched over, scurrying across to a spot on the railing where she could see a little better. No one had noticed her yet, and the soldiers were still getting their bearings. They still hadn't realized one of their own was already down. Alice decided to use the confusion to her advantage. Leaning over the railing, she opened fire at the soldiers on the lower level.

Three soldiers dropped instantly. Alice noted that they seemed to be wearing Kevlar vests, but that wasn't helping the two she had tagged in the legs. The third she nicked in the head, which sent him reeling. The remaining four scurried for cover and returned fire. Alice ducked down, but not before she noticed that they were hiding behind Fudo.

"Fudo," Alice yelled, her voice muffled by her mask, "Please take 'em down!"

Two of the soldiers were instantly picked up by the giant stone golem and slammed into each other. Fudo dropped them and advanced on the third, who was firing wildly on the stone giant. Alice grimaced as the bullets bounced off his stone hide and wished she hadn't ordered him to remove his metallic disguise earlier on. Seeing that things were getting a bit more dicey than she was comfortable with, she decided it was prime time for a hasty retreat, as more soldiers started descending into the bombed-out common area.

Alice sprinted for her room, snatching up her costume and utility belt. She peered around the edge of her doorway. Although she saw the smoky shadows of the soldiers gliding silently in the open, they had not yet figured out she was here. She raced down the hallway to an emergency escape tunnel as gunfire continued to echo behind her. She hoped Fudo would be okay, but wasn't sure how well stone would hold up to modern firearms. Just before leaving, she stopped at a hallway intersection and smashed out a glass panel on the wall with her utility belt. She smiled as she pulled the handle inside. As she slipped through into the exit tunnel and pulled the door closed behind her, the entire complex was drenched in a torrent of water as a loud klaxon began to blare. *That should keep them busy for a bit,* she thought to herself.

After a few minutes, Alice found herself covered in dust, cobwebs and God only knew what else, standing in the forest just outside of Nagoya Castle. Clearly, no one had taken that particular tunnel in a while – but she had placed a timed explosive about halfway down, just in case. Peering through the branches, she could see lights and smoke coming from the castle grounds. In the distance, she heard sirens from the local police and fire. With a sigh, she took stock of what she had left.

Her business clothes – Hell, everything she had brought – was gone. Her reputation as the deadliest woman in the world was certainly sullied. In the old days, the Purge would have demanded that every solider in the room be made into an example, and in her first few years with the Purge, she probably would have done it. But now, she was supposed to be good – and she was really, really bad at it. Add to that her new status as a fugitive and Alice as starting to feel like a rank amateur. In her utility belt, she had a corporate credit card that was probably cancelled and a phone that could detonate if she asked it. She was tired, wounded and half-naked. In another life, this might have been par for the course. Regardless, she knew what needed to be done.

Alice put on her costume and adjusted her mask. Once she was dressed, she looked back towards the lights and smoke coming from the castle. "Sorry, Fudo. I'll fix all of this and be back for you. Promise."

With that, she disappeared into the woods in the direction of downtown.

No more politicking. No more bullshit. It was time for Dyspell to get to work.

Chapter 8

"I'm Sorry"

The mid-Atlantic was pitch black and choppy as Superior Force, the strongest being in the known universe, rocketed overheard in a streak of red and black. He had been enjoying a rare moment of quiet at his favorite café where he had been finishing some edits on his latest writing project. That was when he received the call from Alan Tanner about Chris and the Phoenix.

In under ten minutes, he had changed into his trademark red jumpsuit with black stripes and a red cape. When people asked him how the cape helped him to fly, he usually made up some big words before stunning them senseless with his smile. The truth was, he wasn't sure the cape did anything – except making him look good. As a hero and role-model, he understood the need to maintain a certain level of appearance and professionalism.

Currently, Superior Force was flying over the site where he had been told to meet up with the supply freighter. The freighter kept to a slow circle of about 5 knots around the coordinates for the *Crystal Foundation.* By company policy, it never left, unless there was an emergency.

And right now, there was no supply freighter in sight.

Superior Force reached for the comm device in his ear, speaking loudly to be heard over the raucous sounds of the wind and waves.

"This is Superior Force. I've reached the expedition coordinates, but the supply ship is gone."

The voice on the other end sounded tinny and hollow, but it was unmistakably Alan Tanner's.

"Can you see it on the horizon? Is it possible they left?"

Superior Force focused his eyes on the horizon. If anyone had been watching closely, they would have seen his light blue eyes glow faintly green as he scanned in all directions.

"Negative, but... Blackthorne, I'm smelling something. It's exhaust, oil, carbon... it's faint, but there was a fire around here recently."

Over the comm link, Superior Force could hear Alan cursing to himself.

"I'm going down to see what I can find." Superior Force started towards the water at high speed. Just before he entered, he heard a garbled, "Be careful, Tom."

The water was ice cold and pitch black, but neither of these facts slowed Superior Force as he sped deeper and deeper into the inky abyss. Even with his enhanced vision, he could see only about 500 yards into the blackness around him. Still, he had a good idea of where he was going. Before long, he could taste the chemicals which had been dispersing through the endless ocean currents. With only a moment spent gauging direction, Superior Force sped through the water until he came across the twisted metal husk that had been the *Crystal Foundation*.

A quick scan with his enhanced vision told the hero everything he needed to know. He counted dozens of bodies scattered throughout the rubble, some of which were in shock trooper gear. He saw the scorch marks from explosions and could taste noxious chemical traces in the water from the nanite bomb. Everything was destroyed, everyone was...

Superior Force raced to a pile of debris on his left and grabbed hold of a riveted steel beam. With inhuman strength, he lifted the beam and bent, ripping piles of wreckage away. When the bubbles had disbursed

157

and the silt settled, the body of Chris Ellswood appeared - pinned to what had been the floor of his suite by an Infinity knife.

With a sudden surge of rage and grief, Superior Force reached down and yanked the Infinity knife out of his friend's chest and cast it aside. Almost immediately, Chris's eyes popped open and he started flailing in the darkness. Superior Force let out a small 'oop' of surprise at seeing the dead man suddenly writhing about, but quickly moved to hold him while Chris adjusted to his surroundings.

After a moment, Chris calmed himself. Then, to Superior Force's surprise, he closed his eyes and started emitting a light green glow. Chris looked to the hero, assessed the situation and nodded his thanks. Clutching his chest in pain, Chris scanned the wreckage for himself, and then turned back to his friend. With a thumbs up, he signaled that it was time to surface.

As soon as they broke the surface of the choppy waves, Chris started cursing.

"God damn, worthless sonnovabitch! Tom, they took the Phoenix!"

Tom Clairman (aka Superior Force), scooped Chris up in his arms and started for shore.

"Come on, we need to get you medical care immediately." Tom focused on the shoreline and went as fast as he could without injuring his friend. Chris clutched his chest and coughed up some blood as he held on with his free hand.

"What happened down there? Who did this to you?"

As mad as Chris was, he couldn't help but notice that Tom's voice was unusually level. In fact, it was almost clipped. Then Chris noticed that Tom's eyes were glowing red, and he understood.

"It was a slaughter," Chris said, mindful of his friend's mood, "Shock troops came aboard while we were celebrating. They didn't even want any hostages; they just killed everyone. They got away with the Phoenix, and left me for dead."

"You were dead when I found you," Tom said, his gaze still on the horizon, "I'm not sure I understand why you're alive."

"I mimicked a jellyfish. It pretty much shut me down, but they don't have hearts. The Infinity knife would only come out if my heart stopped beating."

"So why didn't you pull it out?"

"Because, I was shut down. Jellyfish don't have brains, either. The shock of the knife coming out must have reset my system."

Superior Force nodded slightly.

"Your submarine was missing."

Chris seethed. "The bitch took my keys."

Now Superior Force did look at Chris.

"Who did this?"

Chris shook his head. "I don't know her name- she was new. Young, blonde..."

"You slept with her, didn't you?"

"Only a little..." Chris shifted slightly. "She caught me off guard. She claimed she had a friend. The name sounded familiar. You know, like one of our old . . . do you know a Totallus?"

Chris felt Tom's grip tighten slightly. "How are you a member of the Collective Good and not know what a Totallus is?"

Chris shrugged. "You never remember to invite the fish guy to your little get-togethers. I'm adjunct with you thugs, remember? So, do you know what it is or not?"

"Yes, I do. We need to get you to Alan and get you treated. He's going to want to hear this firsthand."

Chris nodded and tried not to focus on the pain in his chest. Already, he could see the shoreline and beyond it, the skyline of New York.

When they arrived at Tanner Industries, a hatch on the roof opened, allowing Superior Force to drift in with his wounded cargo. A med team was standing by with a crash cart and stretcher, ready to get to work on the aquatic hero. Chris grumbled and swatted them away, storming off towards the medical bay on his own. Behind him, the team of medics scurried to keep up.

As Alan Tanner entered the upper docking area of his tower, he noted how calm and still Tom was amidst the bustle around him. As the workers of the tower were busy scurrying around with their reports and their devices, Alan saw not one muscle move on the frame of the Earth's Mightiest Hero. In fact, Alan wasn't even sure the man was breathing.

Even the workers of the tower were noticing the change in mood. Alan watched as they began edging further and further from him, even though he wasn't even glancing in their direction. It was as if they could sense his mood and were acting on some self-preservation instinct.

Alan walked to his friend's side and stood with him for a moment, watching his staff at work.

"So, how is Chris?"

"He has a hole in his chest from a cursed knife, and everyone aboard the *Crystal Foundation* is dead. Everyone. The Phoenix is missing, and a Totallus was involved."

Alan sighed and pinched the bridge of his nose with his fingers.

"Of course. Of course, all of this is happening. This is my day. Come on; let's see who's taking responsibility."

Superior Force looked to Alan. When he noticed that his friend's eyes were glowing red, Alan felt a slight twinge of nervousness. When he spoke, Alan flinched at how cold his invulnerable friend's voice was.

"You know who did this. This was Prometheus."

"Prometheus is dead, old friend."

"He was sucked into a black hole, not killed. We don't know that he's dead! Besides, who else would have a Totallus android?"

Alan thought about it for a moment. "Well, that's the thing. We don't know how many Prometheus made. There could still be dozens. It doesn't mean that Prometheus weaseled his way out of a black hole."

"So you don't know?"

Alan gritted his teeth. "No, but I know someone who might. Come on, let's check on Chris and place a call."

***

Seven floors down in Research and Development, Victoria Green stood with her design team in a small, comfortable conference room as they went over their Q3 patent earnings. It was one of the many tedious jobs that Victoria handled for Alan Tanner, who would sneak out of any official part of day-to-day operations if given the chance. Depending on what day of the week it was, Victoria might wear any number of hats and titles - but to the denizens of Tanner Industries, she was the right hand of the boss. This meant she was, for all intents and purposes, the boss, and she reveled in it.

Victoria was easily the most organized of their community. When a plan was needed and Blackthorne wasn't available, then you could always count on Blackbird for a contingency plan. She was clever, saw every angle and was also Blackthorne's not-so-secret girlfriend.

Victoria didn't like to think about *how* she got her job, but there was no question that she was competent at it, and extremely so. She was known as the woman who got things done, even if some of those things were boring profit meetings.

The monotony of the meeting was broken up by the near-deafening sound of klaxons throughout the halls. The employees in the hallway stopped for a moment, and then hurried towards their designated shelters. Victoria looked to her staff and nodded. "You're excused. Good meeting, everyone." The boardroom nodded and quietly gathered their paperwork as Victoria exited the conference room.

An explosion from several floors up shook the building, and Victoria had to hold the wall to steady herself. While her first instinct was to head up and see what was going on, she knew the procedures better than anyone. She was the senior company official in R&D, so it was up to her to check on the staff and make sure everyone was alright.

When Victoria entered the development wing, she quickly slid back around the corner and glanced in. The room was clear of staff, as it was supposed to be, but in the center of the room were six men dressed head to toe in black shock troop gear. Each one was carrying an automatic weapon, and two of them were carting something under a sheet. The room itself looked ransacked - lockers torn open, tables upended and supplies scattered everywhere. They had arrived quickly and made a large mess for only being there a few moments.

Victoria reached for her utility belt and then cursed to herself; she was wearing her best black business suit, and that meant no real gadgets. All she had was her purse, her regular, not-cool belt, her phone, maybe some gum...

Victoria reached into her purse and took out her phone. She turned it on and went to her locked apps. After entering a 10 digit code, she knelt down, leaned around the corner and tossed the phone across the room.

162

It came to rest at the feet of one of the shock troops, who glanced down curiously.

"PhoneBuddy, detonate!"

The shock trooper was thrown backwards as the phone exploded at his feet. The other soldiers cowered and took a defensive position as Victoria charged in, using the distraction of the explosion to close the distance between them. Two of the shock troops saw her and started firing, but the sprinkler system had kicked in, and the resulting curtain of water made it difficult for them to focus on her form as she sprinted through the room. Using the environment to her advantage, Victoria leapt on top of one of the design tables and slid towards the nearest soldier, crashing down on his head and throat with all of her weight behind her sharply-heeled foot.

As they fell to the ground, Victoria rolled off the trooper as the second soldier opened fire, trying to follow her form as she moved with the now-unconscious soldier's body. As she rolled off the solider, she picked up his automatic weapon. Still low to the ground, Victoria took off in a crouched sprint to hide behind one of the knocked over steel tables beyond her attackers.

"Move! Get the merch out now," one of the shock troops yelled at the two carting the unknown item. The two men rushed the wheeled cart holding the piece of mystery tech towards the service elevator. Victoria leaned out from the side of the table and opened fire, clipping one of the standing soldiers in the chest and shoulder before having to resume hiding. She flinched as she felt the metal table behind her vibrate and bend with the force of the bullets hitting it.

Victoria heard the elevator chime and tried to shoot again, but the remaining soldiers were laying down a suppressing fire on both sides of the table, cutting her off. Cursing, Victoria rounded the far edge of the table just in time to see the service elevator close. As soon as it did, she rushed the controls. Tanner Tower had protocols put in place to prevent just this sort of thing. If you were senior staff, that meant you had the security override for all elevators and doors in the tower.

Victoria nearly crashed into the wall by the elevator, yanking a brushed nickel panel back to reveal a numeric keypad. Before she could enter a code, she noticed a red light flashing beside the controls. A moment later, she realized the light was attached to a small round device that was buried in something that looked like gum on the side of the panel.

Victoria scrambled away, but still found herself thrown into a table by the blast. When she could open her eyes again, she saw the explosion had completely disabled the control panel. Victoria picked herself up, calmly checked herself for shrapnel and then marched over to the unconscious solider she had laid out before. She knelt down, picked the man up by his collar and ripped his helmet off to reveal a pale, scraggly young man with a trail of blood coming from his mouth and nose.

Victoria slapped the man hard across the jaw. "Wake up; I need to talk to you."

The man sputtered and looked around as Victoria slapped him again. Before the man could react, Victoria let him go and put the muzzle of his gun right between his eyes.

"You know those heroes that have a solemn code against killing?"

The soldier nodded slightly, his eyes on the barrel of the gun. She leaned in slightly, placing her blood-red lips right next to his ear.

"I'm not one of them."

The scraggly man paled even further as she pulled back and continued, "Now that we have that settled, you'll answer my questions, and then be taken into custody. If you give me any shit – any at all – I will shoot you in the face. Are we clear?"

The man nodded, his eyes wide with fear.

"What did you come here for?"

The man stared at her for a moment, then glanced at his Kevlar vest. *'Idiot,'* she thought, *'that wouldn't save his face.'*

Victoria pointed the gun slightly to the side of the man's head and let off a round, making the solider visibly jump. The ricochet bounced off the floor and pinged elsewhere as Victoria stood, unflinching. "What did you come here for? Answer me!" Victoria screamed, her gun trained back on the soldier's head as her finger tightened on the trigger.

Before the man could speak, a pouch on the man's vest started beeping. He immediately began scrabbling backward and screaming as he tried in vain to remove the vest, swatting at the pouch as if it were a poisonous spider. In the next moment, a charge went off just above the man's heart, killing him instantly.

Victoria stood there for a moment, not quite processing what had just had just happened, and just what that level of preparation meant. Finally, she dropped the gun and marched determinedly toward the stairs, cursing a blue steak all the while.

***

Alan led the way to the medical facility where Chris was currently being x-rayed by the technicians. Tom stood off to the side, out of the doctor's way, while Alan moved in to examine the wounds on his friend. When Alan saw the gaping hole oozing in the middle of Chris's chest, he let out a long, low whistle.

"So, how are you not passed out right now?"

Chris chuffed and glared at the doctors as they took the x-ray machines away. "I picked a fish that has no pain sensors and adapted its abilities. I feel numb and a little drunk, but it beats feeling this," Chris gestured to the wound that was now being patched up.

Alan nodded, deciding to cut to the chase. "You claim a Totallus was behind this?"

Chris shrugged. "I guess so. I only saw the girl, but something was rocking my platform like it was a damn tinker toy. What the hell is a Totallus, anyway?"

A medic handed Alan a tablet. He glanced at it casually, before starting to read with more attention as something caught his eye. Without looking up, he said, "You look like you've had some nanite exposure recently."

"Probably from the nanite bomb that little bitch used on my staff," Chris growled.

"If that were true, I think you would be dead, too." Alan continued to read, only glancing up occasionally to look at his friend. "A Totallus is a killer android specifically designed to target members of the Collective Good," Alan said while examining the data, "Some were focused on strength, some on speed, nearly all of them could fly. They were cold, mean and tough as Hell to take down. I think we dealt with them while you were still solo. They were mostly dismantled after we took down the Purge, but apparently we missed one."

"I'm sorry," said Tom. Alan and Chris glanced to their friend, who was standing as still as a statue.

"Don't be," said Alan. "I was there, too. Besides, it was my job; I should be apologizing, especially since it was apparently strong enough to dismantle an underwater laboratory."

"Well, that's just craptastic," Chris sighed to himself as the doctor finished wrapping him up. "Meanwhile, my people are dead and we've lost the greatest treasure on Earth. My team was still investigating it; they didn't even have time to tag it with a tracer for us to track it."

"I'm sorry," Tom said again, still not moving.

Alan glanced again at Superior Force. "You couldn't have done anything about it, and you," Alan turned to Chris, "managed to upload enough of the radioactive patterns from the Phoenix that we can get a bead on it."

"It wasn't enough to pinpoint by satellite," said Chris as he sat up.

"True," Alan said, putting the tablet down as he helped the attending medic get his friend off of the exam table, "but each Phoenix emits its own special radiation pattern. It's not a lot, but it is traceable from a short distance. We just need to start a sweep of old areas the Purge used to…"

With no warning, Alan grabbed Chris and flung him out of the way as the room was splashed in a crimson light; a deadly, red-hot laser blasted past where Alan had been standing and obliterated the medic that had been at Chris' side. Shocked, Alan and Chris looked back to see Superior Force, his eyes glowing red and smoking, his face locked in a scowl.

"Tom! What the hell are you doing?" Alan shouted.

"I'm sorry," Tom answered as he fired his laser vision straight at Alan. At the last second, Chris grabbed a metal tray loaded with medical supplies and used it as a makeshift shield, blocking and redirecting some of the blast. Chris screamed as the tray melted in his hands, burning his fingers.

"Run!" Chris shouted and grabbed his stunned friend as the most powerful man in the world started to advance, his eyes still glowing.

"I'm sorry," they heard him say again as they bolted out of the room, laser blasts firing off all around them in random directions. The second they were out the door, the room behind them exploded and alarms began to sound throughout the building. As they scrambled down the hallway, Alan grabbed his belt buckle and pressed a button in its center. Instantly, the lighting in the building went wild, flashing a thousand different patterns every second. Around them, employees screamed

167

and covered their eyes, their free hands going for special silver sunglasses that they all seemed to have in their pockets.

Chris tried to stay focused as Alan handed him a set of silver shades. "Put these on!" Alan shouted.

"Why are you shouting?" Chris asked, just as he covered his ears and let out a cry of pain. The PA system started blasting out what sounded like an insane cacophony of what had to be dozens of different songs, conversations and noises. Alan reached in his pocket and dug out some ear plugs for Chris and himself.

As Chris looked around, he saw that every computer terminal was flashing the same message, over and over: FORCE PROTOCOLS. Chris looked to Alan, who was half-dragging him down the hall to a door with a numeric pad. With a wave of his hand on the opposite side of where the pad was, a red light flashed in the wall and Alan opened the door. Chris looked back to see Superior Force stumbling down the hall, his hands on his ears and his eyes clenched shut. Chris couldn't hear, but from the look of things, he seemed to be screaming in pain.

Alan reached back and grabbed Chris by the arm. He practically threw Chris through the entranceway before diving in after him, narrowly avoiding another laser blast coming down the hall. The doors slid shut with an echoing thud.

Chris looked around and saw a large, metal command center. The lighting was normal, and he couldn't hear the music through the plugs anymore. After taking off the glasses and plugs, he turned to Alan, who was already at a terminal. Chris also noted that they were the only two in the room.

"What the fuck just happened out there, Alan? Tom killed that man?! He was damn well trying to kill us!" From the monitors on the wall, he watched as hidden doorways opened in the hallway they were just. Battle drones he'd never seen before were rolling out in droves, each one firing non-stop on the advancing hero as he continued stumbling down the hallway towards their location.

"Yes, Chris, he did. I would say our friend is having a day, wouldn't you?" Alan worked furiously at his keyboard, watching his own screens and the monitors which showed Superior Force being blasted by no less than a dozen tank-like battle drones. They seemed to be doing little beyond pissing him off even more.

"Whatever you're going to do, do it fast, Alan. He's coming up on us quick, and I don't think he wants to chat."

Alan nodded to a door opposite Chris that slid open, revealing a slick, full-body, black battle suit. The front had a yellow logo of a thorn branch in the center.

"Put on that battle suit. It won't stop him, but it might keep you alive long enough for me to do what I need to."

Chris didn't waste time arguing. On the monitors, he watched as the last of the battle drones was being torn to shreds by Superior Force.

Alan saw this, too. After checking the monitors to make sure no one was left in the hallway, he keyed in a command. Instantly, the room buzzed with the sound of a massive electrical current moving through the building. On the screens, Alan and Chris watched as Superior Force screamed and reared back, his whole body shaking.

"Tom never did like electricity. Are you dressed yet, Chris?"

Chris was putting on the last of the battle suit as Superior Force shrugged off the electricity and started hammering away at the door. With every hit, it buckled further inward.

"There's a red button on the left arm of the suit," Alan said as he stayed focused on the computer in front of him, "Push it four times, and then point both hands in his direction. Do *not* close your fists."

169

Chris pressed the button four times and felt the suit start to vibrate as the door glowed red and melted into a pile of slag, revealing a smoking, shaking Superior Force. Before Chris could ask what the suit was supposed to do, he felt himself get thrown backwards as his suit let loose a massive plasma blast from his outstretched hands. The beam hit Superior Force square in the chest, knocking him off his feet and sending him sailing into the hallway.

Chris tried to turn to face Alan, but found himself frozen. "Something's wrong," he shouted, "my suit won't move!"

"It's out of power. That blast just drained the whole thing." Alan was hovered over his keyboard, watching his screen. On it, a yellow bar was nearly done filling its loading container.

"What?! Why the Hell would I want to do that? I need to be able to fight, dammit!"

"He would have ripped you in half," Alan said, still watching the screen, "I just needed you to buy me 30 seconds."

Both men turned to the doorway, where a whoosh of air signaled that their adversary had taken to flight to cut down on time. With a blast of air, Superior Force zoomed into the room, his eyes nearly dripping with red plasma, his face covered with blood. Chris watched in horror as those glowing red eyes turned towards Alan.

Alan pushed a button on his wrist and covered his ears. A moment later, a high-pitched whine blasted through the room, making Superior Force scream as he clutched his ears. Chris winced in pain, but the suit was protecting him from going deaf. He noticed that Alan was shaking with pain as he clutched his head. After a moment, Superior Force gained his footing and fired a blast of red-hot plasma straight at the PA system in the room, causing it to explode in a shower of sparks. A moment later, he returned his attention to the stumbling human in front of him.

"I'm sorry," Superior Force said, the sound muted by the vibratory hum of power coming from his eyes.

"Alan!" Chris shouted.

Alan looked to the screen in front of him.

The bar was full and glowing green.

Alan slammed the button on the keyboard and dove, but not before the laser blast from Superior Force's eyes sliced through his side and arm, severing a good chunk of flesh in a hot, charred pop. Alan screamed as the building shuddered violently with a loud, bass-like thudding, and then everything went black.

***

Chris was trapped in the battle suit for what felt like an eternity, unable to see or do anything. He could hear muffled sounds; screaming, some running, a general commotion. He heard something crash and someone speaking nearby, but the suit did a decent job of keeping out sound. For a moment, he thought that it was just the suit that had lost power, but then Chris felt someone working his suit from the outside, and after a moment he found his suit loosening and felt hands guiding him out into a dark, crowded room.

Chris looked around and saw technicians already in the darkened lab assessing the damage, each one wearing a large, bright green glow stick around their necks on a lanyard. Where Alan had been standing, Chris saw a melted computer terminal, still smoking in the soft, green light.

Next to the terminal was Alan Tanner, sitting and patiently letting a young female medic bandage his side and arm. He was talking and joking with the young lady, who Chris could see was pretty shaken up. As soon as he was out of the suit, Chris looked around the room and saw, sitting in a chair by the corner, Superior Force. His eyes, nose and ears were bleeding, and he was holding what looked like a wet

171

washcloth to his face. A nervous young medic stood next to him, waiting with another towel.

"What the Hell just happened? Will someone please give me a decent answer before this psycho starts shooting the place up again?!"

Alan gestured for Chris to calm down. "It wasn't his fault. I noticed it when I saw your blood work but I didn't put two and two together until Tom lost control and started… doing what he was doing." Alan glanced to Tom, who looked up with a haunted, wide-eyed look on his face.

"I didn't know," he said in a hoarse whisper, "I didn't know."

Alan nodded. "There were nanites in your blood work, Chris. At first I thought they were some form of parasite used on your staff, but if that were the case, it probably would have killed you. Instead, it was actively trying to interface with your blood cells and couldn't."

"Why not?" Chris nodded a thank you to a young man who handed him a glass of water.

"Because it wasn't geared towards your genetic makeup," Alan said, gesturing to the shaking super hero in the corner, "It was geared towards his."

"You mean it was something designed to attack only Tom? How is that possible? Did you get exposed to something before you found me?"

Tom shook his head. "No…no, I was just looking for you under the water…and then I found you…"

Alan nodded. "The water in the area had been poisoned. At that depth, anything put in the water wouldn't have moved around much, unless there was an explosion, which there was. It scattered the nanites enough to spread them throughout the water. Tom was infected when he approached, and by the time we were in the medical bay, they had multiplied enough to take control of Tom's nervous system."

172

Alan reached with his good arm to his melted computer terminal and picked up a precariously balanced cup of coffee. The heroes and technicians watched as he proceeded to drink the entire cup in one, long swallow.

"Whoever brought that, thank you," Alan said to the room, "but the next one had better be 50% alcohol or you're fired."

"Alan!" The three heroes turned at the sound of a familiar voice. In the doorway stood Victoria Green with a look of shock on her face. Her stunning black business suit was marred with black smudge marks down the front, her hair was pulled back in a ponytail and her purse was slung carelessly on her shoulder. Without so much as a nod to the others, Victoria rushed across the room and nearly tackled Alan in a tight hug, her face buried in his shoulder.

"There was a break-in downstairs in R&D. I tried to stop them, but they got away. They left two behind, but they're both dead - some kind of explosive charge in their vests."

Alan eyed his girlfriend. "Did you ruin your suit in the fight?"

Victoria stepped back and glanced away, self-consciously straightening her blouse. "The elevators were out and they blew the service. The stairways were flooded with workers."

Chris snorted, "And you let that stop you?"

Victoria shot the aquatic hero a cross look. "I climbed the main shaft without my belt, gloves or suit, and I still made it up here before the elevators kicked back on, so go screw yourself." Victoria looked around the room at the damage and took note of her surroundings for the first time. After a moment, she turned to Superior Force and stared.

"*You* did this?"

"It wasn't his fault," Alan said, "He was being controlled, and if anything it was my fault for not immediately tossing both of these idiots through the nearest electromagnetic scanner. Although," he gestured to the still in shock hero in the corner, "I doubt it would have worked on him; his skin is so thick that the only thing that could have really done the job was an EMP. By the way," Alan raised his voice to address the room, "when everything is working again, let everyone in the building know we'll replace their smart devices as soon as possible."

Chris looked around at everyone cleaning up and noticed that they were using electronic devices. He also noticed that now the lights and electronics in the room seemed to be working just fine. "How come nothing in here is fried?"

Alan gestured to Tom in the corner. "Because this entire tower was designed around something like tonight happening. Force Protocols are designed to waylay our friend here in case he ever did anything like what he did tonight. I only enacted the non-lethal codes because tonight wasn't intentional on his part. Every floor of this complex has a safe room similar to this one."

"You built your company headquarters around killing one of your best friends?"

Alan gave Chris a level stare. "I built this place around stopping any one of you. For Tom, I have a mass overstimulation countermeasure designed to wreak havoc with his super senses. For you, I can set the air to 0% humidity and raise the temperature to 115 degrees in two minutes. I have something for each member of the Collective Good, just in case."

"And you don't think that's being a little paranoid?"

Alan looked around the room. "Why, no, Chris. No, I do not. I would say that this constitutes some pretty damn level-headed forward thinking, wouldn't you?" A sandy blonde intern came into the room with a black and white spotted coffee mug and handed it to Alan. Alan nodded, took a sip, and then pointed at the intern.

"You. You get a raise." Alan proceeded to chug the steaming beverage in his hands.

"Alan, how much alcohol is in that?" Victoria asked, eyeing the mug.

"All, dear. All the alcohol is in this. Right now, I am going to focus on getting buzzed and not on the chunk of my arm flesh that was just charbroiled."

"I'm sor..."

"I swear to God, Tom. If you say sorry one more time tonight I will find a way to light you on fire, do you understand? I don't care if you're invulnerable; I will find a goddamned way."

Tom nodded, his face drawn in a long frown.

Alan nodded to himself. "So, first some medicinal beverages. Then I am going to run every scan I can on Tom and find out what they infected him with. Then, I'm going to find the bastards who did this, figure out what they stole and do something decidedly not heroic."

Chris eyed the mug in Alan's hands, and then grabbed the young intern as he tried to scoot away. "Bring me and the big guy in the corner one too, will ya?"

The intern left as Victoria grabbed the bridge of her nose with her fingers and sighed. Beside her, Alan continued to guzzle his drink.

Chapter 9

The Restaurant Is Now Closed

Then

***

Cindy left, waving and smiling. Alice watched her go as a voice said from behind her, "She's *not* shadowing me."

Alice sighed and held the bridge of her nose, a headache threatening already. "Allison, she should learn everything about what we do and that includes your job. She needs to know how to handle the clients, so she's shadowing you."

Allison shook her head. "No, I mean she *really* can't shadow me. I have a meeting with Algerton's Exchange tomorrow and I can't do it with her there."

Alice turned and looked Allison in the eyes. "What can't you do with a fly on the wall?"

Allison looked off for a moment. "I just really need to not be shadowed for this meeting, okay?"

Alice stared at the younger girl as she shuffled under her superior's gaze. Alice watched as Allison kept looking off to the side and adjusting her glasses. Finally Alice sighed and grabbed Allison's arm. "Dammit, Allison, come here." Alice dragged the younger girl into the back room and shut the door. Before Allison could say anything, Alice whirled around and slammed the younger girl against the wall.

"What is going on that I don't know about?"

Allison frowned at the older woman and said, "Just let me go, okay? I've got a 3:30 and…"

Alice pulled back and decked the younger girl, bouncing her head hard off the wall. Before Allison could react, Alice had her hand on the young girl's throat. Allison took a moment to realize the hand was glowing purple. She looked down and then into Alice's eyes.

"You wouldn't…"

"See if I don't? You're lying to me, and I'm not going to put up with it. Now tell me what is going on or I swear to God I will rot your pretty head right off your stump of a neck."

Allison glared at Alice for a moment and then sighed. "Fine."

Alice relaxed and stepped away. Allison wiped some blood from her nose and looked at the floor for a moment. "You know how we've been scoring a lot of clients lately?"

Alice nodded.

"Well, some of it is because we're so good," Allison said, "And some of it is because I've been making deals with our competition."

"What kind of deals?"

Allison paused for a long time.

"What kind of deals, Allison?"

"…The kind where I threaten to kill their families if they don't let go of their key clients."

"And have you?"

Allison just looked at the floor.

"Allison, did you kill anyone so we could have more business?"

Allison nodded. "A little."

Alice stared at Allison for another moment. Then, before Allison knew what was happening, Alice punched her again. As Allison reeled back, Alice grabbed her and pulled her forward, rolling her off a shoulder and throwing her into a display case that had been covered with a blanket for storage. Allison screamed in pain as the case shattered on impact.

"Goddammit, Allison!" Alice was practically shrieking with rage. Allison looked up to see tears in the other woman's eyes. "I've worked so damn hard to keep us safe, to keep a low profile! Do you know what you've done? Do you have any damn idea what could have done to us?!"

"I DID WHAT YOU TAUGHT ME TO!"

Alice froze. Allison sat and sobbed on the floor in front of her aunt. "I did exactly what you taught me to. This is what I know! I can't do what you do, alright? I can't just shut it off like you can. I look around and all I see are ways to kill a person, or how to set a building on fire and make it look natural. I see nothing but how to hurt. That's it, that's... that's me, okay? I don't know anything else..."

Alice watched her niece cry. Allison's entire body heaved with sobs as she sat, slumped in the broken pile of debris left over from the display case. Finally, Alice knelt down and scooped the younger woman into her arms to give her a long hug. "Hey now, hey now, it's okay. Just let it out."

"It's not okay. Dammit," Allison sobbed, "don't you get it? I... I hate you. I hate you for doing this to me!"

"So then, why did you stay?"

"You mean back then?"

Alice pushed her back and met her gaze. "You know what I mean."

Allison started to cry a little. Alice could see the tears running down her cheeks, but this time, the young girl didn't sob, she just sat there and wept. "At first, I didn't know any better. After a while, after I learned more, I hoped... that I could hurt you. I wanted to, but then... you made things complicated. You tried to actually raise me, and you cared about me. No one had shown me that since... you know..."

Alice let out a long sigh. "Allison, I know I was a piss poor substitute for your parents, but I swear to you, I've always tried to do what's best for you. I just... Look, I ran away when I was really young, younger than you are. I didn't have a firm direction in life, no goals, nothing. I was just some shitty, snot-nosed punk that had this evil, scary power. When Prometheus found me and taught me how to use it, I felt good. I felt good about myself and about what I could do. It was messed up, but it was a purpose. I guess... I guess I just wanted to give you something, too. Especially after everything that happened with your parents and all..."

Allison shook her head. "I know that, and you completely suck at doing right, by the way. Still, I know that. I just... I didn't think about what would actually happen later on; I just figured that we needed clients and, well..."

"And now?" Alice stared at the broken girl in front of her and felt herself die a little inside at the failure she had let progress.

"Well, for a girl who used to kill people on contract, I guess I damn well should have known better. I think, God I think I might have a problem."

Alice laughed a bit. "Honey, I think that ship sailed years ago. I'm not saying what you did was right, but do you seriously think that was any worse than any of the things you've done on assignment?"

Allison shook her head. "No... but this feels different."

Alice nodded. "It damn well should. Now, you clean yourself up and get this display case sorted out. Tomorrow, you and I are both going sit down and work out a schedule of activities that... that suits your personality a bit better. Also, you're getting a therapist. You will not fight me on this point."

Allison looked at Alice, her eyes scrunched in confusion. "Wait, you're not handing me over to the cops? Even after what I did? I mean, you do that and you could plead ignorance, if it came to that. I... look; I'll give you an out, okay?"

Alice let out a long breath. "Allison, I am...was...am your legal guardian. I am your aunt in title and believe it or not, I've always tried to act as such. I promised you that no matter how much you hated me, how much you messed up or how bad of a job I did, I would do everything I could to make it up to you, and so far, I've failed spectacularly on every level. No hon, I'm keeping my promise, even if I probably shouldn't."

"I'm sorry, Alice."

Allison sighed and sniffed a little. Alice patted her head. "Get cleaned up; we have work to do in the morning."

"We're stuck together, aren't we?" Allison asked, her eyes closed, her head hung low. Alice stood and stared at the young woman in front of her.

"Yeah, I suppose we are."

"And... and what, we're good guys now?"

Alison sighed. "Let's take things one step at a time."

Now

***

The castle was in ruins. Outside, the local media was having a field day reporting on the act of terror that had occurred at one of Japan's most prized landmarks. Inside was a different story, as the one soldier who had avoided being taken out stood with a small battalion in the ruins of the former super villain lair.

The soldier had removed his mask and was surveying the work done by the others. He was an older man with short, graying hair. His face was lined and tired, but his eyes were sharp. The men moving around him did so with caution, and when he spoke, they stopped to listen.

He motioned for a lieutenant that had just emerged from a tunnel to approach him. With a controlled, even voice, he asked in Japanese, *"Anything, lieutenant?"*

The solider shook his head. *"No, Sir. It looks like she fled through the escape tunnels. We're attempting to track her location now."*

The older man looked around at the damage. *"I just can't believe we missed all this. How long do you suppose this was here? Months? Years? Someone dropped the ball."*

"Sir?" the young soldier asked.

"This whole complex is a testament to how pathetic our own internal security is. This is exactly why I left the service."

The older man watched as a man in a business suit was lowered into the debris. The commanding officer walked over and saluted his employer as the businessman dusted off his shoes. *"Sir."*

Nakajima looked to the soldier and then to the rubble. *"So, did we get her this time?"*

The soldier paused a moment and said, *"No, Sir. She escaped again, but we did manage to capture the golem."*

Nakajima looked at the giant statue behind the soldier. It was frozen in a solid block of ice, a soldier locked in a frozen scream was trapped in its hands. *"How did you accomplish this?"* Nakajima asked.

"I employed LOX grenades while it was distracted. The target is currently neutralized, but may prove hostile when released. I recommend we detonate it immediately."

Nakajima shook his head and smiled at the statue. *"Nonsense. This is a trophy of war, Colonel. We'll just keep this one on ice until we figure out how to shut it down, understood?"*

The older man nodded. *"Sir."*

"In the meantime," Nakajima said, *"I would like you to redouble the guard at my estate. This young lady is going to get desperate soon, and when she does, I have a feeling I'll be having a visitor."*

"Sir," the colonel saluted. Nakajima nodded and the colonel left to direct his troops on handling the golem. Nakajima continued to admire the underground lair as Lotus came up silently behind him, dressed in white and wearing her fox mask.

"You should let this go," she said in her monotone.

Nakajima scoffed. *"This woman has cost me time and money, and she represents a potential threat. I will not have any loose ends for others to pull, even some American whore. Is that understood?"*

"And what of my sister?"

Nakajima looked to Lotus. *"I'm sorry?"*

"My sister. She was at my sister's apartment. Why would she go there, do you think?"

"Obviously to find a hostage to bait you with. She apparently didn't realize that the Dead Talon had already taken her, did she?" Nakajima asked with a small smile.

Lotus stared at Nakajima for a moment before asking, *"When this is over, you will resume searching for her?"*

Nakajima nodded. *"I promised you, didn't I? You'll find your sister. That I am sure of."*

Lotus pinned an appraising glare on her employer from behind her fox mask as he surveyed the carnage, before seamlessly melting away into the shadows.

***

It was 7:00pm and the dinner crowd was drifting in at the Red Bunny. While not a family restaurant, it saw its fair share of business dinners and casual dates. Behind the bar, flat screen televisions played clips of the day's news and sports. As he mixed a drink for a businessman and his purchased date, Yoshi watched a story about an apparent string of micro-earthquakes that struck throughout Nagoya during what appeared to be a terrorist attack.

A young waitress rushed in from the main lobby to where Yoshi was working and signaled for his attention. As soon as they were out of the customer's earshot, the waitress said, *"Sir, we have a problem. Do you remember that pale woman that came here the other day?"*

"What about her?" Yoshi asked, continuing to wipe down a glass.

"She's in the elevator and she's wearing a strange costume."

Yoshi froze, his face drained of blood.

"We need to clear the restaurant before she can..."

Yoshi was interrupted by a heavyset guard flying through the smoked-glass front of the restaurant entrance. In the lobby stood the deadliest woman in the world in full costume, her face a mask of indifference.

"The restaurant is now closed", she called, her echoing voice the only sound. "Everyone who wishes to live will please exit the building."

Without warning, a guard charged her from across the room. In one fluid motion, Alice caught the guard's extended arm, pivoted around and twisted him to the ground. Without even showing any effort, Alice reached around, shifted her weight and gave a sharp jerk. The restaurant winced as a loud crack came from the guards forearm, followed by a blubbery scream from the guard.

"Now, please." Alice was the picture of calm as she dropped the crumpled guard to the floor.

The patrons scurried past her in a silent, cautious rush.

Yoshi positioned himself behind the bar as the waitress staff slowly wandered into the main dining area of the restaurant, placing themselves between Yoshi and Alice. Alice wondered if Yoshi paid them for working double duty. Alice ignored them and focused on the bartender. "Yoshi," Alice said, her voice raised so he could hear, "may I please have a word with you?"

"I'm sorry, Alice; the bar is now closed. Why don't you come back another time?"

"Yeah, that's not going to work for me."

Alice stepped over the broken glass and entered the restaurant. She took two steps before the first waitress charged, her apron whipping around as she twisted in a screaming leap. Alice caught sight of a knife from under the young woman's outfit as she came down. With a quick sidestep, Alice avoided the quick, thin blade and grabbed a plate from a nearby table. Spinning around, Alice shattered the plate across the waitress's face, knocking the young woman out cold.

Two more waitresses came at Alice from either side, each with a knife in hand. Alice watched both ladies approach and shifted to avoid the one on the left as the waitress lunged with a yell. Alice dodged and blocked the waitress's swing with her forearm. The other waitress charged Alice from behind, but Alice spun around, her hand going quickly to her belt and letting out her filament line. In a smooth, twisting motion, she wrapped the second waitress's arm and brought it back and she roped the young woman by the neck. Then she spun and slammed the choking woman into the first waitress, sending both ladies sprawling into a table and shattering it on impact.

Alice sighed. "Okay, then. Let's get this over with."

A fourth waitress moved in, a knife in each hand. Alice walked swiftly towards the young woman. As the waitress swung her knife, Alice grabbed her by the wrist with one hand while punching her in the face with the other, sending the girl flying backwards into a pillar. Yoshi watched as the young woman bounced off the pillar and collapsed to the floor, her face covered in blood.

Alice spun in a slow circle, indicating the room. "While I applaud your little staff of wanna-be female badasses, could you not find any that didn't suck? Really, Yoshi. It's embarrassing."

The last waitress, the young woman who had alerted Yoshi to what was going on, stepped between Alice and her employer. In her hands a well-crafted katana winked in the lighting of the bar. Alice watched as the young woman brought her blade to eye level and started to move in a slow semi-circle.

"They were practice," the young woman said, "I'm for real."

Alice considered the young woman for a moment. "Yes, I'm sure you are." The woman cautiously watched as Alice reached towards her belt and pulled out her cell phone. "Say, you mind if I get a picture of this? You know, before I die and all."

The woman paused for a moment in confusion.

"PhoneBuddy, fire!" Alice yelled out as she pointed the business end of PhoneBuddy towards the young woman. Instantly, a blast of electricity shot across the room and knocked the young woman off her feet and over the bar. Yoshi ducked as the waitress sailed over his head and smashed through the glass shelves of bottles behind him. The smell of ozone and expensive liquor filled the air.

Yoshi looked at the young woman at his feet, stunned at how quickly she'd been put down. "She was my best waitress," he said, his voice practically dripping with disappointment.

"Well, considering the last time she served me I was poisoned – unsuccessfully - that statement doesn't give me much hope for the rest of your staff."

Yoshi looked back to Alice, who was standing calmly on the other side of the bar. He noted that her phone already back in her utility belt. Yoshi regarded the costume and mask. "Is that… did you get a new outfit?"

"Yes. Yes, I did. Thank you for noticing." Alice nodded to show her gratitude, and then lunged for Yoshi. In one swift move, she latched onto his collar and dragged him over the bar. With a practiced ease, she flung him over her shoulder and onto the floor a little harder than necessary. The bartender landed with a cry of pain and a satisfying crack on the hard wood floor.

"So," Alice said as she straddled Yoshi's chest, carefully pinning both of his arms with her knees. "When I came here the first time, I was civil. I asked polite questions, received polite answers and then was poisoned, which was not so polite. I don't like being poisoned, Yoshi. I don't like it one bit."

186

"You...handled it..." Yoshi coughed out.

"Yeah, but it put me in a *really* shitty mood. You see, it sucks, Yoshi. It sucks a lot. You have no idea how painful it is to process complicated toxins and break them down from the inside out. It's... well, here." Alice took her Infinity knife out of her belt and grabbed Yoshi's hand. "I suppose the best analogy I can give someone without any powers would be... it's like having a pissed off woman with super powers and questionable morals slowly slice your fingers off and then feed them to you."

Yoshi's eyes nearly tripled in size. "You wouldn't!"

Alice dug her nails into his wrist, drawing a cry of pain. "You're right, Yoshi. I could always rot them off. That's a different experience altogether. You see, you seem to be forgetting that I practically ran an organization that made mass murder an afternoon activity. Do you have any idea what some our more interesting members would *wear* on casual Fridays?"

"You had casual Fridays?"

"What can I say? I know how to motivate my staff," Alice said as she shifted her weight and braced her knee against Yoshi's throat. "Move and I will remove a finger. Try to fight me and I will remove two fingers. Give me any considerable trouble, and I'll just put my dainty little hand on your face and show you exactly what I can do when I am sufficiently pissed. Do we understand each other?"

Yoshi nodded as best he could.

"Very good," Alice said. She put the knife to Yoshi's hand, drawing a thin line of blood. "Why did you lie to me about the Lotus? You knew where she was the whole time, didn't you?"

"She had been sent on assignment to remove Nakajima," Yoshi sputtered, his eyes on the knife in Alice's hand. "We wanted him gone, but had to get her in place first."

"How did you do it? How did you convince him that hiring an assassin from you was anything other than a bad idea?"

Yoshi paused briefly, his eyes flickering between Alice and the knife. "We used Purge technology and weapons. We confiscated them when you were here and thought it would take suspicion off of us if we made it look like an outside job. We killed one of our top enforcers in a car bombing two hours after we failed to kill Nakajima. He figured we were in this together."

Alice considered Yoshi for a moment. "Go on," she calmly replied.

"We sent the Lotus. We told her to make an example of Nakajima, but then she cut off all communication with us. We sent in another agent, but she murdered him before he could establish contact. She betrayed us, and now serves him."

Alice shook her head. "No, I don't think it's that cut and dry. There's something else here, and I'm starting to think I know what it is. Next question: why did you send those men after me in the park?"

Yoshi shook his head. "I didn't. Those were Nakajima's men, not mine."

"Someone's about to kiss his piano lessons goodbye..." Alice pushed the blade against Yoshi's hand, drawing another rivulet of blood.

"It's the truth! If we wanted you dead, we would have moved against you by now."

"You poisoned me!"

"That was a formality! You're Dyspell; I figured you could handle it."

"That... well, that's just a horrible excuse for poisoning someone!"

"They needed to see we didn't like you! If they thought you were working directly with us, then you wouldn't have been able to meet with Nakajima. We had to do something, and I figured this was as good a thing as any!"

"And *talking to me* wasn't considered? You never once thought, 'gee, I've worked with this woman off and on for years and have a great rapport with her. Maybe I should tell her our plan, and not potentially kill her?' Did that option just never pop up in your horny, lonely, psychotic little brain?"

"Do you remember the people in the restaurant when you came here before?"

Alice thought for a moment. "Yes. One of them was a plant?"

"The old man at the bar," Yoshi said. "He comes in daily and sits right at the counter. He started doing this the day Lotus went to work for Nakajima. He was listening the entire time we were talking. When you left, he got on his cell phone and took off shortly afterwards."

"Huh. Okay, next question: Why did you murder everyone in my hotel?"

"We didn't. That was Nakajima."

Alice glared at Yoshi. Even through the opaque domino mask, Yoshi could feel her stare. "There were children in there, Yoshi. I've got a special corner of Hell waiting for me when I die, but it *isn't* the corner for monsters that murder kids."

"Nakajima knew you were in disguise and he wanted to send a message, so he had the floor purged. It wasn't us. We found out about it when you did."

Alice considered the bartender for a moment, and then took her knee off his throat and stood up. "Why do you want Nakajima dead?"

Yoshi struggled to his feet and coughed as he rubbed his throat. "He's trying to muscle us out of Nagoya. He owns a good portion of the manufacturing here, and he doesn't feel like playing nice anymore. At first, he was obedient and paid his dues, but now he figures he doesn't need us. Other businesses are watching this unfold with great interest; how things go here could have consequences for our holdings throughout Japan. We need him put down and his company broken up, but now he has our best assassin and we can't touch him."

"Okay, so blowing up his factory isn't an option?"

Yoshi shook his head. "We want to take over his business, not destroy it. We need him dead and his empire crippled so we can move in and purchase. We own 30% of his stock already; once he's dead, we can maneuver ourselves into a position of controlling interest."

Alice put her knife away and handed Yoshi a napkin for his hand. Yoshi nodded a thank you and wrapped his bleeding finger up. "Here's my offer," Alice said as Yoshi tended his wound, "I get Nakajima out of the way, you get the controlling interest in Nakajima's company."

"And what do you get, Miss Alice?" Yoshi asked.

"I get Lotus. If everything goes well and she agrees, we leave together; no muss, no fuss. If I die but remove Nakajima, you send Lotus to the US to serve under Alan Tanner at Tanner Industries until he says otherwise. Also, you sign an exclusive deal for distribution, parts and shipping through Tanner Industries for your US-based cellular ventures. Mr. Tanner will give you a fair deal, and you will have a respectable business partner."

Yoshi considered Alice for a moment. "This is an acceptable offer. I will, of course, have to discuss this with my superiors before I can commit."

Alice stared at him for a moment. "Since when does the Black Nail of the Dead Talon answer to anyone? Why do you think I came to you first?"

Yoshi smiled widely. "Miss Alice, you never fail to impress. How did you know?"

Alice shrugged. "I've known ever since we tried to muscle you out of Nagoya years ago. I just didn't think it was worth bringing up until now. Now, where can I find Nakajima when he's not at work?"

"He is almost always holed up in his ranch estate on the western edge of town. The complex is walled, with at least a dozen guards on the perimeter - probably quite a few more right now. Inside, you'll find three roving patrols of six men each, all armed with automatic weapons. The house itself is fortified to be bomb proof, and he keeps a personal guard with him at all times."

Alice crossed her arms in front of her chest and put her chin in her hand. "Okay, okay, no biggie. I'll just need something to distract them. This is difficult, but not impossible. I'll just need to put in a quick call..."

"Alice, why are you doing this?"

Alice looked at Yoshi and shrugged. "The man insulted me, tried to murder me and slaughtered an entire hotel floor just to get my attention. He's made a simple job difficult, and he's interfering with my business back home. If I don't do this, he'll keep trying to get to me and those who work for me. Eventually, he'll succeed, and I'm not having that. Just because I'm retired does *not* mean that I am an easy mark for some no-name, wannabe crime boss."

Yoshi considered the young woman in front of him. "Funny, you don't look at all retired to me."

Alice shifted in her uniform. "Semi-retired. Retired from evil."

"You're on your way to break into a businessman's home and, in all probability, kill him."

Alice stared right back at Yoshi, "This is true, but, on the other hand, he is a very bad man."

191

"I don't think being a hero works like that."

Alice rummaged in her utility belt, pulled out 500 Yen and tossed it on the counter. "Then it's a good thing I'm not a hero. The tip's for the first staff member who wakes up. I'm banking on the one I put through the table."

Alice wound her way through the unconscious staff on the floor as Yoshi gingerly picked up the wadded bill and tucked it in his apron. "Good luck, Dyspell."

Alice walked out without looking back.

Nakajima's house was a decent size by Japanese standards. It was a stretched out, one story ranch done in what looked like white stone with a black shingle roof. The property was surrounded by a solid white stone wall that had only one break in it to allow traffic in and out of the complex. Alice was perched in a tree a block away, using the enhanced lenses of her Domino mask to examine the property. In a branch beside her, Makoto sat, straining to see.

"So, how bad is it?" Makoto struggled to keep his balance, while Alice continued to stare.

"Two guards at the front gate, some security cameras, and I count four guards on the property, all armed. The house is well-lit, and there are several main structures to the complex that could potentially house Nakajima. There's a heliport on the far side, on what looks like a closed pool. Huh."

"Huh?"

Alice shrugged. "Nothing, that's just a nice use of space, that's all. Anyway, my guess is that Nakajima does business in the structure closest to the helicopter to ensure a quick escape. I'm guessing that Lotus is in there tonight, as well."

Makoto nodded. He was dressed in a black spandex suit. Alice noted that in the dark, it did well to hide his less-than-impressive physique.

"Hey, Makoto? There's something I've been meaning to ask you."

"Yes?"

"You and your pack, you're kitsune, right? Fox people?"

Makoto nodded, his face a mask of pride.

Alice bit her lip, not sure how to phrase her next question. "I always thought kitsune were girls in the old stories."

Makoto laughed a bit. "Shifters can come in any gender and any species. For our tribe, the gene passes down easier on the woman's side, hence the stories."

"Oh," Alice said. "Cool. Anyway, that had been bugging me for a bit." She continued to examine the property before shutting off her glasses. "Okay, here's what I need from you and the pack. Can you give me a distraction so I can get in the main entrance?"

Makoto nodded. "I suppose so, but if they open fire, we won't be of much good to you."

Alice grinned. "Makoto, I'm not asking you to go all shifter for me just yet. Did you pass out the bags I brought?"

When Alice had met up with Makoto, she had been delighted to see that eight of the pack had come with him, all dressed in dark clothing, and all looking eager to help. Alice had prepared for this and had packed nearly a dozen prep bags, just in case. Not willing to ask Yoshi for any more help, she had to raid a local sporting goods store. The credit card had been Yoshi's, which thankfully he hadn't noticed was pickpocketed from his person earlier.

Alice may not have felt like asking Yoshi for help, but she saw no harm in *volunteering* it.

Makoto nodded, his face a little uneasy. "I still don't see how what you brought will help us. They have guns, and we don't."

"This is true," Alice said. "Let's get the troops together."

Now, as she and the kitsune did their final prep, she wished that she had more weaponry, planning and safeguards in place. However, considering the short notice, she thought the plan was as solid as it was going to get.

Alice had three members of the pack go to either side of the compound wall while two went to the rear. Makoto and Alice stayed at the front, just out of site of the security cameras. Alice looked to Makoto, who whispered into his phone, "Everyone ready?"

"Ready," came the response from each team. Alice nodded to Makoto, who gripped his phone and said, "Now."

Each team took the compound bow and arrow sets that Alice had handed them and lit a small pouch filled with an explosive gel on the front of their arrows on fire. The chemicals had taken her two hours to measure out and mix, but it was well worth it to the former villainess as she saw the arrow pouches raise like glowing, yellow stars throughout the trees. As one, they shot their arrows over the wall, trying to get off as many as they could. The effect was almost instantaneous; the guards started yelling and running, trying to dodge the arrows, while simultaneously putting out the small fires from the blasts before they could damage the house. Several stuck in the roof of the ranch and spread rapidly, igniting with the tar in the shingles. In a panic, one of the guards pulled the fire alarm.

Alice patted Makoto on the shoulder. "If they leave the compound, take them out. If things get too thick, leave and regroup later. Just keep sending over those arrows!"

Makoto nodded, his face already contorting as he began to change. In a semi-growl, he said, "Good luck!"

"You too," Alice said, as she calmly walked out from their hiding spot, crossed the street and strolled right up to the front gate. Alice wasted no time in grabbing the bars of the gate and focusing her powers, which caused the steel in her hands to rust, flake and then crumble into red dust. One of the guards noticed her and came running as she stepped through. Alice sprinted for the guard and knocked the gun out of his hands before he could get off a shot. Then she slammed the palm of her hand into his face, brought her foot around the back of his leg and sent him crashing to the ground. For good measure, she smashed his face with her elbow, guaranteeing he would stay knocked out.

Alice quickly dragged the unconscious man off to the side and rooted through his clothes until she found a walkie-talkie and a key ring. She slipped both items into her belt and took his automatic weapon before making a beeline for the house.

Inside, Nakajima watched calmly on his monitor system as the fire on the roof gained momentum. He noted that his guards were running around in a panic, and that several that had gone outside the wall had failed to report in. There were sounds of sporadic gunfire, and the sound of the fire alarm was grating as its high-pitched whine screamed through the house.

Nakajima yelled at his head of security, an older man that stood in a black uniform with a pistol at his side. It was the colonel from the castle raid earlier, and he was sporting the same dour expression he had been earlier. *"Is this what you consider ensuring my safety?"* He had a feeling he knew who was behind this. If he was right, the Lotus would pay for her failure.

The colonel didn't even flinch as he watched the monitors. Suddenly, he pointed at one and said, *"Right there. Someone is trying to get into the house."* The colonel wasted no time in ordering his troops to the main entrance as Nakajima watched the monitor. On it, a blurry image of a purple-haired woman in a black skin-tight suit and a domino mask was kicking in his expensive, stained-glass doors.

Nakajima turned around and looked to the Lotus, who until now had been standing quietly at the rear of the room. *"You stay with me,"* he said. He then turned to the guard standing beside him. *"Kogoura! I didn't pay for your team to play around in my entryway! Find her and kill her; I don't care how you do it. We'll cover it up later, just end her!"* Colonel Kenji Kogoura, the commanding officer for Nakajima's security forces, nodded and quickly left the room. Nakajima stood, looked at Lotus and barked, *"You! This is your fault. If you had done your job at the warehouse, she wouldn't be here now!"*

Lotus seemed unfazed by her employer's screaming and continued to watch the monitor. Idly, she said, *"Your guards are losing."* Nakajima turned and watched as the woman in black proceeded to rip through his soldiers like they were made out of tinfoil.

"You will *not* lose this time," he said in halted English, his eyes locked on Lotus. "I want her dead, and in the Pit, do you understand?" The Lotus continued to watch the monitor, giving him the barest of nods. Nakajima started to say more, but something about the Lotus' body language told him that it would not get the desired result. Angrily, he stood and continued to watch his entire security force get taken out by a single intruder.

Chapter 10

"Our arrangement is at an end"

Against her better judgment, Alice was enjoying herself in the lobby. There had been considerably more guards than what Yoshi had told her, but that hadn't come as a huge surprise. She noticed that they didn't seem to want to shoot unless she was alone, so she purposefully put herself in the midst of at least one or two guards while fighting, even going so far as to avoid a knockout blow or two just to keep someone on her.

She was doing well; the lobby was mostly cleared out, save for three remaining guards. She had taken quite a few blows to her upper torso and was seriously starting to feel the burn, but her costume (for the most part) was sealing itself like it was supposed to. She'd only been grazed by two or three bullets; so far, it was a good night.

Alice was engaged with a guard that barely looked old enough to shave while the other two waited nervously with their guns trained on Alice. With a well-placed punch, she connected with the young man square in the nose.

"You bwoke my nwose!" he shouted as Alice snickered.

"What are you? Twelve? Here, hold your hands up higher." Alice reached over and lifted the young man's hands up as the other guards watched, confused.

"Your technique is terrible. You keep letting your arms drop to your side. Look, kid, this isn't a video game, people are gonna hit you in the face if you do this. A lot. There! Now you can block. Go ahead, block me," Alice said as she threw another punch. The young man swatted it away and took a swing, which Alice easily dodged.

"Hey, now, careful there. You almost hit a girl!" Alice yelled. The confused guard stammered a bit.

"I'm...sorry?"

Alice punched him in the nose again. "Don't drop your guard. Geez, you guys are seriously undertrained, you know that?"

Alice was admittedly letting herself get distracted with the young soldier in front of her when suddenly two shots rang out, one hitting the guard she was fighting square in the head, the other knocking Alice back as it went into her arm.

"Okay...that was my fault. That was stupid." Alice breathed as she clutched her bullet wound. Her Kevlar suit was decent, but to Alice's dismay it apparently wasn't as reinforced in the arms as it was in the torso. The bullet made it through the mesh and into her right arm. Alice felt it lodge under the skin and cringed; her right arm was now pretty much useless. She looked up to see an older man with a handgun trained on her person.

"That will be enough, ma'am," Kogoura said in clipped English. Alice noted his calm stance, his even stare and level hand, and cursed to herself; *this* man knew what he was doing. Based on how the other two guards instantly relaxed in the man's presence, Alice guessed that this man was in charge of the security forces.

Alice relaxed a little and nodded. She wasn't stupid; this man had a gun trained on her head and had just shown he wasn't afraid to kill someone. She looked to the dead young man she had been fighting and winced a little; even as a villain, she had always gone out of her way to avoid killing children. This kid was barely old enough to know what he was doing, but because he was here and she was fighting him, he had

198

been executed just to prove a point and end a fight, and that made Alice uneasy.

Kogoura gestured with his firearm for Alice to stand. As she struggled to her feet, she heard one of the guards scream as they fired their guns towards the door. Alice turned in time to see the guard be tackled by a half man, half fox monster that had some dark wet patches of fur across its chest.

Snarling, the kitsune slashed at the other guard and knocked his gun across the room. With a growl and a leap, it caught the other guard and sunk its teeth into his neck. Alice looked to the older man to see he already had his gun trained on the fox monster and was about to fire. She leapt forward, ignoring the pain in her arm as she lunged for the man.

Kogoura noticed her out of the corner of his eye, turned, and fired at Alice as she closed the gap between them. Alice barely registered the searing flash of pain as she grabbed Kogoura's gun with one hand and his face with the other. Normally, Alice would concentrate on the level of power she was using to inflict a calculated amount of damage. Seeing as how Kogoura was already reaching into his belt for a knife as Alice held tight to his face, this was time she just couldn't afford. With a grunt, she forced her powers to the surface and pushed them against the man and the gun at the same time, causing her hands to glow a bright purple.

Kogoura let loose a guttural scream as the gun crumbled to powder in his hands. He backed away, swinging wildly with his knife as he did so. Alice winced as the knife struck home in her side, causing her to lose her focus and stagger backwards as blood poured down the leg of her suit. The blade had been mostly stopped, but the sheer force of the impact had been enough. The blade had managed to work through her suit and penetrated the skin beneath. Alice tried to see how badly she had wounded Kogoura, but he was covering his face with both hands and screaming while crumpled on the floor. From the inhuman sound coming from his throat, she guessed the damage was worse than she had intended.

Alice gripped the knife blade in her side and yanked it out with a cry. Already, her costume was closing around it, but she could feel the warmth spreading in her uniform. The blade hadn't gone in straight so the wound wasn't nearly as deep as it could have been, but it was enough that Alice felt severely diminished. The self-sealing fabric was doing its job, but it could only do so much to stop the blood. With some effort, she walked over to Kogoura and looked down at his writhing form.

"That was for the boy you killed," she said, her voice shaky as she spoke.

Alice then looked over to the fox man as he sat on the floor, looking winded. Alice watched as the fox whimpered and clutched at its chest. "Get to the rest of the pack, and don't change back until you get those out, or you'll be as good as dead, understand?" The kitsune nodded and started to limp towards the door. Alice noted the pants that the fox man was still wearing and recognized them as the bottom portion of Makoto's outfit.

Alice made her way over to one of the guard's automatic weapons and picked it up. As she did, she noticed her mask slipping off the side of her face. When she reached up and touched her temple, her glove came away bloody. Alice blinked in confusion, and then she remembered that she had been shot. The bullet had grazed the side of her head and ripped through her mask. Alice could feel where she had lost a bit of hair on the side of her head, and when she touched it, it stung.

With a grunt, she left the lobby through the same doors the older man had entered through. As she made her way through the home, she noted that the fire alarm had stopped blaring sometime during the fight. It didn't matter, she supposed – the smell of smoke was quickly growing. The pack had done their job and as a result, the house would most likely burn to the ground. Alice knew she only had a few minutes before things got dicey.

After a minute or two of searching, Alice found a set of parlor doors that opened to a large, dimly-lit study, complete with a bar and a wall of windows that looked out over the closed pool and helicopter. The wall of windows was interrupted by a set of glass doors that led to the outside patio. The doors were currently propped open, and the smell of smoke was wafting in. Behind the bar, calmly mixing a drink, was Nakajima. Alice noted the wall of video monitors behind the bar showed the house in various stages of burning, as well as guards still battling the kitsune outside.

"I must admit, I did not expect you to be this much trouble, Miss Alice." Nakajima's voice was calm as he poured a martini into two glasses and added olives to each. "Would you care for a drink? I admit, I lack Yoshi's talent, but I've been told my martinis are just shy of perfect."

Alice shook her head, smiled and pointed her automatic weapon at Nakajima. "No thank you; I didn't come here for a drink."

Nakajima sighed and nodded. "I suspected as much."

Before Alice could react, a throwing star zipped across the room and plunged into Alice's leg, right where she had been struck the day before. Alice screamed and dropped to her good knee, the gun fell from her hands as she crumbled. When she looked towards the shadows at the far side of the room, she saw Lotus standing there in her fox mask and white gi, her hand filled with sharp, shining stars.

"If you take a step," she said in calm, clipped English, "I will throw another."

Alice struggled to her feet and looked to Nakajima. "You wanted to muscle your way into the Dead Talon's territory. Why? Why not just stick with being a businessman?"

Nakajima smiled at his guest. "As a businessman, you never pay out more than you have to. The Talon wanted more than what I thought was reasonable for an operating fee, so I decided it would be better to take their operations for myself."

"So how did you get her to work for you?" Alice gestured to the Lotus.

"She was hired by me, after an assassin tried to kill me in my sleep."

Alice took a step towards the bar and shook her head. "The Dead Talon never sent an assassin, did they?"

A throwing star whizzed across the room, this time planting itself in Alice's right shoulder. Alice stifled a scream and clutched at the now bloody shoulder as her arm went completely dead. "You... staged it, to get them to agree to send her. Why?"

Nakajima gestured to the Lotus, who looked as though she hadn't moved a muscle. "Oh, they sent her, but only because I had my moles and spies suggest that they do. After all, she is well worth the price. She is precise, loyal and follows orders well."

"What did you tell her about Nanami to get her to stay with you, Nakajima?" Alice asked through gritted teeth. The pain from her side was starting to make her feel faint, but she forced herself to focus.

"I am helping her track her sister down," Nakajima said, his voice as calm as his smile. "Lotus knows I wouldn't harm her dear sister, but without my resources, I doubt she would be able to find her."

"Really? Is that why you had her kidnapped and then ruined her reputation after the fact?"

Nakajima laughed a little. "You have a wild imagination. Lotus, give her the Long Kiss and toss her in the Pit. We need to be leaving before things get too hot." Without another word, Nakajima pressed a button on the bar. Alice noted that the floor near the glass wall opened to reveal what looked like a chute.

202

Lotus looked to Nakajima and then back to Alice. For a moment, she paused as if she were considering doing something else. Then without a sound, she calmly walked over to Alice and reached into the folds of her gi. Alice's eyes widened as Lotus brought out a handful of what looked like gray gel. "I'm sorry," she said to Alice as she smeared the gel into her face. Alice didn't even have time to scream before the gel solidified across her mouth and nose. Without wasting a moment, Lotus picked Alice up by her good shoulder and tossed her towards the chute. Alice didn't even have time to react before she tumbled head-first into the blackness.

"Excellent," Nakajima said, "Now, let's round up the others. Lotus, if you would get my bag?"

Nakajima calmly left to collect his things as Lotus looked to the still-open chute. After a moment, she followed her employer out of the room.

***

Alice tumbled down the heavy metal chute and crashed into a soft, foul-smelling inky blackness that seemed to echo slightly with the sound of her landing. Without wasting a moment, she tried pulling at the gel on her face, but found it stuck fast to her skin. The goo wasn't just over her mouth and nose; Lotus had smeared it across the entire lower half of her face, so ripping it off would be next to impossible. Alice tried focusing her powers, but she was shaky, and she could tell from the resistance her powers were giving her that this was a synthetic polymer, which meant breaking it down would take time and energy – both of which Alice did not have.

Under normal circumstances, Alice could hold her breath for up to four minutes. Physically, she was relatively young, in great shape and had practiced for scenarios similar to this, so being cut off from air wasn't an instant concern. This, however, didn't count as 'normal circumstances'.

203

With her injuries, Alice didn't know how much longer she could hold out.

Alice quickly considered her options. She didn't know if she would survive ripping the gel off, so that one was out. Even at her best, she knew that rotting the gel off would take some time. She didn't have a chemical dissolver in her belt (she honestly never saw a need, considering her power set), so there was nothing artificial that could help. That only left one option. Even though her lungs were beginning to burn madly, Alice paused and steadied herself before pulling the Infinity knife from her belt.

Alice felt the world spin around her as she pulled the collar of her suit down and felt her throat for the spot just above the cricothyroid muscle. She blinked as she saw white splashes of light dance across her vision. With her eyes tightly shut, she pressed the point of the knife to her throat.

'I love you, mom.'

The thought flashed through her mind as the knife blade dipped into her skin. Alice felt a gush of warm blood pour out of her throat as the air whooshed in, filling her lungs. Alice nearly started coughing, but focused all her energies on not gaging while her mouth couldn't open. At first, the feeling of breathing through the tiny hole in her throat was disorientating. Once she'd steadied herself, Alice found she could do it, and the trickle of blood began to slow. To keep the hole open, Alice fumbled in her belt until she found what she was looking for, a small, plastic tube. It was her miniature siphoning kit. Normally, it was meant to be used for extracting chemicals, fuel or other liquids. Alice didn't see why it couldn't be used for the opposite as she carefully slid it into the hole in her throat.

Alice wasted no time in checking her belt for a glow stick. After cracking and shaking it, Alice's eyes widened in shock at the sight before her. The Pit, as Nakajima called it, was a storage area under the house that looked to have a garage door at the end of it. On the floor were bodies of office workers, factory employees and many other random, unfortunate people. Each one carelessly murdered and left to rot in the dark. She was momentarily glad for her inability to smell the sickly odor of decay around her. Alice's eyes narrowed as she continued to take stock of her surroundings; she had seen rooms like this before and knew what it meant. It was Nakajima's trophy room, his monument to those who had stood against him.

Alice started to turn towards the hatchway she had slid down, but then stopped as something caught her eye. Bending down for a closer examination, she brought the glow stick close to one of the bodies, and then closed her eyes in a rush of cold anger. After rooting through the pockets of the dead body, she found what she was looking for and headed for the chute.

The shaft was a solid 45 degree angle and incredibly slick, but the gloves of Alice's suit were designed to offer her a firm grip, and her boots provided a sure footing. After several failed attempts, she hauled herself over the edge of the shaft and back into the study, which was quickly filling with smoke.

As she pulled herself up to her knees using a nearby window ledge, she saw that Nakajima and Lotus were already outside and heading for the helicopter, which was powering up for takeoff. Alice quickly assessed the situation. Her leg felt like it was on fire and her arm was useless. Her side was thick with blood and her throat... Alice didn't want to think about her throat. She knew she barely had enough energy to make it out of the house before it burned around her, so she staggered for the glass doors that led out towards the backyard and the helicopter.

Nakajima was already on his cell phone talking to the police when he felt himself get pushed out of the way by Lotus, who whirled around and brought her hand up to catch a projectile that had been flying for her employer's head. They both looked to see Alice collapsed to one knee, her costume torn and bloody, her throat slick with blood and sporting a small plastic tube that moved up and down sporadically. Her eyes were hard and focused, and her purple hair was matted with sweat and blood, but she wasn't glaring at Nakajima.

Lotus met her eyes for a moment, and then noticed the strangeness of the weapon that had been thrown at her boss. Curious, she looked at her hand, and froze as she saw a familiar and cluttered key ring. Hanging from the rungs were several charms, three sets of keys and a pink, coiled wristband that dangled off the side. Lotus took off her fox mask and met Alice's eyes with a solemn nod. Alice, unable to do much of anything else, nodded back.

Nakajima put away his phone and gave a loud, slow clap. "I admire your fortitude, Alice! Not too many people have the guts to do what you did to stay alive. Pity it was a waste of effort." Nakajima pulled out a handgun and pointed it at Alice's head, his mouth curved in a huge grin. That grin turned into a gargled scream of pain as a silver flash sliced through the air in front of him, neatly severing his arm from his body.

Nakajima fell backwards, clutching his bloody stump and howling in pain. Lotus stood over him, a short, bloody blade clenched tightly in her hand. Nakajima looked up at her in outrage and screamed, "What the hell do you think you're doing? You'll never find your whore of a sister now, you bitch!"

Lotus held up her sister's keychain for Nakajima to see.

"Our arrangement is at an end," Lotus said evenly as she advanced on Nakajima, her sword glistening in the light of the raging fire behind her.

The last thing Alice heard before she passed out was the satisfying sound of Nakajima screaming in terror, and then blessed silence as the world went black.

Chapter 11

"Here, I ordered you bacon."

Then

***

Alice had been dreading this meeting for months. She knew it was stupid to feel afraid, but she just couldn't help herself. This was the one thing that she had actively worked to avoid since retiring, but after Allison had found out she had been ducking this meeting, Alice found herself all but forced to go.

Allison had been very adamant on the matter. Alice could still hear the young woman's voice in her head as she remembered their brief conversation earlier. "If I could do it, if I could be in your shoes and do it, I would. I would give anything to have that chance, *so don't you fucking waste it.*" She had said this to Alice shortly before locking her aunt out of *Rare Gems*.

Even then, Alice had wandered around for a good six hours in an effort to dodge what was coming. She was scared, nervous, even borderline terrified, but she couldn't help it; this was something that she had run from for a very long time. Now, standing in front of the old, red brick apartment building, Alice wondered if she had made a big deal of things. She fidgeted a little, stalling as best she could. She adjusted her wig. She checked her makeup. She checked the time. She checked her wig again.

She was ready.

She took the stairs to the apartment, not wanting to rush things by taking the elevator. She took them one at a time. She thought about the last time she had done this, and how that had been a lifetime ago. She thought about what she would say and how she would act. She thought about all of this until she found herself standing in front of a plain, ordinary door that had appeared far too fast for her liking. Alice reached up to knock and then froze as her breath tightened in her throat.

She really wasn't ready.

Fortunately for her, she didn't have to be. At that moment, the door opened to reveal a small, older woman with silver hair and a round, lumpy figure. Her face was wrinkled, but not ancient, and her eyes were alert and wide with surprise. In her arms was a flower print grocery bag and purse. Alice guessed that she was on her way to the market.

They stared at each other for what felt to Alice like a very, very long time. The older woman had momentarily stopped breathing, her eyes looking over every inch of the young woman in front of her. Finally, with a half-whisper, the older woman mustered up a single word.

"Alice?"

Alice was frozen. Her entire body was locked up tighter than a steel rod. She felt herself shaking with fear, sadness and disappointment in herself. She suddenly felt horribly self-conscious as tears started to form in her eyes. With everything she had, she managed a nod.

"Hi mom," she choked out. "I was, well, I was nearby and I thought that, well, I, I thought that..."

Alice got out a small "eek!" as her mother grabbed her and pulled her into the longest, tightest bear hug she could ever remember being in. Alice felt her mother heave and sob as the older woman buried her face in Alice's shoulder. Alice felt herself breaking down as well as her arms wrapped around her mother. There they stayed for a good five minutes before Ms. Gailsone pulled back and said, "Come inside, dear. Please."

"But, you were on your way out..."

Ms. Gailsone glared at her daughter. "For what, chicken wings and bad television? Screw that, my baby girl is home! Get in here and shut the door. Would you like anything to drink? What do you drink? Oh my God, I think I'm going to have a stroke. I need to sit down."

Alice helped her mother to a nearby green velvet chair. The apartment was small, cluttered and filled with books, newspapers, porcelain dolls and photographs covering every free surface. Alice looked for a place to sit and was having difficulty finding one. Her mother noticed and leaned over to another, nearby chair that was piled high with papers. With a heave, she pushed them off onto the floor and pointed at the now-empty seat. "God, I don't even know where to begin! Sit down and talk to me. How... how have you been? What have you been up to? Where have you *been*? Good Lord, you were how old when you left? 15?"

Alice shrugged. "15ish I suppose. Yeah. Anyway, I was... Someone told me where you were and I realized you were really close by, so I thought I would, you know, let you know I wasn't dead and all."

Ms. Gailsone took Alice's hand and stared at her. "I know, dear. I've been following your business. You own that nice little jewelry shop down in Brooklyn, don't you?"

Alice nodded. "*Rare Gems* is a broker, not really a direct shop, but we also do that, too. How did you... How did you know that?"

The older woman smiled. "A young woman came by a couple months ago with some information on you. She strongly hinted that I should stop by, and believe you me, I nearly did a few times, but every time I thought about it, I just... I got nervous and, and backed out. I just didn't know what would happen, but now... I wish I had taken her advice."

Alice stared. "Young gal, auburn hair, red glasses, grumpy?"

"You know her?"

Alice sighed and rubbed the bridge of her nose. "Yes. Yes, I know her. You should have just swung on by."

"I didn't know if I would be welcome. I didn't think it was my place to say anything, so I didn't. I just figured you would, well, you would come by sooner or later."

Alice shrugged. "I guess it's sooner."

Ms. Gailsone sighed and patted her hand. "I just wish it had been because of something more positive, is all."

Alice stared at her mother for a moment. "What do you mean? I was, I mean, yeah, my niece *told* me to come here. She was pretty adamant about it, so I figured I would..."

"You have a niece? You got married? Oh Lord, who is he? Is he nice? Are there grandchildren? **WHERE ARE MY GRANDCHILDREN**? Talk to me!" Ms. Gailsone was nearly bouncing in her seat with a huge smile plastered on her face. Alice blanched and shook her head no.

"NO. No, no mom, it's... Allison, the young woman you met? She's my *adopted* niece. She's a Gailsone, but not through marriage. I never really... I'm single, mom."

Ms. Gailsone slumped in her seat, a look of disappointment on her face. "Oh well, you can't blame a gal for hoping, can you? Still..."

Alice shook her head. "Anyway, what did you mean by something more positive?"

Alice watched her mother stare off to the side for a minute in silence. Finally, the older woman said, "you... really didn't come here for any other reason? You just came because someone made you? Nothing else?"

Alice nodded. "Yeah, I figured it was about time, and Allison has a thing about family, so she was insistent. In fact, she locked me out of the shop to make sure I'd come here."

"I see." Ms. Gailsone sat still for a moment and then winced. Alice watched as her mother jerked in her seat and then seemed to clutch wildly for a moment before latching onto her purse. Alice, confused, sat and watched as her mother fished out a prescription bottle and quickly dry-swallowed several pills. She then closed her eyes and clenched her fist tightly.

Alice reached over and put her hand on her shoulder. "Hey, are you alright? What the he...ck was that?"

Ms. Gailsone shook her head, her eyes still closed as she put her prescription container away. "It's nothing. Just... some heartburn. It'll pass in a moment. Would... would you like to go out to dinner? My treat? We...wow... okay, I'm feeling better. Pills will really kick in after a bit, but... My treat?"

Alice stared at her mother for a moment and then reached over for her purse. Before her mother could stop her, Alice snatched the purse from her hands and started rooting through it until she found the prescription bottle from before. Ms. Gailsone sat quietly as Alice read the label. Then, Alice reached in and fished out several more containers. She held one up to her mother.

"This is Erlotinib. Why is this in your purse?" She put it back and held up another. "Why is Vicodin in your purse? Why did you just down three of them in front of me like they were candy?"

Ms. Gailsone shrugged and said, "It's just... they're just senior medicines, dear. That's all. Now, there is a fabulous café down the street that I am dying to take you to. Let's..."

"Mother," Alice said, her voice level, "I realize we are just in the initial stages of catching up and mending things, but let me lay something out for you that you probably don't realize. I *know* what these are for, mother. I'm not some scared, stupid teenager who doesn't know any better. I know more about chemicals than most, *believe me*, and more than that, I *know* when someone is lying to me. It has been a character

211

trait that has served me very, *very* well. I know that we're just starting out on the whole reconnecting thing, but let's try this whole conversation again as two intelligent, mature women. Now, without the bullshit, why is there Erlotinib in your purse, mother?"

There was a pause as Ms. Gailsone stared at her daughter. "You really shouldn't swear like that."

Alice continued to stare.

Ms. Gailsone squirmed in her chair. "Can't we talk about this over dinner?"

Alice shook her head.

Ms. Gailsone glared. "If you know, then why are you making me say it, young lady?"

Alice closed her eyes and sighed. "Mother. Please. Just... I think I need to hear it, is all. This... is not what I was expecting today."

Ms. Gailsone stared at Alice for a good 30 seconds before she slowly stood up and shuffled to a nearby walkway table. There was a stack of what looked like bills on its surface. She grabbed the paperwork and started filing through it until she found the one she wanted and then handed it to Alice, who took it with a look of confusion on her face.

"Mom, what's..?"

"Read it," she said.

Alice skimmed the document, and then stopped. She then read the document. She then read it again. The older Gailsone sat down and waited patiently as Alice absorbed what was in the letter. Finally, Alice set it down and stared at her mother.

"How advanced is it?" she asked.

"Enough that at this point, chemo may or may not work. The Erlotinib was a gamble by my doctor before we had to try the more extreme route. It's spreading, and my insurance dropped me when I retired, so it's been... a bit of a challenge. I've been doing my best to make those pills there last as long as I could, but sometimes... sometimes it hurts."

"Why didn't you say something? Why didn't you contact me and let me know?" Alice said, her voice rising slightly. She was mad, scared and a little put out. Why *hadn't* she contacted her? Awkward family issues aside, this was serious.

"Because I didn't know what to say, and I didn't want to make you feel like you had to do something," she said softly. Alice stood up and glared.

"Screw that noise. This is serious. Congratulations, you work for me now, and *Rare Gems* has a helluva insurance policy. You're getting treatment, starting tomorrow. You're going to the best doctors, the best specialists, everything. The works. Tomorrow. First thing."

Ms. Gailsone shook her head. "Honey, no, that's, that's okay. You don't have to..."

"If I hadn't been such a bitch, you and I might have found this out sooner and then maybe you wouldn't be in this position. Nope, my stupid ass drug this out, my stupid ass is paying for it. Tomorrow. Tonight, we're going out to dinner. My treat."

Ms. Gailsone shook her head. "No dear, I can't put you out like that. I..."

Alice pounded the table beside her. "Mother. I might have left a teenager, messed up, and very, very stupid and poor, but now... well, I'm older and *extremely* richer. The stupid and messed up are arguable. Now, go grab whatever it is that old people wear when they go out, because you and I are going out."

"Hon, really, I... What do you mean 'old people'?"

"Dorothy May Gailsone, go get your damn shawl and come with me to dinner or I swear I will stop bonding with you this instant. Don't act like you don't have one, I saw it by the door when I came in."

Dorothy stared at her daughter for a moment.

"I'll get my shawl."

Alice nodded. "You do that. You get that shawl. We'll go eat and you can talk to me about this cancer thing or whatever else we would have talked about without… you know. Deal?"

Dorothy May Gailsone looked at her daughter and smiled. "Look at you. You're so strong now. You seem so… confident. It wears well on you."

Alice nodded, her cheeks turning slightly red. "Yes, I went into the world and found myself, or something. I grew up, had some adventures, raised a little Hell and…okay, raised a *lot*, but now I'm… I… why are you staring at me?"

Dorothy was beaming as she looked at her daughter. "It's just… You look beautiful, dear. More than that, you look good."

Alice sniffed a little, grabbed the paperwork from the doctor's office and shoved it in her purse. "Good stock, Ms. Gailsone."

Now

***

When Alice came to, the first thing she realized was that she was in a soft bed, and not a burning house. The next was that she was breathing through her nose, and that her flesh felt pulled tight with itchy bandages. She felt the light, stiff cotton of a hospital gown on her exposed skin, and the air had a slightly dry, stale flavor. When she opened her eyes, she had to squint from the bright fluorescent lighting.

She was in a hospital room. Her arm was connected to an IV drip and there were a host of monitors running beside and behind her bedside. She looked around and noted that she had a room with a window walls that were painted with a pretty, pale grass motif. To the side of her bed was a tray of what appeared to be bacon, eggs, silver-dollar pancakes, toast and juice. On the nightstand on the far end of the room were several large bouquets of flowers, each with a card. Also, there was a stern-looking, late-twenties Japanese woman in a dark green business suit, reading a book in a chair by her bed.

After a moment, she made the connection and tried to talk, but her throat screamed in pain when she did. After biting back some tears and swallowing carefully, Alice tried again, this time in a near-whisper.

"Lotus?"

The woman across from her glanced up, put her book away and calmly stood. She approached Alice and stared down at her prone form for a moment before saying in sharp, alto English, "You must have hit your head in the accident, ma'am. My name is Fukijima Aika. Your secretary, remember?"

Alice blinked several times, processing what the woman had said. Finally, she managed, "What?" before eying the rest of the room to see if she was being filmed.

Aika shook her head. "We are alone; I am here to make sure you are safe. Here, I ordered you bacon. You like bacon, yes?"

Alice again looked to the lady standing beside her. "What?"

Aika sighed a little. "You made a very large mess. No one here has had the gumption to be as direct as you were. Now, everything is in chaos."

Alice sunk back in her bed and did her best to shrug, which she found difficult, considering her arm was in a sling. Aika looked to Alice's arm and nodded. "It was a clean hit; no tendons were cut, but you were already wounded. I wanted you to stay down."

Alice eyed the woman. "You could have just asked."

Aika eyed her right back. "I did. Twice."

"I suppose you did," Alice said, her gaze unwavering, "and yes, I love bacon." Aika moved the tray of food in front of Alice and pressed a button on the side console of the bed. Alice felt the back of the bed rise up, bringing her closer to her food. With her working arm, Alice attempted to open the syrup pouch that came with her breakfast. After trying and failing several times, she placed her index finger on the top of the syrup container and concentrated. Her finger pressed through and plopped into the syrup as the top of the container rotted off.

"Damn," Alice muttered as she poured the syrup over her slightly cold pancakes. Aika stood silently and watched as Alice prepared her food and then took a small bite. Wincing at the feel of food going down her throat, she nearly pushed it away, but then realized how incredibly hungry she was. After a moment, she decided she would just chew until she couldn't tell the difference and risk swallowing again.

"Why didn't you kill me in the warehouse?" Alice asked as she slowly ate her food. She flinched at the sound of her own voice; it was gravelly and coarse, and when she gingerly rubbed her throat, she felt a thick bandage covering what felt like stitches.

216

Aika calmly reached over and helped Alice cut up her food into tiny portions. "You were looking for my sister."

Alice eyed her for a moment. "Really? You killed that young woman, what was her name, Megumi? You killed her pretty quickly in the factory and then you ignored me completely, but then you up and tried to kill me at Nakajima's. I don't get it."

Aika glared at Alice for a moment. "How could I let you leave when you walked in through the front door? You were stupid and careless."

Alice smiled a bit, "I had fox men. What woman wouldn't be careless with an army of fox men?"

"You are lucky to be alive. I did not think you would do what you did."

Alice looked away. "Yeah, I've done a lot of things people wouldn't think to do just to survive. That ranked in my top five terrible things, but it's not number one. In fact, it's not even number three. Still," Alice rubbed her throat, "I never want to do it again."

After a pause, Alice looked to Aika and asked, "Hey, do you know what happened to my fox men? In the study, on the monitors, it looked like they were really getting into it."

Aika shook her head. "The pack is stupid and clumsy. Their leader should be dead after taking a shot like that. Kogoura does not miss, and when he shoots, he shoots to kill."

Alice thought for a moment. "Was that the man who shot the boy in the entrance?"

Aika nodded.

Alice chuffed. "Asshole got what he deserved."

Aika looked away, her face twisted with concern. Finally, she turned to Alice and said, "How did you know Nanami was dead?"

Alice looked at her and saw that her face was strained. This was a woman who had been carrying the weight of the world on her shoulders. She looked worn and drained, and her body screamed that it was only now beginning to relax from endless nights of tension. Alice took one look and understood that Aika had known about her sister for a while - but until those keys were in her hand, she hadn't been sure.

Alice spoke softly, but her eyes stayed hard as she said, "Nakajima doesn't just beat you, he tries to destroy you. He takes and takes until there's nothing left. He killed your sister, but then to rub it in, he had her articles continue to be submitted, but with terrible predictions. He beat me at the warehouse, and then used his pull to try to hurt my company back home. It's what he does."

"What he did." Aika corrected her.

Alice eyed the woman beside her for a moment. "Did." She parroted.

At that moment, the door to Alice's room opened and Victoria Green walked in. Aika immediately took a defensive stance beside Alice's bed, causing Victoria to pause before Alice gently touched Aika's arm and said, "It's okay. She's good people. You are good people, right Vicky?"

Victoria glared at both women for a moment and said, "My mother calls me Vicky. You call me Ms. Green."

"Okay Vicki," Alice said. Aika cleared her throat and moved closer to Alice's side. Victoria raised an eyebrow, but said nothing.

Victoria crossed her arms and slowly walked through Alice's room. "I see you got our flowers," she commented in a crisp, cold voice while nodding to one of the bouquets on the dresser. "Oh, and look; a fresh bouquet from a Mr. Yoshi. That wouldn't be the Yoshi who sits as the Black Claw of the Dead Talon, would it? My, you have some interesting friends. Oh, a bouquet with a card? 'Glad you aren't dead.' And a squiggled picture of a frog. Huh. So, I trust the room is to your liking?"

Alice tried to shrug. "I guess. I've been unconscious for most of my stay."

Victoria eyed the two ladies in the room. "Alright, suppose we cut the crap. What the hell do you think you're doing here, Gailsone?"

Alice looked around for a moment. "Recovering?"

"You murdered one of the most prominent businessmen in Japan, burned his home to the ground, killed his bodyguards and caused millions in property damage to the Nagoya transit system! I want you to give me one good reason why I shouldn't rip up your agreement with the government and have you hauled off in ionic chains!"

"Actually, I killed Nakajima," Aika said, her voice neutral.

Victoria glanced towards the Asian assassin. "I'll get to you in a minute. Fine, that still leaves nearly a dozen counts of murder, arson, reckless endangerment, espionage and terrorism to answer for."

"With the possible exception of that jerk in Nakajima's lobby, I didn't kill anyone," Alice said in a hoarse voice. "I only roughed them up; the pack did the killing. In fact, I specifically told them to leave once they set Nakajima's house on fire." Alice took a shaky drink of her juice and continued. "I had to destroy the subway, or Nakajima would have had me killed once I was caught. Fudo's great, but he was too slow. They would have nabbed me if I hadn't... you know."

"And how do you explain the bombed-out crater on the grounds of Nagoya Castle?"

"That was Nakajima, not me, and honestly, I didn't do anything particularly terrorist-y that I can think of."

"That's . . . yes, you did, and that's not even a word!" Victoria was getting flustered. "I have had to pull a lot of strings to keep you from being arrested, and I just want to know *why*. Why should I do one more thing to keep your pale, worthless ass out of jail?"

219

Alice leveled her gaze at Victoria. "Because," she said in as loud of a voice as she could muster, "I did exactly what Alan wanted me to."

Victoria stared at the crippled woman in front of her and considered her words. "Go on," she said in a cautious voice.

"Alan was losing steam in the Asian market; Nakajima was buying out his business partners left and right. I checked the business news via PhoneBuddy while I was here, and it wasn't too terribly hard to make the connection. Alan had no intention of me actually getting Aika to switch sides; the Lotus is a master assassin who is fiercely loyal to her employer, whoever that may be, until death or vows release her."

Victoria glanced at the Japanese woman as Aika calmly stared back. "Then why is she standing here instead of reporting back to the Talon?"

"Aika? Could you get my belt? Where is my belt?" Aika walked over to the dresser with the flowers across the top and pulled out Alice's utility belt. Wordlessly, she handed it to Alice, who in turn started rooting through its patches until she found her wallet. She fished out a $20 bill and handed it to Aika, who calmly took it and pocketed it, all while never breaking eye contact with Victoria.

"And now, she's on my payroll." Alice said.

"I work for her now," Aika said, her voice completely steady.

Victoria sputtered. "That . . . that doesn't even make any sense!"

Aika continued. "Dyspell found my sister. She could have given up, but she did not, and it nearly killed her. The Dead Talon has agreed that I should repay my debt, so now I work for her."

Alice chimed in. "Alan didn't care about Lotus; he only wanted me to disrupt Nakajima's empire. He knew Lotus was working for him and that if I looked into finding her, I would find out the rest."

"Then why wouldn't he just come out and say it?" Victoria asked.

"Because then he would be culpable. Alan Tanner, the faultless superhero businessman, can't have anything tying back to him. But me? Hell, I'm a supposedly reformed super villain. Why *not* hang me out to dry?"

Aika reached down for a small leather briefcase and handed it to Victoria. "These are Nakajima's papers from the night he had his accident. You will find evidence of a hostile takeover directed towards the Asian electronics partners and subsidiaries of Tanner Industries inside."

Victoria raised an eyebrow at the word 'accident', but took the suitcase and opened it to have a look for herself. After a few moments of reading, she sat down on the edge of the bed, her eyes glued to the documents. The other two women stood (or lay) in silence as Victoria scanned the documents for a solid three minutes before the she started cursing under her breath. Alice and Aika watched as Victoria closed her eyes for a good ten seconds and then stared at Alice.

"I'm sorry."

Alice blinked. "Excuse me?"

Victoria shifted a bit. "I'm sorry. You're right. You're absolutely right. It's all right here. I had suspected this for a while, but this just felt a little too underhanded, even for Alan. I'm just amazed that..."

"Blackbird!" Alice chirped up.

Victoria blinked.

"You're Blackbird," Alice said as she smiled, and then winced from smiling. "I knew when we met at the tower that you were familiar, but right there, that grumbling disdain for Alan, that I *know* I've seen. It's been a while, BB."

Victoria stared angrily at Alice, and then at Aika, who shrugged. "I could tell by your movements. You do nothing to change your stance. It is very noticeable."

"Told you I was awesome," Alice said.

Victoria gripped her forehead with her hand and sat in a chair across the room from the two women. "Fine, yes, whatever. You're both very clever. God! This... this is just like him, you know? When we hired you, I was told it was specifically for the recruitment of new heroes for Open Hand, not for corporate espionage. When he offered to pull you after just one day, I was wondering what was going on, but now I get it; he thought Nakajima knew and your cover was blown. When you asked him to set up that meeting... you should know that he had that penned in for two weeks in his calendar."

Alice sat in silence for a moment while Victoria looked like she was struggling to not punch a hole in the wall. "No offense, but why do you care? Alan just scored a massive boost in the Asian market from his soon-to-be-partnership with the soon-to-be-reformed Nakajima Industries and you got to throw a villain under the bus and still came out on top, so, yay you?" Alice said.

Victoria shot her a glare, stood and straightened her dress. "I understand you stole Alan's corporate card?"

Alice nodded and clumsily fished it out of her belt. "It's in there, feel free."

Victoria picked up the leather suitcase and checked to make sure she had everything she needed. "I was supposed to cancel it. I am ordering you, as your immediate supervisor, to use that card for as much food, alcohol and male entertainment as your body can tolerate before going into shock. Also, feel free to book a flight home on whatever airline you prefer."

"I have a 10-foot-tall golem somewhere; he'll need special accommodations," Alice said.

"Then buy a damn jet," Victoria snapped. "I'll expect you at Tanner Tower in one week, and this time, I'm picking your assignment." She then turned her attention to Aika, who had been standing stock still with a look of boredom on her face. "You," Victoria said, her voice hard, "will need to sign a declaration of commitment to the Open Hand Act as well as paperwork linking you to the Collective Good, otherwise you will be arrested the moment you set foot on American soil, understand?"

Aika nodded.

"You're heroes now, so try to act like it." Alice watched as her new supervisor briskly walked out of the hospital room.

Aika turned to Alice. "I like her."

Alice looked to Aika and then at the credit card she had slipped out of her belt. She played with it between her fingers idly. "Yeah, me too. I feel bad I tried to kill her, once."

"I don't," Aika said.

"By the way, do you know where they put my golem?"

"There's an insulated warehouse near the Toyota plant on the edge of the city. Your frozen golem waits for you there."

"Cool, thanks." Alice smiled to herself and slipped the credit card back into her belt before she drifted off to sleep, her breakfast forgotten and cold on the tray beside her bed. Aika took the belt and put it away, tucked Alice in and resumed reading her book as the morning ticked lazily along.

***

The large cathedral of steel and glass had been dark for a long time. Once it had buzzed with the hum of electronics and glowed with the faint, blue light of computer screens, but for two years, it had remained dormant under a mile of ice, trapped in the blackness of a forgotten glacier.

The deafening silence of the dusty room was cut by the splitting hiss of a hydraulic door coming to life, allowing light to spill into the ghostly chamber and flicker off the dead screens. The light was interrupted by two shadows; a small one and a huge one as their owners moved with confidence into the room.

Anna walked to the center-facing console and swiped a keycard that hung from her red and black jumpsuit's belt. After a moment, a small green light flickered on, followed by the entire forward bank of monitors as they hummed to life and began processing their startup procedures. One by one, the various machines of the great steel hall flickered to life until the entire chamber was bathed in cold, off-blue light.

Anna looked around the cavernous bridge and smiled to herself. The structure had been built to be two stories, but the top tier stopped midway to the front, allowing for a balcony-like setting for the view ahead. In front of her, Anna saw the great glass wall of tiled blocks that reflected the glow of the interior structure.

"This never looked like a bridge to me," Anna said to her compatriot as she stared at the glass wall in front of her. "The glass always made this look like more of a church. I guess that was on purpose, wasn't it?"

Silence greeted Anna, but she didn't mind. Her partner wasn't much for small talk.

"Totallus," Anna called to the second figure in the room. Totallus had entered and then stood off to the side, waiting idly for some direction from his mistress. He looked to Anna, his face completely indifferent. "I want the main systems powered up and operational in 24 hours. I want her sky-worthy in five days. Once we get our power supply figured out, I want to be able to launch at a moment's notice. We'll need to alter the bridge for the medical harness, but other than that, it looks like once we get enough power to the engines for a low-orbit launch, we should be good to go."

Totallus nodded. "Yes, Mistress," the smooth, dark-skinned giant said in his hollow, emotionless voice.

"I want to know the minute the Collector is operational, understand?"

"It can be operational any time you would like, Mistress."

Anna paused, considering the giant's words. "Is it compact enough that someone like you could wear it?"

Totallus nodded. "Someone like me could wear it just fine, Mistress."

Anna smiled to herself. "Then make it work. Phase One went beautifully; now we need to get a move on with Phase Two."

"Yes, Mistress," Totallus said again.

Alice stood for a moment and let herself take it all in. She felt a sudden rush of euphoria, as though everything had been practice up until that moment, but suddenly it was real and it was happening. She was standing on the bridge of the *Metatron*, the most powerful weapon that had ever been created by the hand of man, and she was in command.

"He will need attention," Totallus said, cutting into Anna's moment. "We should be there when he wakes up."

"If you insist. Honestly, I doubt he even knows what's going on; but fine, whatever, we'll play nursemaid until we get everything rolling."

"Why are you so cruel to him?"

Anna chuffed, "Probably because he keeps calling me Alice while drifting in and out of a delusional state."

Totallus said nothing as Anna stared out the black windows. Finally, she said, "We need him, don't we?"

Totallus nodded. "Yes, Mistress."

Anna rubbed the bridge of her nose. "I want the Collector ready to go as soon as possible. That right there is your top priority. I want to be in Phase Two and see some dead heroes, or I'm going to lose my temper. By the way, how are the Newbies?"

"They are getting settled in."

"Fine, great, I'll meet with them tomorrow."

Totallus nodded and made his way towards the door. "Totallus?" Anna called, bringing the giant to a halt. "I assume you have a list of all employees that were recruited under...her, correct?"

Totallus nodded.

"Good," Anna said, rubbing her chin in thought, "I want them liquidated. Put them in a cargo bay; tell them it's a training exercise or something. I don't know, but open the hatch and flood it. I don't want anyone on my staff that has past loyalties, and that starts today."

"That will leave us underhanded, Mistress." Totallus said without turning around.

"That's not going to matter much once we get some new recruits, now is it? Now move it, and let me know when you're finished. I'll go hook up the geezer."

Totallus nodded and turned to leave, but then stopped. "I received a report on a coded frequency during our descent, Mistress. It concerns Dyspell."

Anna froze. When she spoke, her voice was quiet and strained. "Go on."

"She has been sighted in Nagoya in costume. Apparently, she has killed Nakajima Toshino and assisted the Dead Talon in redistributing his assets. We have lost a foothold."

Anna didn't scream, stomp or raise her voice, but Totallus noted that she was visibly shaking as she spoke. "How did she know? How did that bitch even know we were there?"

"I'm not sure, Mistress. Because of her interference, we are down 30% on financial assets. This will make recruiting more difficult."

Anna shot him a cross look. "That's why you were so concerned about our numbers. I don't care; kill them all. She is not going to ruin this for me, I promise you. I am going to burn everything she has ever touched to the ground and when I'm done, I'll kill her with my bare hands. Then we'll see who is better, won't we?"

"There was one more thing. We recovered a body from Nakajima's estate. He is badly injured, but he should live, provided he receives treatment."

"And why do I care?" Anna asked.

"It's Kenji Kogoura."

Anna thought to herself for a moment. "Fine, tend him. We could use someone with his experience working directly with us. I'll speak to him when he's better. You're dismissed, Totallus."

Without a word, Totallus bowed slightly and left Anna by herself on the bridge. She took one more long look around before allowing a giggle to escape her. "I'm going to be better than you ever were," she said to the air around her. "I'm going to do what you never could, and when I'm done, I'll force you to admit that I'm the best - right before I kill you."

As Anna walked off the bridge of the *Metatron*, her chilling laugh echoed throughout the cold, metallic corridors of the most terrible weapon in the world.

Chapter 12

Madison Square Garden

Then

***

The 67th Precinct was used to its share of crazies, drug-addicts, psychopaths and other various forms of criminal. It was the first, the crazies, which they were most accustomed to, so much so that Officer Justin Simms didn't even look up from his mountain of paperwork when a young, female voice cleared its throat and said, "Hello, I'd like to register under the Open Hand Act."

Officer Simms saw what looked like a female form in a trench coat in front of his desk out of his peripheral vision, but didn't even bother to look up as he said, "Yeah, okay, whatever. Look, go talk to Officer Dakota about two doors down the hall if you're looking for a hot and a cot, okay? I'm busy here."

The young woman stood in front of the desk for a moment and waited for the officer to finally look up. After a moment, she sighed, took off her wig and tucked it into her coat pocket. "I would like to register for the Open Hand Act, please. I'm a super criminal and I am seeking government promised asylum."

Officer Simms chucked and adjusted his weight in his seat. Without looking up, he said, "Sure you are, sweetie. Look, I've got a lot of paperwork to do, so why don't you go play super villain somewhere else, okay?"

Alice glanced at the older, larger man sitting in the small, creaking metal and plastic chair in front of her and sighed. Calmly, she reached out and put her hand on the stack of papers in front of the police officer and focused. A moment later, a bright purple light formed around her hand and the stack of papers, and a moment after that, the papers rotted away to nothing.

"There, now that you're finished, can you please tell me who to talk to about the Open Hand Act?" Alice was smiling. She had read that cops liked it when women smiled.

Officer Simms looked at the spot where the stack of papers had been for a moment and then at the woman in front of him. It took all of two seconds for his brain to register the purple hair, pale skin and the rotting power. With a jerked leap out of his chair, the policeman pulled his gun, pointed it at Alice's head and screamed, "FREEZE! DOWN ON THE GROUND! DOWN ON THE GROUND, NOW!"

Alice calmly went to the ground with her hands behind her back. Around her, the police department was exploding with screams of shock, panic and fear. On top of her, she felt at least six grown men tackle her already prone form as they scrambled to put her in handcuffs. '*Huh*,' she thought, '*This part isn't so bad.*'

After waiting in a small, smelly, mirrored room with a plain wood table and a cold cup of coffee for what felt like hours, Alice was rewarded with a visit from a balding, overweight detective. He had a thick, bushy moustache and a coffee stain on his yellow shirt. He came in glaring and sat down across from Alice, who burst out laughing.

"I'm sorry, is something amusing you, Miss?" the Detective asked.

Alice tried to calm herself between snorts of laughter, but was having a hard time. "I'm sorry, it's just... did they pluck you from the set of a crime drama? You *have* to know how you look. Oh my God, this is, am I being pranked?"

The Detective stared for a moment and then said in an angry voice, "I'm Detective Paulmer. I've been assigned to handle your case, Miss..?"

"Gailsone. Annalicia May Gailsone, but call me Alice. I brought all my identifying paperwork for today in my purse."

The Detective took out a pad of paper and a pen. "I am to understand that you are here to turn yourself in? That you are in fact the woman known as Diespell?"

Alice glared. "Dys. Dyspell. Like dispelling a rumor. Where did you get Diespell? God, that sounds terrible. And no, by the way, I'm not turning myself in, unless I have to when I sign the Open Hand Act, in which case I am turning myself in."

"We'll get to that. You admit that you are... Dyspell, criminal leader and mastermind behind the Purge?"

"I admit that I was second-in-command of the Purge, but that sounds nice, too." Alice smiled. The Detective did not.

"Are you willing to provide a confession of your crimes? You realize you have the right to an attorney, if you choose."

Alice shrugged. "You realize I could have just up and killed everyone here, if I had chosen, right?" Detective Paulmer stared, wide-eyed as he went for his gun. Alice waved him down with her cuffed hands. "Joke! Joke! Geez... Anyway, I'm cool. I'm here for the Open Hand Act and to, well, for lack of a better word, purge my record. So, how do I get started on the whole straight and narrow thing?"

Behind the mirrored wall of the interrogation room, Alan Tanner stood with the precinct chief. The understandably nervous police officer asked, "Are we safe with her like this? Isn't she dangerous?"

Alan chuckled. "She's *extremely* dangerous, and more to the point, it would take her two seconds to break out of there. Still, she came asking for the Open Hand Act, and part of the law says that anyone, even her, can apply. "

The Chief looked at Alan and gestured back to the glass. "Even her?"

Alan nodded. "I actually wrote the law with her in mind. I figured that if it applied to her, it could apply to anyone, so yes, even her…"

Alan watched as Alice tried to drink her coffee while still wearing handcuffs. She tried twice and the set the cup down. A moment later, her wrists glowed purple and the cuffs rusted away. She calmly picked up her coffee cup and sipped it while Detective Paulmer jumped up and back in shock.

"…Provided that she can behave herself," Alan said, half-muttering.

"But why her? Why now? How do we know this isn't some kind of trick?" The Chief was wringing his hands, and rightly so. The woman in the next room was firmly outside his level of expertise.

Alan smiled a little and took a folded piece of paper out of his pocket. He looked at the treatment report in his hands that the hospital he sat on the board for had been generous enough to provide.

"I don't think it's a trick," he said calmly. "I don't think it's a trick at all."

***

"This is a trick, right?"

Allison stood stock still as Alice grinned and showed off her Open Hand ID card. Allison didn't rip the card up or crumple it as she examined it, but Alice saw that she was starting to shake. The young assistant had been worried about her aunt, considering the older woman had been missing for 24 hours. While Allison knew Alice was a big girl, she was always leery of something happening. She had visions of SWAT teams in riot gear finding them and taking her down, or maybe an incident involving a disgruntled hero that happened to find out who she was.

This, however, was about as far down the list as she could imagine.

"Nope! I'm a legitimate girl. Legitimately! Isn't that cool?"

Alice took the card from Allison and put it in her wallet. Allison just stood there shaking with anger.

"What. The. Fuck? You went to the COPS? What is wrong with you? Did you have a death wish?"

Alice patted her niece on the shoulder and smiled. "Would you relax? They obviously didn't arrest me and this whole Open Hand thing is real, so what's the big deal?"

"What's the big... what if it had been a trap? What if you had been arrested? What... Alice, what about *me*?"

Alice stopped and stared at her niece. Allison was no longer yelling, and Alice saw the younger woman's lip quivering.

"I can't *do* this alone. I'm doing better, but... this is hard, you know? This whole 'normal' thing. I... what if they had taken you? I need you here. I can't... I don't know what to do. Didn't you think about...well... about..."

Alice took Allison by the shoulders. "Are you looking for the word, 'family?'"

Allison shuffled her feet. Alice smiled and drew the young, tense woman into a hug.

"Hon," she said, "that was *exactly* why I did it."

Alice felt the younger woman shudder in her arms. She hugged Allison tighter and rocked her slightly. "Hey, it's okay. It's okay."

"Goddammit, it is not okay! You could have... after all the crap you put me through about keeping a low profile, about keeping our heads down, and you didn't even tell me! You could have...oh God, you could have..."

Allison was not a crier. In fact, if you called her a crier, there was a good chance she would unload a clip in your face and then light you on fire.

So Alice held her clearly not-crying niece as she not-cried into her shoulder for a good five minutes.

Once she was done, Allison stepped back and wiped her nose. "Sorry. I... It's been a while, is all. Would you excuse me?"

Alice nodded as Allison headed up to the top floor of *Rare Gems*. A moment later, Alice heard the sound of gunshots coming from the training range.

"That's my girl," Alice said with a smile as she proceeded to get the shop ready for the day.

Now

***

The weather was warm as three figures gathered in the cluttered yet beautiful Okuno-in cemetery. Alice sat in her wheelchair, dressed in a black pantsuit with oversized sunglasses covering much of her bruised face. Her wig looked dull in the afternoon light as she gazed thoughtfully at the well-manicured lawn at her feet. Beside her, Aika stood dressed in a traditional white kimono as a Shinto priest laid the recovered remains of Nanami to rest. Yoshi stood to the side, his head bowed in respect as the priest finished up his ceremony.

When it was over, Yoshi walked to Aika, bowed deeply and presented her with an envelope. Aika, completely emotionless, took it and nodded stiffly back as Yoshi turned and walked away. After a moment of watching him step carefully out of the cemetery, Aika turned back to Alice and started pushing her chair towards the exit.

"You did not have to come," Aika said quietly.

"The hell I didn't," Alice said. "Your sister wasn't like us; she just got caught up in our world's stupid games. She was young and not involved, and she did not deserve this. Besides, I nearly died for this woman. I felt like this was needed."

"You did not nearly die for her."

Alice sighed a bit. The rough stone path under her chair made the trip a bit bumpy, but she didn't mind. She was just glad to be outside.

"Okay, fine. It wasn't just for her."

They continued on, the tour groups in the cemetery keeping a respectful distance. Faintly, Alice heard the sound of cameras clicking on the breeze and repressed a grimace.

"So, did Yoshi just hand you your retirement papers?"

235

"Something like that," Aika said, "I asked him for my pension. The Dead Talon has been investing my earnings for years. He was giving me my portfolio and access to my accounts."

"That's a good thing, right? Being rich is good?"

Aika sighed. "It means more. It is . . . symbolic. My association with the Dead Talon is at an end. They will never invest in me again, which means they will never welcome me back. I am finished in Japan."

Alice closed her eyes. She knew Yoshi was pissed about Aika's defection. To the Dead Talon, her reasons – any reasons – were both unimportant and insulting. Alice knew that Aika had gotten off easy. The Dead Talon weren't known for letting people walk away; but this wasn't just anybody, and Yoshi had made a promise.

"I'm sorry if I cost you your job," Alice said quietly.

Aika shook her head. "It wasn't you; I was marked the second I went to work for Nakajima. I could have stayed with the Dead Talon and protected their automotive and electronic interests, or simply killed Nakajima and been done with it. But I wanted to know about Nanami. Yoshi was within his rights to kill me for that."

Alice nodded. "So, were you spared because of your years of loyal service, or because of the deal Yoshi struck with me?"

"Both," Aika said, "I work for you, now. Not Blackbird, or the American government. I hope this is an arrangement we can live with."

"...Aika, do you know why I was so important in the Purge?"

"I have my suspicions," Aika said as they continued on.

"I'm not a very nice person. I don't play well with others. I don't like authority and I don't trust people if I can help it. I've done some truly awful things just because I could, but that's not why I was second-in-command."

236

Aika nodded, even though Alice couldn't see her.

"I have never failed an assignment, Aika. Never. No matter how terrible it was or what it cost me, I did the job and I did it well. Maybe not the way people thought it should be done, no. But I always finish what I start, and I take care of those that take care of me.

"Your sister was nice to me once, and while that may not mean a lot to most people, it meant something to me. I have always taken care of my own. Despite everything I've done in the past, I have never sold out a teammate or left a soldier behind, and I never plan on doing so."

Aika stopped pushing Alice, came around and knelt in front of her in her gi. When she spoke, Alice felt a chill go down her spine.

"No one has ever done anything like what you did for me. No one has ever tried. I will follow you until I die."

Alice stared back, not knowing what to say. She took off her sunglasses and looked Aika in the eyes. "Thank you, Aika-san. I am honored."

Aika got up and resumed pushing. "You don't sound serious when you sound serious," she said casually.

"Screw you. Now, let's collect Fudo and get the hell out of here. There's still a bit of unfinished business at home I need to attend to."

"Do you have any idea how racist and off the mark that name is for that golem?" Aika asked, her voice still deadpan.

Alice shrugged. "Hey, when we're stateside, who's gonna care?"

The two women left the cemetery in silence. Around them, the tour groups continued quietly on.

***

The apartment of Steve Burmer was a small, cluttered, dusty cave of technical drawings, sci-fi DVDs and haphazard computer parts. The floor

237

was only visible in a few small patches, which made walking through the room nearly impossible. Fortunately for Steve, walking was no longer an issue.

As Steve floated in through his front door, he didn't bother letting his eyes adjust to the darkness of his tiny high-rise loft. He was exhausted from taking inventory at Tanner Tower after the heist; On top of that, for the last 12 hours, he had led his division in revamping the tower's automated defense systems. Unfortunately, tomorrow looked to be no better, and his team was completely spent. While Steve would have loved to devote some time to his video games, or even a microwave pizza, his only focus was on getting out of his harness, having a bath and crawling into bed.

"Hey, Steve," a crisp voice cut through the darkness. Steve screamed and floated backwards into a wall, knocking a shelf of paperbacks onto the already messy sea of trash.

From the darkness, Alice emerged. She wore a floor-length black trench coat that skimmed her toned figure closely. Her mask was gone and she had foregone the wig, her deep purple mane seeming to glow in the faint moonlight. Steve could see that she was moving slowly, and that her throat was still bandaged.

"It's you... God, you scared the crap out of me!" Steve stammered as he righted himself. With his hands still shaking, Steve tried to glide towards the bookshelf that he had just knocked over. "Not that I'm complaining, but what brings you here? I mean, it's pretty late, and I'm pretty sure this constitutes breaking and entering." Steve paused. "Did my tech work okay for you?"

Alice nodded, her face calm. "Your tech works great. There's a young bar bunny in Nagoya who now pisses herself in terror whenever someone yells at a cell phone."

Steve grinned and nodded. "That's awesome. I know it sounded dumb, but PhoneBuddy was one of my finer inventions. I'm just glad it worked out for you."

Alice nodded. "Yeah, your little toys helped out, the suit especially. I tell ya, if it wasn't for those self-sealing fabrics, I would be *extremely* dead right now, so... thanks for that."

Steve nodded and smiled. "Not a problem. I just..."

"Kind of odd, though," Alice continued, "I got shot and stabbed, and you know what, this suit did jack-all to stop it. For a Kevlar weave, this behaved more like nylon, let me tell you. In fact, it did such a poor job at blocking things that had someone landed a shot at my heart, I don't think it would have done a thing to stop it."

Steve adjusted his glasses, a frown now on his face. "I highly doubt that. My tech *works*, and I designed that suit myself. If it doesn't..."

"Madison Square Garden."

Steve froze. Alice noted the light had caught his glasses just so, causing a solid splash of light to reflect back at her.

"It was you, wasn't it? The hostage I took that night to escape. I dropped you nearly 50 feet to get Blackthorne to stop chasing me. I just figured he caught you."

Steve stared at her for a moment in silence, his helpful, good guy persona quickly replaced by something much darker. His voice dropped an octave as his shoulders straightened. "It was 85 feet, actually."

Alice shrugged. "My bad, I was never the best with physics. Anyway, I am just floored that you went to such trouble to have me killed. I mean, I get it. You were pretty messed up, but still..."

"No. No, no, no. Breaking a leg or ripping up your face is pretty messed up. Accidently setting someone on fire or getting in a car wreck is pretty messed up. You *paralyzed* me, Alice. You put me in this…thing! And why? Because you were and are a self-serving, vicious bitch who destroyed more lives than you even care to count. You'll understand if that causes some resentment on my part."

Alice crossed her arms and shrugged. "I understand. Hell, if I were you, I'd be angry, too. I don't know about getting selling out my boss or trying to kill his employees angry, but I'd be angry."

Steve took off his glasses and spread his hands wide with a smirk. "I'm afraid I don't know what you're talking about."

Alice shot him a level glare. "No one but Tanner's men knew I would be in Nagoya, but not five minutes after I visit my first contact, Nakajima's men were already after me. They knew I was there ahead of time, Steve. Only a handful of people knew who I was and what I was doing. Alan wasn't going to sell me out that early in the game, Victoria is a stone-cold bitch, but she's not evil . . . so, that pretty much left *you*."

"You can't prove it. You can't prove anything," Steve said, his voice slightly raised.

"Don't have to," Alice said. "Steve, I think Alan is going to be extremely interested in how his calendar was programmed for a meeting between me and Nakajima that he didn't even know about. That . . . God, that was genius. I was trying to figure out how he had made that meeting happen so easily. Let me guess, Alan put you on it at the last minute? Told you to hack something and fit me in?"

Steve stared silently as Alice continued. "It was a neat idea; make it look like Nakajima didn't know I was coming. But he did know, Steve. The problem with your scheme was that Nakajima was too protective of his person. He had the Lotus watching him at all times. His house was guarded by a private army of mercenaries. There was no way a man that paranoid was going to agree to meet with a former super villain; but there he was, ready to go. I didn't even question how convenient it all was at the time, but once he had my secret base bombed, I started to smell a rat."

"Alan had me set the meeting up, just like you said," Steve said, "I just made Nakajima think that he had penciled you in. When it comes to hacking, I'm the best, Alice."

Alice shook her head. "And when it comes to Alan Tanner, Victoria Green is the best. She lives and breathes that man's schedule. Did you really think she wouldn't notice that little meeting was already in place before I asked for it?"

Steve frowned. "That's still not enough to go on, you know."

Alice nodded. "I know. Honestly, I thought it was pretty thin myself. I'm no great detective, Steve, but I know one thing better than anyone, and that's people. I can read a person better than anyone I know, and I can read you right now, Steve. You're body language changed the moment I started this conversation. Hell, you practically started vibrating with hate the moment I mentioned the Garden. Your motivation on this was pretty clear; I'm just surprised Alan let you work with me."

"Alan believes in change, Alice. Maybe you should, too. I'm willing to, provided you leave here now; otherwise, I'm going to have to call the authorities. Now, wouldn't that be a fun conversation for our boss?"

Alice smiled at Steve and shook her head as she held up her phone. "Steve, he already knew I was here. You all knew where I was as long as I was above ground. Remember, you told me yourself that this was a GPS tracking device. How else could Nakajima's men have just magically appeared twice?"

Steve paled as Alice admired the phone. "Like you said, you're the best. Tell me, how many people would have known how to hack this phones frequency without your help, Steve?"

241

Steve slowly shook his head, his mouth curled back into a tight smile. "Not too many."

"And tell me, where did you get such advanced tech for a cell phone? Last time I checked, Alan didn't work in wireless communications as a main market, but someone else we know *did*. Did you really think Alan wouldn't notice what you were doing?"

"Alan tends to forget a lot of things when he buries his head in a bottle," Steve said, his hands slowly going towards a small side panel on his floating harness, "For all his talk, the man wouldn't know what day it was if Victoria didn't tell him. Still, I'm impressed that you remembered me, and that you figured this out all by yourself."

"How much did he pay you, Steve?" Alice asked as she slid her hands in her coat pockets.

Steve smirked. "Nakajima set me up pretty damn well, but to be honest, I would have done this for free. You're a blight, Dyspell. Let me ask you just one question. It's an easy one. How many people died during your first mission as a "hero"? If it's under a dozen, I'll call Tanner tonight and admit everything."

Alice stared at him in silence.

"I see. How about under twenty five? Fifty? Do you even know? You don't, do you? How many families are mourning tonight just because you set foot on Japanese soil? You can walk around with your pretty little head held high and act like a changed woman, but you and I both know you're a monster."

Alice continued to stare. He was right, and she knew it – but whatever she was had been crafted and cast in stone long ago.

Steve reached for the control panel on his harness, but before he could press any of his buttons, the harness suddenly shut down and Steve crashed to the ground. Panicked, Steve scrambled for his controls, but nothing was working. Wide-eyed, he glared at Alice and yelled, "What did you do?!"

Alice pulled her belt buckle out of her pocket and held the mini-EMP up for Steve to see. "Your tech really does work great. Thanks for that."

Steve screamed at her and started throwing anything he could reach at Alice, who calmly stepped past the flying debris to the door. Steve did his best to hit her as she made to leave, yelling and cursing the whole time. One item, a glass mug that he had carelessly dropped on the floor, found his hand. Grinning, he chucked it as hard as he could at her head...

...Only to see a gloved hand reach out of the darkness and catch it.

Steve blanched as Blackthorne oozed out of the shadows in his apartment. The yellow eyes of his mask narrowed in a smoldering, hateful stare as he glided towards the crippled tech. Steve cowered as his employer towered over him and growled.

"I trusted you. I took you in, gave you the best medical care I could and the best job I had. I gave you anything you asked for and this . . . *this* is how you repay me?"

"I'm sorry. I'm so sorry . . ." Steve choked out.

"I've heard a lot of that lately. You know, Steve, it just isn't doing it for me anymore," Blackthorne ground out as he bent and dragged Steve off the floor by his collar. Alice quietly shut the door behind herself and headed home.

Chapter 13

Customs

The sun was still hiding behind the clouds as Alice walked into *Rare Gems* and greeted her staff. "Good morning, everyone," she said as she held up an orange and brown box, "I brought doughnuts."

Douglas looked up from examining a small stone before placing it on a yellow cloth on the counter. Cindy smiled and nodded as Allison took one look at her employer and said, "What the hell happened to you?"

Alice was dressed in a white blouse and a dark brown pencil skirt. While she could walk, her body was still black and blue, and her arm and throat were still bandaged. "Customs," she shrugged as she placed the doughnuts in Cindy's waiting arms.

Allison looked out the front window. "And what's with the giant statue out front? You're into Japanese art now? I came in to open the shop and that . . . *thing* was just standing there."

Alice smiled a little. "Don't mind him. Fudo is our newest security system."

Allison looked behind Alice as Aika drifted in, dressed in a simple green business jacket, slacks and a light silk shirt. The two women stared at each other for several moments. Alice regarded their exchange while trying to look like she wasn't.

"Welcome to *Rare Gems*. Can I help you, or were you just planning to whip out that blade in your boot and start killing people?"

Aika arched one thin black eyebrow. "That depends. What are you planning on doing with the knife in your slip?"

Allison glared. "I always wondered how good you were, you know? When we were in Asia, I begged to go on detail with you."

Aika shrugged, "Maybe you will find out one day."

Alice sighed and held her forehead with her hand. "Allison, will you calm down? Do you have to do this every time I bring someone into the shop? Yes, we know who she is and yes, she's all big and bad. Now quit posturing and make her feel welcome, will you? She's staying with us."

"For how long?" Allison asked, eyes widening in disbelief.

"Forever, I guess."

"Oh, no," Allison said as she gritted her teeth. "You go to Japan for a week and trade me out for the new model? Is that how this works?"

Alice rubbed the bridge of her nose. "Oh my God, will you calm down? She's working with us now. Just... you didn't have a good time in Germany, did you?"

Allison let her guard drop and straightened her glasses. "It was...professional, and very boring. No. I'm... I'm admittedly not having the best week."

All three ladies continued to stare at each other as Douglas gathered his gems and quietly put them away. With a practiced ease, he took the box from Cindy's hands and dug out a bear claw. "Allison? Bear claw."

Allison glanced at Douglas and then back at Aika.

Douglas sniffed the bear claw. "It smells wonderful."

Allison glanced at Douglas again.

Douglas started to walk away. "Very well. I suppose it's mine, then."

Allison glanced at Aika one more time. "Dammit, fine," she muttered and chased after Douglas, who was chuckling to himself.

Aika drifted over to Alice, who had moved to inspect a transaction log behind the counter. "What was that about?"

Alice glanced at Allison, and then back at Aika. "Customs," she said and then went back to checking the log.

A moment later, the antique bell above the door rang as Alan Tanner walked through the door. Cindy smiled, automatically starting her customary greeting before realizing who he was. "Hello and welcome to Rare . . . oh-my-God-you're-Alan-Tanner-hello!" she said in one impressive breath. Alan gently shook her extended hand as he flashed her a warm smile.

"Thank you," he said in a strong, slightly deep voice. Cindy grinned sheepishly back. Behind her, Alice cleared her throat. Cindy jumped a bit and turned to face her boss.

"Cindy?" Alice asked as Cindy cleared her throat.

"Yes, ma'am?"

Alice pointed over her shoulder with her thumb at the door Douglas and Allison had retreated through.

"Bear claw."

"Yes, ma'am," Cindy said, her face red. Alan watched as the young receptionist scurried away.

"That's a neat trick," he commented idly as he admired the store. Alice shrugged.

"That was nothing. If you'd asked, she probably would have rolled over," Alice said. Alan chuckled a bit and nodded to Aika. The assassin merely stared back. Alan noted that her body was completely still; she didn't even appear to be breathing.

He shivered a little and turned back to Alice, who was standing against her front counter. She stood, eyes expressionless with arms crossed over her chest, looking decidedly *not* like she was going to roll over.

Alan pointed towards the front of the shop. "So, is that the golem out front that I paid to have shipped from Japan?"

Alice nodded, "Yep."

Alan sighed a little, "You're still upset about the other evening, aren't you?"

Alice nodded, "Very good, Mr. Tanner. You don't make the big bucks for nothing."

"Look, I'm sorry about Steve," Alan said, "I really didn't know, Alice. Yes, I wanted you to disrupt things on Nakajima's end, but I wouldn't have sent you if I didn't think you could handle it. I was just impressed that you not only did the job, but brought back the Lotus as well."

"I didn't bring her, she came with." Alice wasn't moving. Alan noted that she was leaning against her counter and that her face held the pinched look of someone in pain. He knew that she had been badly injured, just as he knew that she didn't want to look weak in front of him. For a moment, he found himself admiring the ambitious, frighteningly tenacious young woman in front of him before snapping back to business.

"You were right about my intentions," Alan said, his face losing a bit of the charm that Alice had noted earlier. "I wasn't lying when I said I wanted to put a team together, but it's not just for good PR. Alice, this is a touchy time. There are things we need done that heroes just can't do, but we need them done all the same. We need a clandestine team, one that isn't afraid to get its hands dirty. That was why I picked you; you know this game. You know what it takes to win it, and you have the resolve to do it. I need you to do the things the other heroes would be blacklisted for, and that need is pretty strong right now."

247

"In other words, you need people with a touch of evil in them to do what you'll fall short of." Alice said calmly. Alan stared and gave a small nod.

"A bit melodramatic, but yes. That about sums it up."

"What about my mother?" Alice asked, her voice level.

Alan sighed. "I wasn't lying about that, either. We found the Phoenix, only to have someone swoop in and murder everyone on the deep-sea platform it was being stored on that night. They took out the entire complex, nearly killed Poseidon and then poisoned Superior Force."

Alice broke her poker face for a moment and let her eyes go slightly wide. "Seriously? Who was it?"

Alan shook his head. "We don't know, but we were hoping you did. A young blonde, late 20's, athletic?"

"That really doesn't narrow it down, Alan."

Alan sighed before he continued. "There was a Totallus, too."

Alice froze. "That's... well, I guess it's not impossible. Oh God, was it blonde? Was the blonde the Totallus?"

Alan shook his head. "No, I don't think so. No one got a good look at it, but Chris seems to think it was male."

Alice let out a breath. "Okay. Okay. That helps narrow it down. After Pittsburg, there would have been as many as four Totallus units unaccounted for."

"Just four?" Alan asked.

Alice closed her eyes. "I hope it was four. There was a fifth, but she had . . . problems. I want to say she was destroyed when the *Argent* went down."

Alan nodded. He remembered the *Argent*, the floating fortress that he and the rest of the Collective Good had stormed that night in Pittsburg. Most of it had been obliterated by a miniature black hole, but some pieces had managed to take out a neighborhood or two as they fell to earth in flaming chunks.

Alice continued, "The poison that infected Superior Force, was it nanite-based?"

Alan nodded. Alice chuckled to herself as Alan shot her a cross glare. "What's so funny?"

Alice shook her head. "That was my idea. I always thought if we used nanites to poison him from the inside we would have a better chance of taking him down. So, what was stolen?"

Alan froze and stared at the injured jewelry store owner. "How did you know there was a theft?"

"Because," Alice said with a frown, "I know this plan. You're describing what sounds like my Red Rook scenario. I came up with it years ago, but we had other issues on the table to deal with. Plus, we could never get the nanites to work properly. I guess someone took my ball and ran with it. Step one was to use Superior Force as a carrier for a nanite-based virus that would shut down his mental faculties and make him lash out blindly. We got it to work in rats and chimps, but we always had problems with people."

"So what was step 2?"

"Well, we didn't want step 1 to go to waste. I figured we could always use a rampaging God-man as a good distraction for a major crime, some kind of theft or assassination. It was supposed to be for something that the big guy would have been likely to stop."

"Like a theft from Tanner Industries?"

Alice nodded. "Yeah, that would fit. You've got a lot of fun toys, boss."

"Alice," Alan spoke softly as Douglas and Allison reemerged from the back, pastries in hand. "What would you have stolen, if it were you?"

Alice shrugged. "At the time, Prometheus had a plan for an energy collector that would give him immortality. He was about a third of the way into it when he figured he could do it better by harnessing antimatter, hence the black hole bomb."

"So did it work?"

Alice gave him a level glare. "Do you see him around? No, Alan, I'm pretty sure that when he was compacted into microns, it was solid enough proof that it didn't work."

"Alice," Alan said, "I've never known you to not have a solid plan to go with your actions. So when you were laying out your whole nanite trap… what was the rest of the Red Rook scenario?"

"At the time? To kill or incapacitate the Collective Good and ultimately unleash an army of immortal soldiers on the United States. Well, there or Canada, depending on my mood. But now, who knows?"

Alan stared off into space for a moment, lost in thought. Finally he nodded and patted Alice on the shoulder. "Thanks, Alice. You did great out there. I'm serious; you impressed the hell out of me. I think this is going to be a fine arrangement for both of us. By the way, here's your pay for a completed mission."

Alan took a folded, yellow check out of his pocket and handed it to Alice, who promptly handed it to Aika without breaking eye contact with Alan.

"A folded check? This is how you pay your employees? Is this the 70's? Am I on a construction crew?"

Alan shook his head. "Your pay was submitted by electronic deposit. This is a bonus commission on the Nakajima merger. You set it up, so… your bonus."

"That's really sweet, but that's not what I did the job for. Alan, I wasn't kidding in your office. You made a deal, and I expect you to honor it."

Alan looked Alice in the eye. "I keep my word, Miss Gailsone. Your mother will be healed, I promise. If I have to rip the planet apart, I will find that Phoenix and bring whoever took it to justice."

Alice nodded and said, "Fine, I can accept that. In the meantime, you're going to do something for me as collateral."

Alan nodded. "What can I do? If you like, I can set your mother up with the finest cancer research centers money can afford."

Alice nodded. "Go on…"

Alan stared for a moment. "And pay for her treatments."

Alice nodded. "Go on…"

Alan stared at her blankly. "Aside from magically finding the Phoenix right this moment, what more can I do?"

Alice smiled. "I'll talk to Victoria about clearing some time on your calendar. My next assignment is going to have my input, and believe me, there will be alcohol, food and hedonism or our arrangement is officially off."

"That sounds like a vacation, Alice."

Alice pointed to her throat. "Alan, have you ever had to give yourself an emergency tracheotomy after being shot and stabbed multiple times?"

Alan shifted his weight and looked off to the side. "Alice, that's… you know every assignment is different, and…"

"Emergency. Tracheotomy. Alan, I didn't even know if you *could* do that to yourself until I did it. My next assignment is going to be one I have direct input on, and then we look for this blonde and her wind-up toy. Now, you take care, Mr. Tanner."

Alan regarded Alice for a moment, smiled a little and nodded. Without another word, he turned and left the store as Alice turned to Aika.

"Hey, how much did he pay us?" Alice asked.

Aika stared at the check in her hands for a moment, and then handed it to Allison, who had wandered out from the back to see what was going on. Allison stared clapped a hand over her mouth, muttering, "Ho... Holy shit, boss."

Alice nodded. "Good. I measure currency in swears, and that feels right for this weeks' worth of work. By the way, I want that money deposited immediately. As soon as it's in our account, contact Victoria Green at Tanner Industries and see about a patient that was admitted the same night I was. It was a gunshot victim. Young, early 20's, answered to Makoto. I want his hospital stay covered completely."

Allison took the check to the register and slipped it in. "So what now? Are you a good guy, or what?"

Alice turned and smiled at the women in her shop. "Didn't you hear? Apparently, I'm on the Blacklist."

Aika nodded and asked, "And you are okay with this?"

Alice shrugged. "Why not? Now, let's show you your new room. Allison, please show Aika her new room upstairs, and for the love of God, quit glaring at her. She's with us now."

Alice watched as her two grumpiest employees headed towards the back room and the stairway leading to the upper levels of the building. She then settled into a chair behind the counter and watched the morning traffic go by.

"So, I'm a good guy now."

Outside, the morning traffic carried on, oblivious.

Afterword

This is the first of a series of Gailsone books. As of this publication, the second volume, *Red Rook*, is now available. Also, there are now several short stories available to fill the gap between the first and second novel. You can find them on the Kindle store and printed in the collection, *Black Days*.

These books were written when I realized that I had no shortage of male hero stories to share with my son, but came up short on female hero stories. I wanted to show them all that there could be an adventure story involving a female lead that didn't revolve around romance. In my mind, the characters in the Gailsone universe are strong because they're strong, not because they're women or men. Alice is determined and driven, Alan Tanner is terrifying in how own right, and Allison... You haven't begun to see what she can do when pushed. Fortunately, I rectify this lack of knowledge about the younger Gailsone in the next chapter of this story.

This book wasn't written for a particular audience. It was written because I wanted to tell a story, and I wanted to tell one I would be happy to share with all four of my kids (when they're each old enough. Some of this is a bit adult).

And now, a preview for what's coming next...

EXTRA: The following is a sneak peek at the next volume in the Gailsone series, *Gailsone: Red Rook*.

On a slightly busy sidewalk with the sun just starting to creep down the sides of the buildings around her, Allison Gailsone counted to ten, leveled her temper, and downed the last of the contents of her large, paper coffee cup before wadding it up and tossing it in a nearby trashcan. She was standing outside *Rare Gems* and staring with her arms crossed at the latest addition to the property; a giant, stone Japanese golem that, despite Allison's best efforts, didn't seem to want to do much of anything.

Most people would think that the addition of a giant stone statue to the front of their property would simply be a decoration, but according to Allison's aunt and employer, this was a centuries-old war machine designed to unquestioningly obey its master. Since its master was currently on vacation, Fudo (the current name for the golem) was instructed to follow Allison's commands for the time being.

This sounded good to Allison in theory, but after going over every command she could think of, the novelty of a giant stone tank on legs had worn thin. Allison clenched her fists at her side and tried not to get too worked up. She had been standing outside for over 20 minutes talking to the giant stone statue in an effort to get it to move, but so far, nothing had happened. While 20 minutes may not seem like a significant amount of time, Allison was not one that was considered to be patient.

Allison, while not normally comfortable with taking charge, was acting manager for *Rare Gems* while Alice was away. Allison was many things and while she wasn't the best at managing a business, she was good at adapting to situations and rolling with change. To the dread of her coworkers, this made her an ideal choice for the role of pseudo-boss. She was dressed in a simple white blouse with a dark brown vest and matching slacks. Her shoes were flat, brown pumps that were good for running (just in case), and her thin, red-rimmed glasses were currently sliding down her nose in protest of their home continually wrinkling. Her shoulder-length auburn hair was in its signature pony tail, which swished slightly as she shook her head in frustration.

Beside Allison stood her fellow employee and kind-of-friend Cindy, who had come in early to help open the store. The young, blonde saleswoman munched on a bagel and watched with some amusement at Allison looked over the list of commands left to her in a sticky-note.

"Fudo, move your right arm," Allison loudly commanded. Cindy watched the golem stand stock still.

"Maybe you need to say some magic words or something?" Cindy asked between bites.

Allison glared at Cindy. "Don't be a bitch. This thing works, otherwise, it wouldn't be here." Allison looked again at the list of commands. Maybe she needed to stress certain words...

"No, seriously," Cindy continued, "Isn't the boss, like, magic or something?"

Allison paused and considered it. "True, but she's not... You know how you hear about fantastic wizards and witches and people with an unbridled mastery of the mystic arts?"

"Yeah?"

"Yeah, she's not one of those. She can barely use magic to warm a pop tart without binge vomiting from the side-effects, so I really don't think she did anything super-special to make this thing work."

Allison started to attempt to make the golem move again and then paused. "Cindy?"

"Yeah?"

"How did you know about Alice being… special?"

Cindy shrugged. "She told me a little about it when she came back from her trip. I asked her how she got so messed up and then got healed so fast. She told me some stuff, I guess."

"Some stuff, you guess," Allison repeated. She liked Cindy well enough, but sometimes she wanted to strangle the girl for her lack of a vocabulary.

Cindy shrugged and sipped a coffee while Allison went back to deciphering her employer's handwriting. The street was just waking up, and this corner of Brooklyn was usually bustling by 9:00 AM, so it wasn't uncommon to hear car horns, street vendors, loud music, children screaming, cars skidding to a stop…

Allison snapped out of what she was doing to look down the street. At the end of the block, she saw what looked like three large men of questionable intent in drab, forgettable clothing grab what appeared to be an 11 year old girl and throw her in the back of a black sedan. Allison only caught a little of it, but she had worked as a terrorist long enough in her former life to recognize a classic grab-n-dash when it was happening. Two of the men had drug the screaming girl into the car while the third, a large, balding man of what looked to be Mid-Eastern descent, looked up and down the block to see if anyone saw what had happened. The car was already running, and the moment the third man hopped in, the door slammed shut and the car peeled off into traffic.

"Oh, oh *Hell* no, not on my street," Allison muttered as she dropped her coffee and reached behind her. Tucked neatly into her back waistline was her favorite travel gun, a small, fully loaded Beretta. There were better guns and there were stronger guns, but Allison liked how this one wore with her wardrobe, and the smallness of the gun worked well for her somewhat petite hands. Cindy stopped in mid-conversation as her acting manager drew a firearm in front of her.

"Okay, I can be more specific!" Cindy yelped as Allison ignored her fellow employee and stepped forward into the street. Cindy stood and watched with some confusion and fascination as Allison slipped effortlessly into her old training.

Allison only had a few moments to gauge distance, speed and trajectory. Inwardly, she was already cursing, as the car was roaring down the street towards her at a high speed. Thankfully, it was still early enough that traffic wasn't a major problem. She only had a few seconds and one or two shots at most to stop the car. She drew a bead, steadied herself and took a deep breath.

One of the first things Alice had taught her was how to fire a gun. Alice could still remember being on an indoor firing range in one of the East Coast warehouse fronts owned by the Purge. She could still smell the sawdust and paint from the facility and feel the cold, concrete floor under her shoes. Most of all, she could remember holding the gun in her small, sweating hands while Alice stood behind her, holding her shoulders and calmly talking her through the process.

"You don't swing it around, you don't hold it sideways and you don't rush to make the shot. You take aim, keep your arm bent, put your free hand underneath your weapon hand to steady it and take a deep breath. You keep both eyes open, you stay focused and you wait until the gun is firmly pointed at the target before shooting. This isn't a game and that isn't a toy, and a calm shooter will always win out over a panicked one."

Even ten years later, whenever she drew her gun, she could still hear those words.

Allison cleared her mind, steadied her arm and focused on the left front tire of the car. She only had a moment to take the shot. Time slowed down, her breathing steadied...

And then she watched as Fudo charged into the street, its shoulder cocked in front of it like a football player holding the ball and dashing towards the end zone. The golem slammed into the side of the speeding car full force, sending the vehicle flying sideways and spinning through the air. It rolled onto its roof and skidded in a loud, grinding shower of sparks into the oncoming traffic lane. Fudo stood calmly in the middle of the road, its body turned towards the now totaled sedan.

Allison and Cindy stood motionless, still processing what they had just seen.

"Did Alice write 'smash kidnappers car' anywhere on that sticky note?" Cindy asked in a small voice.

"It's possible; her handwriting is really hard to read." Allison deadpanned back.

With her gun still drawn and pointed towards the sedan, Allison quickly approached the destroyed car. Cautiously, she stepped widely around Fudo. She gave her attention to the now-immobile golem for only a moment before focusing back on the car. As she approached, the side door to the sedan lurched open with a groan and the driver, a smaller, bald man in his mid-40's, climbed out. His face was covered in blood and he seemed disoriented. Allison kept her gun trained on him and waited to see what he would do.

A panicked, young voice screaming "help me!" from inside the car snapped Allison's attention back to the sedan. She trained her gun on the back door of the sedan and cautiously reached out to open it. After a few tugs, the door came open and a small, shaking young girl tumbled out.

She was about 11 or 12, Allison wasn't quite sure. She had long, dark brown hair that went halfway down her back. Her pink hairband was slightly askew, and Allison could see a gash across the top of her head from the wreck. The girl was dressed in a puffy, silver coat that was decidedly out of season and slightly too big for her. Underneath, Allison could see a stained, sequin tank top. The girl had a short, black shirt and fishnet stockings that were torn. Her shoes were slightly oversized furry

258

boots. She looked extremely out of place for her age, and as Allison looked at her, the petite former-terrorist felt a surge of hate start to well inside of her. Not at the girl, but at what her outfit signaled.

"Are you okay?" Allison asked, her gun still trained on the sedan. The young girl looked up, saw the gun and scrambled back. Allison didn't take her eyes off the car for a moment. "How many are still in there?"

The girl blinked for a minute and then looked at the car. "Um… four? I think… I think four."

The bald man made it to his feet, looked at Allison and started to reach into his jacket. Immediately, Allison turned her pistol towards him and let off two rounds into his chest and one in his head. The man dropped backwards and crumpled to the ground, dead.

"…Three?" The young girl said. Allison, while focused, smiled slightly.

A moment later, the Mid-Eastern man climbed out of the same back door the young girl had climbed out of, a gun in his hand. Before he could even focus on Allison, she let off a round into his hand that knocked the gun away. The man screamed and pulled his hand into himself. He tightly clutched his wounded arm with his still-working one and sobbed at the pain.

"You. Any others inside?" Allison addressed the sobbing man as he rocked a bit on his knees and clutched his bleeding hand.

"Fuck you…" the man muttered as he glared at her.

Allison sighed. In the distance, she could already hear police sirens. Without another word, Allison casually put a round into the man's upper thigh. The man howled in pain and rolled backwards as he clutched his leg and let out a noise not unlike a dog being tortured.

"Any others inside?" Allison calmly asked again.

The man nodded, his eyes squeezed shut and his teeth clenched in pain. Allison knelt down and looked into the car from where she was. Inside, she could see two other men, both completely still with blood pouring down their heads.

Allison walked around the crying man and found his gun on the street. She kicked it over to where he was lying and pointed her pistol at him again.

"Pick it up," she said, her voice eerily calm.

"No...no please...God..." There was blood pooling on the pavement under the man. Allison made a 'ttt' sound and pointed her gun at his head.

"Why did you want this little girl?" Allison asked.

The man looked at Allison and then at the young girl standing off to the side, behind her.

Allison's eyes widened as the man suddenly lunged for the gun on the ground and brought it up to take aim at the girl. The girl closed her eyes and screamed as two shots rang out, but to her surprise, she didn't feel anything. After a moment, she opened her eyes and looked. There, on the ground was the man, dead. There was a hole in the middle of his head and another where his heart was. Allison had already tucked her gun back into her waistline and had moved beside the young girl. The girl watched as Allison got down on one knee and examined her closely.

"Are you okay?" Allison asked. The girl looked at Allison and then at the bodies behind her, and then tensed up. Allison shot out an arm and latched onto the young girl before she could move.

"If I wanted you dead, you'd be dead, sweetie. Now, I get it, you're scared and want to bolt, but you're gonna stay right here and help me explain to the nice policemen that are about to pull up that I just saved your life, got it? You were minding your own business, walking down the street and these nasty men grabbed you. These dead men we have never seen before. Right?"

The girl looked at Allison for a moment and considered her options. Behind her, the girl could hear police sirens loudly blaring and cars screeching to a halt. She looked at Allison a moment longer and then nodded.

"You got a name?" Allison asked as the sound of slamming car doors and screaming could be heard all around them.

"I'm Holly," the young girl said.

"I'm Allison. Let's go talk to the police now, okay Holly?"

Allison stood as the police rushed the scene. Holly turned to face the officers and felt a hand take hers. She looked up to see Allison standing beside her, facing forward. Holly noted that the older woman was a good head taller than she was.

"Hello officers," Allison said calmly, her voice as level as a lake at dawn. "Thank God you're here. There was almost a kidnapping."

Look for *Gailsone: Red Rook*, out now on Kindle and in paperback!

Made in the USA
Middletown, DE
08 May 2022

65486366R00156